NIKKI MARMERY

On
Wilder
Seas

The Woman on the
Golden Hind

Legend Press Ltd, 51 Gower Street, London, WC1E 6HJ
info@legend-paperbooks.co.uk | www.legendpress.co.uk

Print ISBN 978-1-78955-113-6
Ebook ISBN 978-1-78955-114-3
Set in Times. Printing Managed by Jellyfish Solutions Ltd
Cover design by Simon Levy. | www.simonlevyassociates.co.uk

Nikki Marmery has been shortlisted for the Myriad Editions First Drafts Competition and the Historical Novel Society's New Novel Award. She previously worked as a journalist at Incisive Media.

Nikki lives in Amersham with her husband and three children.

Follow Nikki
@nikkimarmery

America
or
India Nova
from the
Typus Orbis Terrarum
1570
Anian
Nova Albion
Acapulc
Burneo
Mindanao
Celebes
Nova
Guinney
Mar
Del Zur
Terra Australis
Nondum

Book One

NOVA HISPANIA

MARCH – MAY, 1579

MARCH, 1579

ACAPULCO

16°50'N

I

On the day the treasures of the East are unloaded in the harbour of Acapulco, the feria begins. When the cloves, cinnamon and nutmegs, musky sandalwood and camphor oil, the silks, porcelains, ebony-wood and elephants'-teeth carvings – when all has been weighed, taxed and released to the merchants, the husks of the galleons inspected for contraband and sent on to the shipyard for repairs – when the scurvy-sore crew are released at last to pray thanks for their lives: only then can the Fair of the Manila Galleons begin.

Now, the scorched and dusty town doubles in size. Here come the arrieros, three-legged with their staffs, leading mule-trains down the treacherous mountain path. In iron-wheeled carts come the merchants of México and Jalapa, shaded under rich awnings. Soldiers to protect the cargo, and the Viceroy's officials to inspect, oversee and record. On foot come the Indio hawkers and begging friars, the gamblers and the whores. By sea, the masters of the Lima ships come to fill their holds with silks to cover the calves and perfumes to scent the temples of lusty Limeños.

And here too, come I, borne here on a Lima ship, unwilling and unasked. I slip through the crowd, among these knaves and sinners, past prodding elbows and bony knees, squeezing myself wherever there is space, to bid and barter, as they do, for the cargo laid out upon tables, rugs and stalls.

Yes, I will fight for these treasures too, because only a fool sees the sun and does not ask why it is there. My grandmother was right in this as in most things. I know the sun is there to warm and delight me, as I know what can be bought here for ten pesos may be sold in the ports of Guayaquil, Paita and Lima for twenty.

If I am careful, that is. For it is not permitted. Everything I earn belongs by right to Don Francisco, since all that I am, my labour and my body, are his, may the Virgin spit on his sword and the Devil shit in his face. But if I am not discovered, it gains me some few pesos to put with the little I have in my pouch. One day it will be enough to pass to an agent to buy my freedom.

And I must be quick about it, for soon we sail. The bell of the *Cacafuego* rings out from the harbour. Already, her banners and pennants are raised and kicking at the wind. The red and white cross of the King of Spain flutters from the topmast. The marineros leap like monkeys about the rigging.

I run. To the back of the plaza, beyond the Hospital de Nuestra Señora de la Consolación. I push past merchants snatching, haggling, outbidding – past porters and slaves stumbling under the weight of their parcels, the painted women weaving their way, bold-eyed, through the crowd. Past the children squealing with delight at the acrobats tumbling on the wooded hill, and the Indio musicians, whose song of harps and flutes floats above it all. But the scaffold stops me. Two slaves await there today. Both men at least – not children. Chained by collar and cuffs, ready for boiling fat to be poured upon their naked flesh. Runaways, then. Caught running for their freedom in the hidden places of the mountains. Their eyes are fixed there now: on the steel-grey rock rising behind the town and beyond; to the unseen narrow passes and secret valleys that would have shielded them.

I will not look. I fly. Past the torture of the slaves, to the alley where the meanest merchants linger. To the stall of the mestizo Felipe, who will keep some offcuts for me. I see him through the crowd from afar. Fuller in the belly than when I saw him last: he prospers. Bales of Chinese silks, cottons of Luzon and muslins from India overflow from three full barrel tops.

"Maria!" He welcomes me with outstretched arms and I fold into him. He still smells of the long voyage from Manila: the sour sweat crusted into his linen and the pitch that can never be got out of canvas.

I pull away from the stench of his armpit. "What have you for me?"

"Nothing, moza, I thought you dead. Where were you last year?"

I do not wish to think of where I was last year. I reach out to feel a beautiful silk of emerald green. "God has been good to you, Felipe."

"*I* have been good to me."

"How much for a piece of this?"

He snatches it away. "I cannot discount that," he shakes his head. "I have a family." He raises his brow and I realise I have not asked.

"How is Nicolás?"

"Well," he nods. "He misses you." He looks both ways to see who is about.

"Come back with the ship," he urges. "Give your master the slip."

I fold my arms. Four times I have made the crossing to or from Manila and four times I made my peace to die. Twice I sailed in a fleet that lost a ship and all who were in it. Twelve weeks or more of the eternal grey sea and unblinking horizon. And what is the point? Nicolás is all very well. He is a dear sweet child but he is not my own. And Manila is no different from Acapulco, or México, Veracruz or Valperizo. I am a slave in every corner of this New World.

Felipe shrugs. "This one I can give you for eight pesos."

He offers me a bolt of black silk. "A little embroidery, make a mantle of it. You can sell it in Lima for fifteen."

I scowl at him. "Four."

"Five," he smiles. "And this – for your hair." He shows me a length of calico.

I eye it greedily. My hair has been uncovered, at the mercy of every marinero who would tug and grab at it, since Gaspar the cooper pulled off my silken wrap and threw it in the sea.

I take it and gather up my salt-stiff curls into a fine double-knot at my forehead. Such relief. I fish out five coins from the pouch at my waist, poking about to check how many remain. Some forty, or thereabouts. One hundred and twenty I will need, this far from the North Ocean ports — and that is if Don Francisco will take the money for my freedom, which I cannot think likely. I fold the silk and put it inside. On second thoughts, I tuck the pouch inside the waist of my skirt and arrange my camisa to hide it.

The bell rings out again from the *Cacafuego* and I embrace Felipe. I hold his head to my breast as if he were dear Nicolás, and I run. Into the back alleys, between the crude fishermen's huts of mud and straw. Past the marineros waiting outside the whorehouse. Around to the harbour – battling through the soldiers on patrol and the custom-men signing off each bale and package that leaves the port – to where the ship sits, laden and heavy in the water.

I watch her awhile. She rides close to the harbour wall, moored to an ancient ceiba tree. A tall ship: so high is the forecastle she looks like she will fall into the sea. Don Francisco is on the maindeck – I can tell his gait anywhere. He walks slowly, head down, as if he picks his way through a mess of dripped tar. Every now and then he raises his eyes to look about: behind the gallery, down the hatches. He is looking for me.

If I had the courage of the men on the scaffold, I would race the other way. Up the path to the mountains. To find the Cimarrones who live out their lives freely in hidden jungle forts. Or I would sail with Felipe, back to Manila, where there is at least dear Nicolás to caress and spoil. But I am short on courage, as I am of most things.

"Well there, negra!" I freeze as I am pulled back into the alley from behind. A filthy hand over my mouth, and the stench of fish-breath and wine in my face. By all God's whores, it is Pascual, the pilot of the *Cacafuego*.

"What do you here?" he sneers. He releases my mouth to push my head back sharp by the chin, searching with his other hand inside my skirts. He cannot resist the opportunity to force his fingers hard inside me, bending me double with the pain. I close my eyes and bite down on my tongue. "Ay!" he brings out my pouch. "You keep two treasures inside your skirts."

Pascual takes out the silk, and pours the coins into his palm. "I wonder," he says. "Does Don Francisco know of this? Is it possible you trade on his account? For these small and paltry sums?"

I hum to block out his noise. I know what is coming.

"Or, more likely, you steal from him. Withholding from your owner his rightful earnings." He pockets my forty pesos, folds the silk inside his doublet and hands me back my empty pouch.

"But do not fear. I will save you the whip, negrita. I will not tell him."

He leads me, pulling hard by the wrist, deeper into the maze of huts and stables. He pulls me into a storehouse through a door that creaks on one hinge. I take in the room in one glance. A donkey roped in the corner. Empty mule-packs stacked by the door. Straw covers the floor, where he pushes me now, my cheek cracking against the stone.

The donkey blinks at me, his long lashes sweeping lazily. His tail switches backwards and forwards, shooing away the flies. Behind me, Pascual, drunk and stumbling, struggles with his breeches.

I count in my head. Not the Spanish numbers. My own

tongue. Kink, cherink, chasas. The only words I have left. Yaunaleih, chamatra, chamatrakink. Everything else is gone into the fog, with the face of my mother and many other things.

I am up to cubach, and much vexed that I cannot remember what comes after, when I notice the hook of an arriero's staff poking from beneath the straw. I do not think. I respond in the instant. As the ass' tail dispatches a fly. With one move I grasp the staff and swing it back to meet with a pleasing crack the side of Pascual's head. He is knocked to the floor, curled and howling like a baby, and I am up, wielding the staff in my hands, before he can raise himself. He moans, a trail of blood pouring from his temple, and pooling into the straw. I back out towards the door. The donkey screeches. Pascual looks to it in surprise, and I rush in and strike him hard across the back for good measure.

I run, as fast as the wind, out of the storehouse, back through the narrow alleys, not stopping until I am at the harbour, by the gnarled and lizard-like roots of the old ceiba tree. Beside its spiny trunk, I collect my breath.

I watch, still panting, as the last porters leave the loaded ship. A black-frocked inquisitor follows them, carrying off the forbidden books he has found. So it will be a dull voyage. No tales of Orlando beneath the mainsail after prayers. No *Araucana* sung to the strings of a guitarra. Two thousand leagues of *Lives of the Saints* and *Histories of the Popes*.

I cast my eyes one last time to the mountains: to the steep and narrow path leading out of Acapulco. Already, the first mule-trains have started, rising from the fields of hemp, through wooded slopes thick with brazilwood trees, on the long road back to México.

But it cannot be helped. I have no choice. Dizzied, holding tight the rope, I climb the swaying ramp onto the maindeck of the *Cacafuego*.

"There you are," says Don Francisco when he spies me. He looks me up and down. "Clean yourself, what's happened to you?" He does not wait for an answer. I put my hand to my face and realise I am bleeding, where Pascual threw me to the floor.

Around me, the men scurry into action. The maestre's whistle shrieks across the deck. The marineros chant as they haul aboard the anchors. The great sails are unfurled from the yards above. They roar as they fill, full-bellied with the wind. The ramp is hoisted, then lowered, as Pascual comes running from the storehouse just in time, red of face, and bloodied of the head. The mooring rope is coiled aboard.

In Don Francisco's cabin in the sterncastle, I wash the blood from my cheek and elbows with stinging sea water.

I check to see if a solitary peso remains hidden in my pouch, but it is flat. Empty as a virgin's womb. What God has seen fit to provide, that vile cabrón has taken away. I fold it back into my skirts.

As we glide past Isla de la Roqueta in the bay, a pair of black-necked geese dance on a flat grey rock by the water's edge. They hiss and bark at each other. A mating pair. Not mountain nor sea can contain them. They arrive in Acapulco every October, in time for All Souls Day, as if they return with the dead from the grave, to visit the living and feast. And every springtime they return – to wherever it is they go – soaring as one arrow-headed flock. Into the north, where the Spaniards hold no power. Soon it will be time for them to leave. Would that they could take me with them.

But here I am. Shut up in the creaking prison of the *Cacafuego*, under the watchful eye of Don Francisco and these other vicious men, bound once again for Lima. Wretched Lima: the place of my worst and most lasting misery.

APRIL, 1579

ZONZONATE

13°50'N

2

Three years have I been on the *Cacafuego*, first with Gonzalo and now with Don Francisco, changing hands with the ship alongside the sails and the cooking-pots as if I were part of its furniture. Twice in every year we make the same journey: from Acapulco to Callao de Lima, then Valperizo and back again. So I know exactly where we are. That waterfall: a ribbon of silver, curling down the vine-covered cliff, this means we are near Zonzonate. Six weeks' sail from Lima.

I hold my belly. Have I imagined it? It is no different. But I feel it now as I did before. Thus far, just the faintness. But the rest will come. The hunger, and yet the fullness. The sickness, and the ripening of the noisome smells of the ships. A life, expanding inside me. Filling me. Till I must expel it in agony at the very knife-edge of life and death. And after all this, he will take it from me, as he did before. *A ship is no place for a baby*, he will say.

The handle at the door shakes, and I have time enough to prepare my face before he comes in. So slow, as always. He is like the tree-monkey the Spaniards call perezoso because they are so lazy.

"I did not expect you so soon, your Grace."

"We were disturbed," he says, eyes hidden under his heavy brow.

I see he was not disturbed before eating since there is a fresh spot of grease on his waistcoat, which will be the devil to scrub out. For the love of God, who wears white silk at sea?

"Have you eaten?" He does not wait for a reply, but throws a leg of Guinney-fowl to me, which I am lucky to catch before it hits the dust of the floor. The meat is good. Not over-burned. Dressed with honey.

"The captain was called to the lookout," he says. "A ship has changed course towards us."

"Perhaps it brings a letter? From his Excellency?" Maybe we can turn back – and this time, yes! I will run into the hills.

But no. "It is no Spanish ship."

What else can it be? From Portingale? But they cannot be mistook, with their sails of triangles, not Spanish squares.

Don Francisco opens the trunk by the bed and he pulls out linen shifts, bales of silk and taffeta, tossing it all around him. Only one thing is he mindful of: a bag of yellow silk tied with a red velvet ribbon. He picks it up like the Holy Grail itself and sets it on the table.

The heavier things: the bars of silver as long as my forearm, bags of coin, dishes of Cathay porcelain, these he leaves in the trunk.

I cannot watch him making this mess, which will be mine to clear away, so I lean out the window. The breeze is cool. I nibble at the honeyed meat to make it last and I watch the land pass by.

Thick jungles rise into mountain peaks. Yellow cliffs stand straight from the shore as if cut with a shovel. A wide river roils the sea where they meet, waves tipped with white foam. How fine and empty it falls upon the eye. But it is in the chokehold of the Spaniards in every direction. I suck the last of the meat from the bone and throw it into the sea. A fine arc it makes, the water bubbling as the fish come up to see it. Above, watching the little fish, gulls circle. Somewhere out there, watching from below, are the tiburóns, who wait for greater prizes than little fish or the leg of a fowl.

There is no sign of a ship, from Portingale or otherwise.

When I turn back he is still unloading the chests.

"You search for something, your Grace?" I pick up and fold the cloths he has thrown down.

"Damned eyeglass."

Of course it is where it always is: on the high shelf, which he cannot see because always he is looking down. He takes it from me without a word.

He is distracted, so I dare to ask: "What troubles you, your Grace?"

He does not answer. I touch his arm.

"Nothing. Only..."

"Only?"

"The ship that pursues... It is so very low."

Ay, and now I understand. Because although he has the ways of a lazy tree-monkey who has never before been ashipboard, he has been in this New World many years. Like me, he arrived eleven years since, though the manner of his arrival was quite different. He came with the flota of 1568, which fought the English at San Juan de Ulúa, and later he was at Panama in the days of the Corsair, so he has a natural horror of the Luteranos.

But it cannot be. They cannot cross the mountains, and they cannot pass the Southern Straits, which are deadly even to the Spaniards, who have the charts and roteiros of every ship that has passed them yet.

So it is quite impossible for the English dogs to fetch in these waters.

3

Cacafuego means Fireshitter. She is named for the power of her great guns. But when it comes, so sudden is the attack, so unexpected in these waters, we fire not a single shot.

It is night and the moon sits low and yellow upon the water. When he leaves to consult with the captain, I follow Don Francisco to the foredeck, so I am there when the ship, narrow and low, glides alongside us in the darkness.

"Who are you?" the steersman calls out. "From where do you hail?"

His words fall into the silence.

The maestre's whistle brings the crew running. Up from below, high into the fighting-tops. It sends the lumbering gunners to the gun deck, linstocks in hand. But there is no time.

Of a sudden there is thunder and smoke. Shot rains down on us, sending dust from the burning timbers exploding into the air. Don Francisco yells: "Run!" and I do not wait to be told again. My ears feel like they will burst. Barely can I breathe through the choking smoke. I feel my way, holding onto the gunwale until I reach the sterncastle, bruising my shins against posts and stumbling over hawsers coiled like snakes in the darkness.

Safe in the cabin, I crouch in the bed, listening. But as quickly as it arrived, the thunder retreats.

Footsteps run past the cabin. I open the door to a crack just in time to see the pirates board, leaping out of the smoke of their arquebus-fire and onto the *Cacafuego* as if they are spirits from the other world. Such command they have, they make merry – bowing low to Captain Anton in asking for his keys and to Don Francisco for his sword, instead of taking them. The marineros are stunned into stillness. They do nothing. Lift not a finger.

It is like a scene from a comedia in procession in Ciudad de México – save that the captain and Don Francisco look very truly frit, much better than the players at Corpus Christi with wide-open mouths, hands pulling at their hair and eyebrows painted high on foreheads. And I am mighty frit too, because I know this language they speak. It is a hard tongue, the sound of a crow calling. Harder than Castilian, and I remember some of these words, though I have not heard them for many years.

The pirates rope the two ships together and lead Captain Anton and Don Francisco across planks onto their own foredeck, where a small fair man waits. He holds his hands behind his back and nods sharply, as he greets them. Don Francisco's head is down, still looking where to put his feet that will not hold steady.

Malhaya Dios, they are taken below. Never did I think the day would come when I would wish that man were beside me.

From the gallery outside the cabin, the marineros watch and curse.

"Tis he, brothers. You know it: the English Corsair."

A young boy, voice shaking, prays: "Holy body, true friend of mariners, San Telmo, help us and save us from harm."

"The cuntbitten devil," says the first.

"He's a Luterano, not a devil," says another.

"Worse – he'll damn our souls for eternity."

The boy moans. "Our Lady of the Fair Seas, succour us now in our hour of need!"

An older man barks: "Fuck your soul and fuck Our Lady.

My bones are what I fear for. He'll put us afire, is what he'll do."

And the sign of how frit they truly are, these ungodly men of the sea: now they pray, rubbing the heathen fig amulets around their necks. I close the door on them and sit on the bed, rocking on my haunches.

They do not know they are lucky for not being women. There is worse that will happen to me before I am damned or burned or drowned.

I am still trembling when he comes in. A thousand little explosions in my breast like a line of gunpowder taking fire.

The wind rises from the south. We drift. After the attack, they towed us far from land. The hawsers tying the ships together snap tight.

At dawn, they come on deck, hard voices calling. The sound of sword against breastplate, an arquebus lock pulled back. They leap aboard. A dozen of them or thereabouts. One low voice, which commands: "Find the silver, she is stuffed full of it." English, but the tongue of a Spaniard. "You – to the cabins. You – the steward's store. We need grain, meat, water and wine."

They say, the Spaniards, that opals bring their bearer foresight. I do not say that. I say she called to me. That is why, of all the precious things strewn about the cabin, I take and hide just one: the yellow silk bag. *Take me*, she said. So I did. I tuck her into the pouch beneath my skirts and return to the bed, for there is nowhere to hide.

So that is where I am: arms wrapped tight around my knees, waiting for the gunpowder to take the fire, when the door opens.

But the first moment I see him, the surprise melts the fear. The powder fizzles out in the middle of the line.

This is not what I expected.

He is tall and wide across the shoulders. He blocks out the

morning sun as he stands in the doorway, squinting into the gloom. His Spanish is fluent: "May I enter?"

As the light floods in with him, I see his high cheekbones, his skin clear and smooth.

But that is not what is surprising.

His linen is clean. His breeches are of taffeta, not canvas. He wears a leather jerkin and a scarlet cap, the colour of a papagayo. His beard is close cut. He wears a ruby ring on one forefinger. The sword at his hip is in a fine gilt scabbard. This is not the English Corsair.

And never, in all my life, have I seen an Affrican dressed like this.

4

"My name is Diego," he says. "Of Santiago de Cuba."

I do not know what to say. So I say nothing.

"En nombre sea de Dios." He bows. "This is the cabin of Don Francisco de Zarate?"

I nod. A terrible thing to lose one's wits. I pinch at my knees to recover them.

"You will not be harmed." He inclines his head as if to receive my grateful thanks. "We will hold the ship for a day only. Two, if the winds go against us."

His eye falls and lingers greedily on the half-emptied chests and trunks. So much to ask. So much I would know. But the words will not come. I feel the pain in my knees where my nails have dug in.

"I see that I disturb you. I will not keep you long." He takes off his cap and places it carefully on the table.

"Your captain –" I stumble over the words. "Is he the English Corsair?"

He crosses his arms as he leans back against the table. His eyes dance. "He is not a corsair. He is the Queen of England's envoy."

"The Queen's pirate, I heard."

"If you like. We are none of us masters of what others call us. Are we – ?" He asks it like a question, with his palm held out to me, and I understand – too late – that he asks for my name.

He goes on. "We take what we are owed and what we need. No more. As for you – what do they call you? De qué tierra?"

For a moment, I think of saying my real name, a thing I have not done for many years. But then I hear the Englishmen, laughing as they steal food and treasure away to their ship, and it recalls to me their countrymen, the first of my misfortunes. So I say: "Maria. Of nowhere."

"Well, Maria of Nowhere," he laughs. "May I?" He gestures to the chests on the floor.

"You have the man, you may as well have his things." I sit forward to watch. Each yard of cloth, each wrap of Cathay silk, he sets apart to see what is underneath.

"Will you kill him?" I did not mean to sound so eager.

"Not unless my General discovers he is related to the Viceroy." He does not look up. "Is he?"

I pause a moment too long. "No."

He raises one brow. "Then we will not hang him."

"Your General?" I ask. "Then you are soldiers?"

The lines around his eyes deepen as he smiles. "Of sorts."

"What is his grievance against the Viceroy?" How *dare* any man grieve the Viceroy.

He perches low on his heels, perfect in balance. I notice for the first time he is barefoot, though dressed like a gentleman in all other ways. "An ancient score," he says at last. "He did my General a grave injustice some years ago."

"At San Juan de Ulúa?"

He looks up. "You know the history."

There is not a man, woman nor child in New Spain who does not. "I was there. I saw it – the battle. From Veracruz."

"Then you know Don Martín Enríquez is a murderous villain who does not keep his word."

He fixes me with his furious eye as if I am Don Martín himself. I sink back into the bed and pull my knees tighter.

He returns to the chests. There is a system to his search:

the silks and cloths he puts to one side, the coin and treasures to another. He lifts each piece of Cathay porcelain with tender care.

"And Don Francisco," he asks lightly, as if he passes the time of day. "Is he a kind master?"

Never have I thought on it. God and all his whores know how I loathe him for what he has taken from me. But that is not to be spoken of. "One devil is very like another," I say instead.

He seems not to hear. He leans out of the door and whistles sharply. Footsteps come running, two men peer in. I pull the coverlet over me.

"Take these," Diego says in English, gesturing to the chests. "Have a care with that one, Pyke. It's porcelain. The General will want it for his wife."

The man called Pyke runs his eyes up and down my body under the linen. A dirty, evil-looking man, he smells as if he has come directly from the bilges. "What about her?" he leers, his tongue showing through the gaps in his teeth. "Can I take her for *my* wife?"

Diego strikes him hard across the ear. "Pendejo!" To me, he says in Castilian: "Forgive him. He has been at sea too long."

I cannot believe it. A black man cannot strike a white man. In New Spain he would lose his hand. More likely, his life.

But Pyke does not fight back. He drops to his knees, blood marking his cheek where Diego's ring cracked the skin. He fastens the trunk, and he and the other Englishman pull it, scratching, across the boards and over the stoop.

"How long have you been at sea?" I ask when they are gone.

"A year. And then some."

"From where did you sail?"

"Plymouth."

"Then you have been to England?"

"By the Virgin, your voice has returned!" he cries. "Yes, I have lived there some years with my General."

"As... his man?"

He nods. He does not look up because he has found the plata and his eyes are shining.

"Then you are free?"

He nods, a bar of silver in each hand, weighing it, assessing its worth. He has not a scar, nor a brand, nor the burn marks of hot-oil torture. He is whole, complete. Truly, I think. A man could not look more free.

"And this is what you do with your freedom?" My arm sweeps over the emptied chests, the valuables strewn over the floor. "Pirating. Pickery?"

Madre de Dios why did I say this? It is nothing to me whoever takes these things. He lays down the silver and strides towards me. I wince as he brings his face a spit from mine. "A thief knows a thief, as a wolf knows a wolf. Has Don Francisco mined this silver? Woven these silks?"

He grips my shoulder, hard. "And what of you? How did he come by you? Did he buy you at an auction? Win you in a game of dice?"

So close is he to the truth, I will not look at him. Don Francisco's face rises before me, fearsome in lust, as it was the first I ever saw of him, when he came aboard the *Cacafuego* to take his prize. The ship and all it contained – including me. Two years now. Won in a game of cards.

"I choose this life," Diego rages. "I fought to have it. And I am no worse than devils like your *master*, who are thieves in all but name."

The door slams open and the Englishmen fall back in.

"Ho, Diego," cackles Pyke, as he sees me kneeling, head bowed, Diego holding me by the shoulder. "Even you cannot disobey the General." He wags his finger. "No wenches!"

Diego glares at him. He loads the remaining boxes and chests into their arms, and barks: "See to the rest of the passenger cabins. Then the hold."

The Englishmen stagger out under their burdens.

When he turns back, his eyes are closed. "Forgive me," he says, sitting on the bed. "I did not mean the insult. I know nothing of your…" He struggles for the word. "Situation."

Still, I will not meet his eye.

"Are you safe – while he is with us?"

I straighten the linen at my shoulder where he pulled at it. "I look after myself."

"I do not doubt it."

He is almost out of the door when he turns back. "Come with us."

I am struck dumb again with the surprise.

His eyes blaze. The fury seems to burn off him.

"I know Englishmen," I say at last. "It was they who took me – the first time."

I thought he did not hear me before, but he repeats my words back to me now. "One devil is very like another," he says. "And this devil, at the least, no longer stomachs slavery. I will have my share of the ship's profit when we return, like any other man."

I look out the window so he cannot see the calculation behind my eyes.

"Which way do you sail?" I ask, as if it is of very small importance to me.

"The Devil alone knows the General's design." He nods. "But we are done with New Spain. We sail home – one way or another."

5

The next day is a Sunday.

At the priory in Veracruz, Fray Calvo told me the English deny the Almighty God. That they are heretics, who roam the world to sow in it the Pernicious Poisons of their Apostasy. I imagined them in the very act of digging furrows, scattering their seeds and watering them with great diligence and care.

But here they are instead making much of the holy day. The boys were up before dawn, scrubbing the decks. Gun-barrels shine brighter through the gunports when they are done. They garland their ship, climbing into the fighting-tops to fasten banners with the likenesses of dragons that fly and roar as the wind whips them to life.

What else did the friars tell me that was not true?

Mid-morning come the trumpeters, in tabards of yellow and red to match the paintwork of the ship. Then come the gentlemen in their finest garments: feathers in caps and cloaks, spite the heat. Sailors in canvas breeches and pitch-stained smocks. Now, the two prisoners. Still not tied nor shackled.

By my faith, they smile, their heads in close with the Englishman beside them: he who stood on deck, owl-eyed in command, the night they attacked. He wears a cap laced with gold trim. Hands behind his back. Every now and again he points to something in proud ownership, or steps aside, courtly-mannered, to let them pass.

A flash of red by the planks roped to both ships – Diego's cap. He waits to bring them over.

From the pirates' ship comes a shout: a boy runs across the deck. "Your arms!" He kneels at Don Francisco and Captain Anton's feet and lets fall their swords. His dress is curious. Fine clothes: a ruffle at his neck and sleeves, no dirty smock like the other boys. Don Francisco takes no notice of the boys on the *Cacafuego*, save to kick or shove them. But he takes his sword on bended knee and pats the boy's shoulder, smiling.

All too soon, they are here.

"All on deck!" calls Diego, as he leaps aboard. "Everybody must receive our General."

I am not everybody. I know that. But I slip out of the door.

Behind the foremast, I watch the men line up. The captain and Don Francisco follow Diego aboard. Between them, a shimmer of gold – this General.

They walk to the far end, backs to me, so I slip to the maindeck and stand in line. Por amor de Dios, it is Gaspar, the scoundrel cooper.

He sneers at me. "Still with us negra? Thought you'd jumped."

I look beyond. They come down the line: the captain and Don Francisco alongside the General, telling him each man's name and office. Diego puts coins in the marineros' palms, to the fury of Captain Anton.

As they near, I hear the words. The General speaks haltingly, in the Spanish of a child. Diego breaks in when he falters.

My apologies.

Forgive me, friend.

The General regrets we have taken you from your course.

"Tis only our great need," the General tells the steward.

"Since we are prevented – by your Viceroy – from fetching our own water and food."

"And silver," mutters Gaspar.

He stops at Pascual. "Ah – the pilot."

"A simple seaman," says Pascual, the fool. He still wears the mark of my staff on his temple. How it pleases me to see it.

"You are Pascual de Chaves?" asks the General, consulting a curled paper in his hand. "The ship's register names you as pilot."

Pascual's shoulders sink. "Indeed. I know... something... of navigation."

"I need you," the General nods. "You will come with me."

Pascual looks to Captain Anton.

"The General is in charge here," barks Diego. "You will come with us or we will hang you."

The General moves on. "I do not take men against their will," he calls back. "You will be paid."

I leaned forward to see this business, and now they see me. Too late, I jerk back into line. The captain frowns. Don Francisco hisses: "Be gone, girl."

I feel heavy. As if a ball of lead in my heart holds me down. I put my shaking hands behind me.

The General comes closer.

He is not far above my height, we are near level. His eyes are gunmetal grey: hard, unsmiling. His hair is the colour of straw. Skin burned red. Beard flecked with copper. His nose is small, like the beak of a hawk.

It seems to me I know him already. Not just the reports of him, whispered by Spanish sailors in fearful voices in every port of the North and South Seas. Also his face: the cocked line of his chin. Perhaps it is the disdain.

He looks down his nose at me. "A girl! And what is your office? Are you the missing pilot?" He turns to Captain Anton, beaming. The captain forces a smile.

Diego frowns. He says with a nod of his head: "Maria is the... companion... of Don Francisco."

The General crosses his arms. "You must forgive me. I have deprived you of his company. I am sure it has been only a minor... what is the word, Diego?"

"Inconvenience? Imposition?"

He prefers his own word after all. "A minor... loss."

I have kept my eyes on the boards, to stay steady. But I look up now. In English, stumbling over the sounds I am unused to, I say: "I find I could bear it."

He looks at me like I am a great curiosity.

I open my mouth but Don Francisco pinches my arm. "This is not your place, girl."

The General brushes him away. "Let her speak."

"General –" *What am I doing?* I breathe out, slowly. I start again. "You must know that after this defeat, no longer can we call this ship the *Cacafuego*."

I look at the floor. I know the English, like the Spaniards, think meekness a virtue. In women.

He lifts my chin, his fingers cold to the touch. "Why not?"

"Because we fired not a shot. With the power of your guns, your ship has rightly earned that name."

His smile does not fit his face. "Indeed! We should take that honour. But then – what would you call this – the ship of Don Francisco de Zarate?" He slaps his shoulder. Don Francisco looks skyward to master his fury.

I stop. But I am ready with it, straight-faced, eyes locked on his: "The *Cacaplata*." By which I mean: she shits silver. "For you have taken every bar of it."

For a moment I think it has gone very badly. They look at me with horror. Don Francisco's face burns with anger. Captain Anton shakes, his arms stiff all the way to balled fists. The sailors stare. Gaspar grunts like the pig that he is. And then the General laughs. He tips back his head and he roars. The lace around his neck flutters as his chest heaves. Diego looks at him in surprise, the edges of his mouth curling upwards. Captain Anton looks set to burst.

When the General has righted himself, I hold him direct in

the eye. I must have the right words. "Forgive my boldness, General. Where do you sail?"

"I cannot reveal my design. Not before our Spanish friends." He slaps the horrified Don Francisco again. "We are – regretfully – unwelcome. Here in their treasure garden."

He speaks in curious stops and starts. As if he has to will himself anew to finish each sentence.

"But you leave New Spain?"

"Aye. We return to England. And what, pray, is your interest in my great venture?"

Don Francisco's eyes warn me. Captain Anton shakes his head. I must say it quickly before I lose the courage.

"Take me with you." I reach into my skirts for the yellow silk bag. "I can pay." I pour out the jewel into my palm. It sits there, big as a walnut, flashing gold and orange shards of light around the deck.

"That belongs to the Viceroy!" shouts Don Francisco, stepping forward as Diego's sword flies up to bar him.

The General picks it up. "Even better. For he owes me a great deal. Two birds with one stone." He holds it to the sun and it changes colour again. Blues and yellows, a beautiful pale green, shine from it. "Or is it three birds?" he smiles, turning from the flashing stone back to me.

"Please." I cannot mask my fear now, for I will be given up for the tiburóns – or worse, the common sailors – if he doesn't take me.

"Take me with you," I beg him. "Now!"

6

There is always a price to pay when you leave the land of the dead.

Persefoni paid for it every year, returning to Hades for six months in every twelve. Orfeus paid for it with his wife Evrydiki. Ishtar the Queen of Heaven sacrificed her husband Tammuz.

Ay, I know the Greeks and the Babylons – and plenty more besides. Fray Calvo kept a full library at the priory as well as slaves and he was a generous man, allowing the one possession to profit from the other.

The smell of his books: the musty, animal scent of the bindings, the bitter odour of the ink. How I loved that smell from the very first. How Fray Calvo laughed when he saw me trying to *hear* the books myself by putting the open pages to my ears. I thought it by some magic that the pages spoke, rather that the words came from the mouth of the reader.

He laughed. But still, he taught me to read. On Sundays after the midday meal. Nourishment for the body and for the soul, he said.

I wonder what it will cost me, my escape. A jewel that wasn't mine to give will not be enough. I wonder when I will be called upon to pay it.

For it is a week now, near enough, I have been on this

English ship. A week since I left the *Cacafuego*, Don Francisco standing on the quarterdeck, his mouth open and closing like a catfish caught in a basket, his body carried this way and that by the mob as they struggled for a sight of his troubles.

Gaspar shouting: "Yer eel's slipping away!"

Alonso the carpenter laughing: "With your riches in her fist!"

Jeering too, from the Englishmen as I came aboard, holding tight to Diego's arm, the General walking ahead to take applause for his victory.

"Behold!" he says, triumphant. "The spoil from the *Cacaplata*!"

He takes my jest for his own. The men, hanging from the ropes and ratlines, standing on the gunwales and yards to see for the better, laugh and roar in their great cheer.

"For God's pain!" they call when they see Pascual. "He's took another pilot!"

"He switches 'em like 'orses!"

They see me behind Pascual, though I curl into myself to disappear.

"And what you got there, General? A proper wench! A fine prize!"

"Such an age since we 'ad fresh meat."

They think I am a thing they have stolen. Like the silver and the grain and the charts, and the roteiro guides, and everything else they take from the Spaniards. Rather have I stolen myself. But little comfort is that, when the hands come out as I pass. As they did on the *Cacafuego*, the Manila galleons – on every ship I have sailed in: the hands in my hair, on my back, pinching hard my rear, pawing at my skirts.

My heart beats like it would escape from my chest. I had thought to grab my mantle when I left Don Francisco's cabin, and I pull it over my shoulders to cover myself. All I have with me, save the clothes on my back and my empty pouch, still tucked into my skirt.

One man stands apart. A tall man, dressed in black. He

glares down his long nose at me, his mouth pressed to a thin line, blood drained from his lips. He looks like nothing so much as an angry crow. As I pass, he meets my flickering eye with fury, then turns and pushes his way through the mob.

"Back to your watches," beams the General. "Come, Maria," he beckons to me. "Diego will show you where to lay a bed mat."

I follow them down the steps into gloomy, bitter darkness. We are in the armoury, I see when my eyes bend to the low light. Muskets and arquebuses are piled up against one wall. Some of these I recognise from the *Cacafuego*. Others I have not seen before. Crossbows: these, Englishmen alone use. They look ancient, like something in a painting in the grand houses of Ciudad de México.

The General opens a door into a cramped space, though brighter, filled with laughing, preening officers. "Here is the Great Cabin."

I peer beyond him. A table of oak takes up most of the space. Draped in Turkey-carpets, with silver dishes of fruits and sweetmeats upon it. My belly growls. Around the table sit a dozen gentlemen, all talking at once. One relieves himself into a pot in the corner.

I go to follow the General inside but he stops me. He throws the yellow silk bag to Diego. "Put this in my cabin." He nods sharply at me and closes the door.

Diego leads me to another stairway leading down. Deeper gloom. The gun deck, I smell from the bitter saltpetre. Some little light filters in through the hatches on the maindeck, and I see the cannon, lined up at the closed gunports. I follow Diego through makeshift chambers parted by boards. Past a manger, hens scratching and pecking at the planks. Bodies lie sleeping wherever there is space enough on the floor. "The larboard men," Diego kicks a wayward leg as he passes. "At the changing of the watch, the starboard men will take their beds and they will rise to their business."

He darts into a cupboard and brings out a lumpen roll of

stuffed cloth. "You're in luck!" he grins. "Whyte's. He died last week."

He shows me, farther into the bow, to a narrow space on the floor: a corner made by the curve of the hull and an unused gun carriage. "As good a place as any," he sniffs.

I look about. I take in the distance to the stair – the narrow and dark places about this spot. The shadows where a man may lurk behind the posts. "Where do you sleep?" I ask.

"In the General's cabin." He looks upwards and astern. "Off the quarterdeck."

"Is there—"

He shakes his head. "The only private cabin in the ship. Even the gentlemen sleep in the armoury."

He unrolls the mat, and I stare at it, in all its meanness and discomfort. A biter leaps out from it. *What have I done? What have I done?* I have given up the haven of a cabin – for this.

He sits and pats the mat beside him. "You know," he says, bringing out the opal from the yellow silk bag, "you didn't need to steal this. He would have taken you anyway. To spite the Spaniard."

I sit beside him. "I wanted it. I wanted to take something from him."

He nods, raises one brow. "Heaven favours worthy desires."

Even in this dim light the opal works its magic, sending out rainbow shards to pierce the darkness. Motes of dust dance in its beams of red, orange and sparkling gold.

"What is it?" he asks.

I sigh, not looking at it. "The Glory of Cortés," I tell him. "A fire-opal. The conquistador Cortés took it from the Aztecas."

"Why did Don Francisco have it?"

"He was taking it to Lima, to the Viceroy of Perou. To show him and beg loan of his mine-builders."

"Then there are more? They will build opal mines in New Spain?"

"Plenty," I nod. "Mountains full of them." Worse luck for the poor souls they will send in to dig them out.

I stare at the pattern my feet make on the boards and back at Diego, lost in his treasure. I have little desire to share its secret with this man, but I don't want him to leave. I do not care to be left alone here yet.

I lean in. He smells musty: of the dried leaves in a cigarro. "This one is special." I turn it for him. "See the face carved into it."

He peers, eyes narrowed, his great shoulders hunched over it. The ship rolls. A dim ray of light falls upon it from an uncovered gunport, and I feel the intake of his breath on my cheek when he sees it: the face of the Sun God, carved into the stone by an ancient jewel worker.

"Putana di Dio," he whispers.

"It was sacred to them. The Spaniards took it. And everything else."

"Naturally," he grins. His face is become ugly. Lit with greed. "I find it is sacred to me too."

His knee splays wide and pushes into the tender flesh of my thigh. I shift a little, not too far.

"Still," he says, head to one side, to look at it from another angle. "It is a beauty. And with it you will buy your freedom."

"How so? I have given it to him already."

"He will take you to England."

England? "What use is that to me?"

"Because while they are happy to murder and kidnap and sell us like beasts of burden elsewhere, it is not lawful to keep a slave in England."

"Is that true?"

"It was their judgement in law," Diego says, turning the stone in his fingers. "That the air of England is *too pure an air for a slave to breathe*."

He says the last words with the tongue of an Englishman, but with bitterness.

I blink. Then that is why she called to me, through the stone.

"I have always been lucky," I tell him. The Fortunate One, my grandmother called me.

He puts the opal back in its silk bag, draws the ribbon and stands, crouching, one arm holding onto the timbers above him in the lowness of the deck. "There is no luck," he says, as if chiding a child. "You sail your own ship." He strides away, towards the stair, holding the gem in the silk bag closed tight in his fist.

He is wrong, of course. A man can sail his own ship. A woman must put herself in the way of one sailing in the right direction.

7

One night I have spent, wide-eyed and stiff-backed hard against the gun carriage. I have not left this spot. I cannot sleep for the tuneless sailors' songs, the rats scratching about my feet and the fear of what will happen to me. Nor have I tended to the most basic of my needs. But I can hold it no longer.

I stand and stride, faster than is natural, towards the stern. The ship sails easy – only a gentle roll. In the shadows to both sides, men watch from the darkness. There are whistles, the same catcalls and foul language. Different words, but the same meaning. I am now a whore and no longer puta, a blackamoor and not a negra. They are the same men, the same cabrones. I must be wary of them at all times.

I reach the stairway, and climb into the armoury, and up again, into the open deck. Deep lungfuls I breathe in, of the clear and rushing air. The spray is cool on my face, the salt is fresh and cleansing. The wind rises from behind me, whipping up my hair that escapes its binding. The sun warms my arms. I blink with the brightness.

Up another short stairway is the quarterdeck, where Diego said the General sleeps. I eye it with envy: how far and apart it is from the common men. Outside his cabin is the whipstaff, driving down through the decks to the great rudder steering us below. The solitary man on duty there nods at me.

From across the ship peals the bell that rings at the turning of the hourglass. A boy sings out:

Another turn / Let fall the sands,
Keep faith in God / And busy hands.

Then he calls: "Last turn before the change of watch!"

So soon all will be in commotion: the men at their leisure rushing up from below and those in the rigging and on deck dropping down to their beds. A sailor emerges from the gallery around the quarterdeck, pulling up his breeches. There must be the privies. I push past him, and barely make it in time to the holes cut into the planks.

I stand and arrange my skirts. Returning from the gallery, I survey the ship. It is not unlike the *Cacafuego*: a little town of business and industry. Men race up the ratlines above me, fast and sure. Barefoot and shirtless, they haul themselves along the yards to unfurl the sails. There are men at the topsail: tiny figures who look as if they could topple to the decks if there came but one high wave.

Around me, in the waist and on the foredeck, boys scrub the planks, and mend the ropes. From the hutches come bellows and curses, creaks and scratches. Mariners come up the steps, bent under the barrels of gunpowder on their shoulders. They stagger to where men sit sifting and drying it in the sun. Others bring weapons to a great pile on the foredeck, where the boys are at work cleaning them of the salt that will spoil them.

A vile stench hits me in the face as I see the men gutting fish, working fast as fishwives, putting the flesh to one side, guts, bones and heads kept back for boiling. Others shell peas and beans. I cover my nose, and see walking among them, the crow-like man in black I saw when first I came. He carries a book, his thumb holding his place until he gets past the foul smell of the fish. He takes it up again, reading as he walks, lips moving.

It feels – normal. The gulls ride the wind, as usual. The waves have the same froth on their peaks. The men are busy. There is nothing to fear.

I go below. Down to the dark shadows of the armoury. I peer into the Great Cabin and shrink back when I see it is full.

The General sits in his chair, feet up against the edge of the table. He drinks from a silver cup. Next to him a fair-haired gentleman. He leans on one arm, a cloud of golden hair falling towards the table like a lion's mane. Spite his unruly locks, he keeps his moustaches finely trimmed and he strokes them now, his forefinger barely able to keep from the tips of them.

The boy I saw from the *Cacafuego* carrying Don Francisco's sword is there. He serves the wine. He goes to pour a cup for Diego, who takes the jug from him, muttering, and pours his own. As he hands it back to the boy, Diego looks up and startles when he spies me, nearly dropping the jug. I too am surprised to see him there: among the Englishmen. Served by the page. Sitting next to the General. No one else looks up. I creep back into the shadows.

I am bold now. How fine of humour they are. How easy they keep their weapons here in the armoury: stacked against the wall, unsecured and open to all. How easy Diego is among them. A ship of discipline and good cheer.

I descend again to the gun deck. I must find something to do here. I cannot be idle. Beyond the manger, I find the steward's store behind an unlocked door. Barrels are stacked along each side, smaller crates and boxes on top of them. Something thick and black oozes from a barrel dropping thickly onto the floor below. There are chests of flour, sacks of beans and wheels of cheese that reek like old clogs. A bag of kola nuts to keep the water fresh. And – how curious. Here is a mortar – of wood, as we made them in Guinney, not stone as they fashion them in the New World – and two oar-like pestles. Five full sacks of rice, though we had none in the ration yesterday – eating instead of moulden bread, foul beans and the hard galleta they took from the *Cacafuego* that must be soaked in water before it can be swallowed.

I dip my hand into the rice and feel it running through my fingers, the pleasing roll of the grains in my palm. I wonder if it was taken from my country. It is what they do, the slaving ships, before they cross the ocean. Do these grains have in them the memory of the soil and rains of Guinney? Who sowed the seeds? Flooded the fields? Harvested the grains? Where are they now, these women? For it is women's work, the rice.

I tuck some grains into my hair behind my ear, as my grandmother did when I was taken from her. It was all she had to give: the seeds of my homeland, to take with me into the New World. It is of her I am thinking – of the last I ever saw of her face, her arms outstretched towards me, howling my name, *Macaia! Macaia!* – when something comes at me from behind, winds me in the stomach, and pulls me back, onto the floor.

Hands on me: one grabbing and squeezing my breast hard, another, foul-smelling, over my mouth and nose.

"What do you, witch? Poison our food?"

I bite down hard on the palm over my mouth. He howls in pain. I go to jump up, but another comes from the darkness and holds my legs down on the floor.

"Close your screeching, Pyke," shouts the man at my legs. Pyke hisses at him and pins my arms back. They carry me through the gun deck. Down one stairway, then another, my head first, like a carcass from the butcher's table. Down into the bowels of the ship.

"Hold still, blackamoor bitch," Pyke growls, ale strong on his breath. "Why has the General brought you here, if not for our pleasure?"

So dark. A musty smell – damp and the growing stench of the bilges. More cramped even than the gun deck. The sound of the pumps is deafening: a continual rattle and clank that pounds the head.

They stop when they can go no further – breathless, holding me only loosely now. I narrow my eyes to see better in the dark, search out the little light that shows the way to the steps.

What is the use of fighting? I know what is coming. There are only two of them. It will not kill me.

Above the sound of the pumps, something scrapes behind me – metal on metal. Dark as night though it is, I see we are by the prison. A thick door. Pascual's face at the bars. He rattles against them with a spoon.

"Bring her in here," he shouts in Castilian. "I'll show the bitch what for."

Footsteps from the stair: more of them. Coming to see the sport.

They crowd the low space like rats in the darkness, jostling for a sight of me. Heads crack against the beams. Their excitement rises. One brings a candle, the better to see by. Boys crawl through men's legs to the front, cheering and pumping fists in the air. I catch the eye of a thin lad sitting on his knees at the front. He blinks at me through a lock of black hair that falls over his eyes, open-mouthed like a simpleton.

Pyke and the other villain are at my head and feet, resting after their effort, sure of their prize. At Pyke's hip, his dagger shines in the low light.

Pascual rattles the bars. The pumps clank and clutter my senses. The men howl like wolves, hammering hilts of their knives against the boards. The boys cheer and whoop. Pascual scrapes the bars faster, laughing. *Nasty slut!* someone shouts. *Fuck the sorry jade!*

There comes a moment every time this happens. When you are taken, as other men look on. Sometimes one will help. Hold back an arm. *Let the wench be.* Sometimes they will not. You come to feel it – sharp behind the breastbone. The moment you know if a man will step in – and the beat of your heart that tells you he will not. Like the final drop of sand in an hourglass.

These men will not help me. I am on my own.

But I think also it is sport they hunger for – and I can give them that.

With my feet on the floor I bring my head sharp into Pyke's. I meet my mark, for there is the crunch of bone and a grunt like a pig under the knife.

I shoot my feet hard and fast into the groin of the man at my legs. He screams the high-pitched howl of a wounded dog and sinks to the boards.

The men roar with laughter. *She's hammered you good in the ballokes, Bonner!*

Pascual scrapes the bars faster, laughing.

I stand and face the mob of men. A wall of muscle and hard bone between me and the stair. At the front, the thin lad stares. He jerks his head towards the midship. His eyes follow the same direction, and back again. There, in the gloom, beyond the barrels piled high between me and my escape: another stair leading up.

I run. A hand grabs at my ankle and brings me down, hard on my elbows. I scramble for a barrel. My fingers graze its iron hoop. Another hand on my ankle, pulling me back, and then I reach it: the tiny gap between the iron and the timber, that I can – just – hook with the tip of my middle finger. It hovers on the very edge – until the ship dives, and rights it – and then rises, and I can pull it crashing down to roll behind me. A thud, a cry, the hand loosens on my foot and I run, pushing back more barrels as I go.

Crashes and screaming above the clank of the pumps. Pascual scrapes the bars, howling.

I reach the stair and turn: the whole mob of them, arms flailing, knees kicking, cries of pain and fury.

I do not stop. Up into the gun deck, using my hands ahead of my feet in the lowness of the space, back through the shadowy caverns of the ship. Past the store, the pecking hens, past the cannon – to the shaft of light that shows the way to the steps. Into the armoury, and beyond to the light and air of the foredeck as fast as the spirit of the wind.

8

The sky is low. It rumbles. Black clouds turn in on themselves in fury. Rain hammers the deck like a drum. It pours from the heavens, driving into me from every angle. In thick, fat drops it rebounds from the boards. It sluices across the deck with every rise and fall of the ship. I could not be wetter if I were in the sea.

What have I done? I have made of myself a coney in a trap. Within this ship and without, for no doubt the Spaniards' warships are raised against us now – and I, a runaway. And now I am sure of it: I have a baby in my belly that these men will be as little pleased to find among them as was Don Francisco.

The sickness roils my stomach and muddles my head. I cannot tell which way we sail, what is sea and what is sky. The confusion of my mind and the world around me is complete.

Soon the sun will set and take with it what little light there is. But I cannot go back down below. How long will it take to reach England? How long can I stay like this?

Through the driving rain, something moves by the stairway to the armoury. The hatch lifts. I pull my soaked mantle over my head and squint. A hand beckons. A pale face, luminous in the gloom. It blinks, impatient. The hand waves again.

I creep nearer. It is the thin boy who helped me in the hold.

"Come," he calls, over the drumbeat of the rain. "You'll be washed overboard."

"And serve myself up to the wolves?"

He wrinkles his nose. "Come. Into the armoury. Out the rain at least. Chaplain's here." He jerks his head down towards the Great Cabin. "They won't come for you in sight nor sound of him."

Ship boys learn quick enough where is safety. I shift myself to the stair and drop as a sodden heap into the armoury.

I cannot say it is dry in here. The water seeps into everything. The timbers are damp to touch. But mercifully no rainfall. It hammers above our heads now like shot against the boards. I wring out the water from my hair and clothes.

"Which one's the chaplain?" I ask the boy, peering through the open crack of the door to the Great Cabin.

He points to the man in black who reads as he walks. "Him that looks like he's eating a lime."

For the first time since I have been on this ship, I come close to laughing. The chaplain sits on a hard chair in the corner, away from the others. He wears a continual frown, whosoever he looks at. The gentlemen seem to disappoint and vex him in equal measure.

"Where are you from?" the boy asks. He does not ask my name.

"Here and there about."

"I'm Thomas," he says. "Carpenter's boy."

I nod.

"You can't sleep on deck in this rain," he looks up to the hatch.

"And I cannot sleep below," I snap at him.

"You can," he nods shyly. "Stay close to me."

"And you will fight them off?" I look pointedly at his thin arms.

"I do well enough."

This I cannot believe, for he has bruises on his flesh where the sleeves of his smock fall short.

"Come. I'll show you." He goes to the stair to descend.

"You said to stay near the chaplain—" I start.

"Be calmed. We stay close enough."

He disappears down the stairs. I take one look at the door to the Great Cabin and I follow.

"First," Thomas holds up one pale finger, "you go no further. At night, the gentlemen sleep above, so stay here beside me." He shows me his bed mat, behind the stairway, backed by the mizzen mast, and barricaded on all other sides by broken posts and yards he has gathered like a magpie.

"Second," he says, pulling at my sodden skirts, "lose these. Better, stitch them into breeches, which cannot be got up. I have needle and thread. At night, you tie a fast knot in the waist."

I look at him. "And this works?"

He shrugs. "It gives you more time."

I pull on his elbow to make him face me. "They use you like this?" This child of ten. Perhaps older: his eyes are sunk and weary.

He pulls away from me to sit on the mat. I sit beside him. "The Spaniards break a man on the capstan for such a sin. They crush every bone in his body and throw him into the sea. You should tell the General."

"Boy before me told," he scoffs. "He found himself in the sea instead." He looks up at me and seems younger than before. "Tale-bearing angers the men. Still, I must live alongside them."

"Have you no friend, no protector?"

"Only Him above. Who cares not a turd for such as me."

He scrambles around beneath his bedding to bring out a little bird half-carved from a peg. He takes his knife to it now, marking the feathers.

"Why did you help me in the hold?"

He makes a deep cut with the knife to mark the edge of the wing. "I didn't like it." He shakes a shaving of wood to the floor. "I thought I would, but I didn't."

I sit with him while he carves in silence. He is right. It is a good spot. A full view of the deck all the way to the bow. The stairway above us, the mizzen mast at our backs. And the gentlemen, as he says, within spitting distance above. For all the good that may do us.

We hide here in the shadows, we two, when evening prayers calls the men to the maindeck. The rain has stopped, the ship sails steady. The men thunder up the stairs above our heads, giving us no notice at all in the darkness. One hundred and more feet, leathered or bared depending on their rank, slap against the steps in a cloud of dust. When they are gone it is quiet as the grave. Just the creaking of the ship, the scratching of the rats and Thomas' knife working the peg.

"Are you from Aethiopia?" he asks without looking up.

"Guinney," I tell him. "Least, that's what Englishmen call it."

"You look like the Queen of Sheba. She was Aethiopian."

I know the story. *I am black and I am comely*, she said. I saw a picture of her once in Ciudad de México. The only time I ever saw a black woman painted with oils. But he gave her golden hair, the painter. In any case, I think she never hid under a stairway with the rats.

After prayers and the changing of the watch, the men return and settle down for the night. They fall to their dice and their carvings. Some of them have books and they try to read in the moonlight breaking through the gunports. Presently four men return to the stairway, bearing strange instruments of wood and metal. Well dressed in linen shirts. Grumbling and dragging their feet.

"Who are they?" I hiss at Thomas.

"Musicians."

"For the General?"

He nods. "They play in the Great Cabin in the eventide. For him and the gentlemen."

I watch them ascend into the armoury. The idea emerges, full-grown. The Queen of Sheba never waited for Solomon to come to her. She went to him in all her finery. I see a better way to preserve myself than stitching my body into breeches.

9

Where there is music there is dancing, and where there is dancing is a man who will do what he can for me.

I was trained to dance before I could walk. Saba, my father's aged aunt, led the girls' training. At first, in the village, and later, in the sacred grove deep in the forest. Old men still talked of the beauty and grace she possessed in her youth. By the time I was passed into her care, lines like knife wounds marked her face and she walked with stiffness in her knees.

She trained us for hours at a time, sometimes throughout the night, never sleeping unless we had mastered a step. We danced till our legs felt on fire, slow to leap away when Saba switched our calves with a sapling.

Dance is transformation, she barked as she switched. Through dance you become women. Through dance you call up your new lives.

I never completed my training. There was no time. Am I then a woman?

Through dance, she said, as we girls moved as one, minds and bodies in unity, knees bending at the same time, hips low and swaying, you cleave together. You weave yourselves into one cloth, tight and binding. You belong to each other.

What would Saba say if she saw what I did? Brazen, dancing alone, as if I am above other women. Dancing for one man. To provoke his lust and not his respect. I belong with no other women. I am a loose thread. Yarn unwoven.

He watched me with wide and blinking eyes, his pewter cup held at his cheek but never to his lips. I kept my eyes low, lifting them now and again, only to his. I cannot but imagine the face of the ever-angry chaplain, the lion-haired man, or the other gentlemen. Diego, I saw only when I left, commanded by the General to repair to his cabin to *recover* from my *exertions*. He held the door for me, glancing fixedly away.

So here I find myself. In the General's cabin. A place of safety, away from the wolves. From most of them. One unwanted man is better than a pack.

The cabin is small, but well-situated – off the raised quarterdeck, where the common men are not permitted. There is one bed. A slim thing, yet made of wood, with a feather-mattress and not an unrolled mat. Two chests, one small table, bolted to the floor, a chair and one uneven stool, which will not stay steady, even when the sea is calm. Two glazed windows on either side let in a goodly deal of light, but no fresh air, which is much needed for it is close and stale.

It smells musty – of animal hides, and I see why. Books, there are, everywhere. Piled on the polished boards, and more on a lipped shelf by the door. Here there are instruments too: an astrolabe, like Pascual used on the *Cacafuego*. Other devices hang from nails on the walls. On the table is a globe made of bronze with the pole star, fashioned in silver, passing above it.

Pictures are fixed to every wall. Fine pictures, in inks and painted colours: sea-cliffs, yellow sands and the mouths of rivers drawn very like to life. Two oiled portraits: of the General, and the English Queen, face each other on opposite walls.

Here, I have met the page, and I discover why he is dressed richly for a ship boy, and why Don Francisco was so careful to show him fine manners. And why, come to that, he is free to enter the General's cabin without a knock.

They are kin: cousins, as the page, John, likes to remind me, at every opportunity. Which is often, since he comes here whenever he can be sure to find me alone. When the General is inspecting the ropes on deck with Diego, or with the chaplain before prayers in the waist.

He looks to be about fourteen years of age. His hair falls in dark curls to his narrow shoulders. There is even a likeness between them, now I know to look for it. In the jaw and in the nose – not in the eyes, for John's are dark and smiling.

His first voyage at sea, he says. He tells me of his mother, who did not want him to sail, and his sisters who waved him away with their underskirts held high against the blue of the sky so he saw them for miles as he walked the lonely path to the sea. Of his father, who is dead, and his famous cousin who is something like a deity.

He is a talker, this boy. He gushes like an open leak in the bilges.

"It must have made it easier on your mother," I say, looking at the General's stern face in the portrait above us. "That you sail with kin."

He shakes his head. "Not a bit of it. She said she knows well what sort of 'ventures he seeks and she didn't want me to have a finger of 'em."

I look at him in surprise. "Why do you disobey your mother?"

"*He* needs me." He nods at the General's portrait with pride. "Well – not me. But my drawings. For the logbook."

For they are his, these fine pictures about the cabin – save I suppose, the oiled portraits. A fine painter for a boy. He draws the coast and the marks of the land, the curious creatures and the people they encounter. "When we get home, the Queen herself will see them." He puffs his boyish chest. "D'you want to see more?" He kneels at the sea-chest at the foot of the bed before I say yes.

He brings them out, placing them with care on the table. I take the unsteady stool, and sit with him, rocking with the rise and fall of the sea.

Here are pitch-dark cliffs soaring above the red-and-yellow

ship testing monstrous waves. Indios wearing skirts of feathers, carrying bows and arrows and pikes. This one, of sea-wolves warming their bellies in the sun, is so like to life I could be watching them through the window.

Here are the creatures I saw in Perou. A great herd of them looking up at me. I realise I have been gazing at it a while when he says: "You like the camel-sheep."

"Is that what they are?"

"D'you not think? The bodies of sheep, but long necks. Have you been to Perou?"

I shake my head.

"Everywhere they are there. Mighty strange – and strong. They spit like sailors. Indians use 'em as we do horses. Tasty too."

"You *ate* them?"

"So hungry we was by then. Nothing but dried pengwyn-meat for a month."

"What's a pengwyn?"

"A big fowl." He holds out his hand at the height of his waist. "With a white head. Can't fly nor run to save their sorry skins. I got one here somewhere."

He rustles the papers and finds it. A fat bird on hind legs like a dog begging for scraps. Head too small for its body, orange ears hunched into his neck.

A picture curls behind the pengwyn. A battle: a building afire. Soldiers on a flat roof aim muskets at men running away. Coming from the building, a man carries a wounded comrade on his back. Dark blood drips from a gash in his thigh. Eyes closed, his head lolls back.

"That's for me," John's eyes flash. He takes it, but with care. "It's not for the logbook. I drew it from my head. I weren't there."

"It is the General – the wounded man?"

"At Nombre de Dios," he nods. "Where he made his fortune. Came back with so much Spanish silver he used it as ballast. Near enough killed him though."

It is not possible to mistake the man carrying him, striding through the musket-wielding Spaniards. "And Diego saved him?"

He nods, running his fist into the corners to make it lie flat. "He wouldn't leave the treasure house, though the Spaniards were at the door. Diego carried him away. They were together always, after that," says John. "Seven years since."

He stares at the image. The corners are flat now, but still he presses them with his fist. He puts it facing downwards, at the very bottom of the chest. The General, I wager, does not know of this picture, nor would he be glad of it.

John takes up the other paintings from the table. He puts them in the chest and closes it. He sits for a moment, swaying with the roll of the ship then asks: "Can I draw *you*?"

"Why?"

"Cos you're – diff'rent."

He unrolls his leather case and takes out a quill and ink.

"Are there often… women here?" I ask him. "You take on girls at port, perhaps?"

He shakes his head. "General says lustfulness is a sin and we're doing God's work. You're the only one. By Jis, he's never had a *woman* in his cabin."

He raises his brow at me, then back to the page. He holds the quill so low on the nib it looks like the marks come direct from his hand.

Already he has made good an image of my hair, loose and uncovered, here in the cabin. So admired it was at home, for it is strong and thick. My mother oiled and combed it at night till it shone.

John draws with great skill the curls about my face and makes two quick lines between my brows.

I did not know till I saw it that I am so angry.

10

One week have I been in the General's bed.

He uses me as he sees fit, of course. But he seems not to profit greatly by it. He tires of me already. And then what? He will turn me back down below. Or worse.

When Diego has served the gentlemen their eventide meal, he comes up to prepare the cabin. For two, sometimes three turns of the hourglass, we are alone. The men call to each other from the ropes and yards. Music from the English instruments – viol and pipe, John tells me – drifts up from the Great Cabin below. The men coming up for the dog-watch sing psalms, those going down, their lusty ditties. I think of Thomas below the stairs. I should not have left him there alone.

We talk, Diego and I. We dance around the edges of what we will not say. He asks about the places I have been: of Acapulco and Manila and Perou. He tells me of Cuba, where he was born, and Tierra Firme, where he joined the General. He tells me of the men aboard the ship, those who are amiable, and those I must keep from as if they are rid with plague. I do not tell him I have some experience myself of these matters.

Mostly, he talks about the General: of his genius for navigation, his daring in battle and the vast riches in his hold that will bring honour and glory – ay and to every man who returns with him – when he sails home to England.

Then the music below will stop. There will be a count of two-score and ten before the General himself appears in the cabin. He will nod to me a curt *good even* and exchange a friendly word with Diego. He will wash his hands and his face with water from the ewer in a bowl, and pick at his teeth with his silver toothpicker. Then we three will bed us down for the night: two in the bed and one on the floor.

Tonight, Diego comes before the music has even started. His hands are empty. No sweetmeat for me, not a date nor dainty from the General's table in his usual way.

I look up from the bed where I sit patching a smock. The light is low: only one candle. My eyes tire. I blink. "Good even."

He closes the door and says, still turned from me: "I told you before we are done with New Spain. But we will make one more stop."

I put down the needle. "Where?"

I go to the window, but it is dark. The cloud is low and the moon yet to rise. My heart races. I count in my head. Seven days' sail from Zonzonate.

"Guatulco," he says. "Why are you so frit?"

"I am not frit," I pace to the bed. I pick up the needle again, though my hand shakes too much to hold it.

Below in the Great Cabin, the viol player plucks his strings in tuning. The melody starts, rising and falling like the wind.

"Only that – I am known there."

I give up the sewing and sit on my hands to steady them. "So?"

He straightens the cabin, picking up books from the floor to put on the shelf, or in neater piles on the boards. He takes from the table the bronze globe I have been toying with and puts it back on the shelf by the astrolabe.

"You know the penalty for a runaway," I tell him. "Worse! Now, I am a runaway found with heretics."

"They have no power here."

"And if they take the ship?"

"They won't." He gathers up the charts and other papers and puts them into the General's sea-chest.

From outside comes the final call for the change of the watch, the boy's voice reedy and wavering. Footsteps run from the gun deck up through the waist, a heavy man leaps down from a yard.

"They don't expect us," says Diego. "They are defenceless. Barely are they men. They are gutless – like women." He shoots me a glance I cannot decipher. "Soft as ripe figs. We do as we please."

More musicians have joined the viol: a pipe and drum. A fast and merry jig. Laughter. Jugs clink as they meet the table. I have not been called upon to dance there since the General claimed me for his own.

I take up the needle and smock to put in the chest by the window.

In truth, they do rest easy now, the Spaniards. The Indios no longer fight back. The Cimarrones who escaped slavery keep in their booby-trapped forts in the mountains. Enemies with guns and shot are mighty rare.

But still my mind runs. "There is a judge in Guatulco, a vicious devil. He has the running of the town. Slaves hauled to the whipping post for no reason. I was there not three weeks ago and on the gibbet was a girl-child."

Diego stops at the shelf. His hand falls, his shoulder bone sinking beneath his bared skin.

"And what if the General puts me ashore in Guatulco?" I cannot stop my fretting now. "I am done for."

Diego turns slowly to face me. "I am sure you know how to soften a vicious judge. Open your legs for him and all will be well. I fancy *your* skin will not be burned with boiling oil."

I flinch as though he has hit me.

"You will land on your feet – after some time on your back," he nods towards the bed. "As you have here."

This is the cause for his fury? I slam the chest closed.

"*You* left me to those wolves." I stab a finger to the decks below. "What can I do? If he turns me out of here –"

Diego glares at me. Below in the Great Cabin, feet take to the boards. The jig whirls faster.

Diego stands so close I smell the grease on him from the ropes and the smell of cigarros on his breath. I brace myself for the blow. I can almost feel the sting of it biting my cheek. But he hisses at me instead. Barely can I hear him above the music and the feet thumping below.

"He is not a monster. I thought you a wily wench, when first I saw you. Find something else to keep you here." He turns and is gone with a slam of the door.

Something else?

Por vida de Dios, I have nothing else!

Fuck him to the Virgin in Heaven and back, this man who is so blind.

Below, the music comes to an end. The General will be here soon. I start counting.

APRIL, 1579

GUATULCO

15°40'N

II

The ship shakes with every firing of the cannon. Black smoke hangs around the windows. How is it possible the ship still sails? This is no warship. Barely is she seaworthy. I cover my ears but the gun-roar shudders through me.

Below, metal scrapes as swords and arquebuses are hauled up from the armoury. Men curse and holler as they carry barrels of powder up the narrow stairs.

Lift it you turd!

Get you to the Devil.

Shouting from the deck, as the men call to each other for help with their armour.

Christ Jesus that pinches!

It is Easter on Sunday. To think! They make war in Holy Week.

Pulleys creak and ropes snap as they ready the launch. Men leap aboard, weapons and armour crashing. As the guns die, I hear their idle chatter as they wait to leave. Not frit. Not worried at all about the battle to come.

Do you think they have wine? We've had none since Valperizo.

I've a mind for wine and a woman. General's not sharing his about.

It must have been like this – men high in jest and merry-making – when they made ready to take my village. They were Englishmen too, though I never knew of such a place as England then.

They too would have dressed for battle on their ship, at anchor in the bay. Helped each other with the straps on their leather jerkins. Laughed at the badly-fitting helmets that came down over their eyes.

Nor did they come in fear of death, for they knew we could not match their weapons. Our bowsmen were our pride. Expert marksmen. Arrows dipped with poison that killed a man in minutes. Useless, against gunpowder and shot.

I was but a child. Trembling and crying. Huddled with my sisters, my brother and grandmother, we waited for the terror to come to us.

The thought of it makes the very walls close in on me. The cabin is at once my mother's house, again in flames. I step out onto the quarterdeck.

Such a commotion as I have ever seen on a ship. Weapons everywhere. Piled high in the pinnace and on the deck. The men gather round, picking out what they will take. Above me men carry crossbows and arquebuses into the fighting-tops.

The boys are at work in the waist. They fashion little balls of hemp to stuff with nails and other flesh-ripping metals. They roll them in a paste of gunpowder, pitch and sulphur, ready to light with fire and throw at the Spaniards. Diego comes to fill a sack with them. For the first time since ever I saw him he wears boots – great leather over-boots reaching above his knees. The boys test a hemp-ball now to show him. It explodes above the sea, sending up a torrent of water like fire from a volcano.

These others Diego loads into his sack will find their mark on the ships in the harbour and the houses and people in the town. I close the door.

Never will I get used to these sounds: the whistle of shot and the roar of the guns.

When I think of the day I first heard them, it comes to me only in silence. I see but the images. The palm thatch of the roof above us in flames. Black smoke billowing down and all around. My mother, wide-eyed. The open mouth of my brother, baby Fode, as though he howls in silence. My sister Dura wiping the stinging smoke from her eye.

Then, the first sight of the devils when they tore down the hanging at our door and broke in, laughing.

Their bodies shone, lit by the flames. Armour, I know now: mere corselets and helmets. Then, I thought them idols made of metal, come to life. Great beards like weeds masked half their faces, the rest burned raw by the sun.

The weapons, we had not seen before. They signified nothing. It was their feet that drew our eyes. Such dirty boots they wore, thick with mud. They had come through the swamp, which way we thought none could ever come. They stamped the oozing mess on the clean rushes on the floor. Bringing filth inside a house: unthinkable. We stared at their feet in horror, no thought nor understanding of what was to come.

From the open deck outside the cabin, a trumpet sounds. "To God and Saint George! The day will be ours!" calls the General. A single shot from a culverin, a great splintering crack and clap of thunder from the shore, and a cheer from the Englishmen.

Now the gunfire begins in earnest and at once the sounds of that other day come back to me too. The pounding, as though the world was ending. Thunder as the living trunks of our vast barricade fell. Screaming as they burst in. Crackling as fire-burning arrows fell upon each dwelling: on the galleries and porticoes, the roofs and the fences. The sound was so big, it filled everything.

We were safe, the elders said. We had survived sieges before. This time we had been besieged for many months, but we had rice enough in our pantries and water in the wells for many more. The swamp was impassable. Our barricade unbreachable – a living wall of trees and vines woven together over decades.

An impossible barrier, they said. Only devils could break it.

But they did not know our enemies had made a bargain with devils. Had met a very devil army, sweeping in from the sea on floating forts of timber. Had led the metal-shining devils to where we waited behind our barricade.

I curl between the bed and sea-chest, my head tight into my knees to stop the smell that comes to me now as it did that first day: bitter gunpowder. I cannot tell if the stench that follows – of burning, charred wood and thatch and flesh – is in my head or here and now.

How much time has passed, I do not know.

Through the window I see the pinnace is gone. Smoke billows from the smashed broadsides of a ship in the harbour. Faint cries and the clash of metal from the shore. Amid the whistle of the shot, the peal of a church bell.

The gunfire from the land wanes. There is instead – singing. The view from the window is too low. *What is happening?* I open the door a crack. The deck is empty, save for one man, standing with his back to the commotion on the shore.

I step outside. The breeze cools my hot cheek. The sand laid to guard against fire scratches my feet.

The man looks up. It is he: the gentleman with the brown velvet cap. He holds my gaze with a scowl and I freeze.

The upper deck. Only the General and his close men go there. I dart to the steps. From here, the sounds are clearer. The bell has stopped. The voices carried on the wind are of triumph and merriment. No more shot nor gunfire. The man with the velvet cap goes below.

From the treetops that surround the town, parrots caw and monkeys hoot. Faint singing comes from below, where houses lie between the hills and the sea. There is but one tall building – the church. Beside it, the wide courthouse. Low dwellings of stone surround the plaza, flat-roofed storehouses line the path into the forest. The thatch on them all is afire. Doors hang off hinges, smashed and broken.

In the plaza, the Englishmen roll barrels towards the shore. A mob gathers on the north side of the church, a clear view from where I stand. The gunner Fludd is easy to mark for his cap – made of *camel hair* he says, and surely does it reek of some animal. He dips – Madre de Dios it is a chalice – into a barrel and drinks from it.

Something moves in a clearing in the woods above the town and I see ten, a dozen people there, looking down to their burning homes. In the plaza, Diego leads prisoners down the steps of the courthouse, followed by Englishmen pushing them forward at the points of their swords.

Por Dios, I am in it to the neck if he puts me ashore after this.

As I scan the paths and open spaces of the town, a shadow falls beside me onto the gunwale. I do not need to turn, I know well who it is. I thought him ashore, but he alone has the habit of creeping silently about the ship. He comes one step further. The board creaks. I turn as if I have only just understood he is there.

"General," I say, trying for brightness.

He looks past me to the town, arms behind him. As if he were a passer-by taking in a fine view.

He waits, not owning me till he is ready. All in his own time.

"Well, Maria!" He turns to me at last. "Do you – enjoy the scene?"

A cry from the shore draws my eye: a mob of many heads and limbs. The men at the edge kick and punch at whoever is in the midst of it. From the feet of the mob, a figure crawls out on arms and knees. He staggers before he is knocked over again. Two men hold him down as another aims a kick at his head.

"You see now – how God provides – for Englishmen," the General says, in his halting way.

I do not tell him it looks as if the Englishmen provide for themselves. Instead, I dare to ask: "Will we leave now?"

"Nay. I have some business first. With the authorities."

My heart sinks.

"Here they come now." He gestures to the shore, where the

pinnace is setting off. Diego and the prisoners are at the bow, more men, chests, barrels and weapons are loaded behind. On the shore a second group of men wait with piles of plunder for the pinnace to return. I see Thomas among them, hopping from one foot to the other on the hot stones.

"And you must come with me." The General puts out his arm.

The thought chills my blood for I have seen who is among the prisoners in the pinnace. "Why?"

"Because they will not expect it."

12

The boat draws near. A shadow passes over Diego's face when he sees me beside the General. We have not spoken since our quarrel. He ropes the boat alongside the ship and puts out a hand to the first prisoner. "Come see our General. He is a good man."

It is he, the judge. Even fatter than I remember. He tries to stand, refusing Diego's hand to steady himself, though he shakes like a newborn goat. He turns to the man in priest's frock behind him: "Mark it, Padre! I go aboard only under threat of violence." He points a ruby-jewelled finger to where we wait on the foredeck.

"There will be no violence," Diego says. "My General wants only to talk with you."

The judge climbs up. He looks from the General, to me, and back again, rooted to the spot so the priest who comes next must nudge him out of the way.

The sight of him makes me want to sink into the boards.

"You think it fit," the judge spits, "to welcome the representative of his Excellency the Viceroy of New Spain with your whore by your side? In Holy Week!"

The General looks down his nose at the judge. "Carey –" he invites the man with the golden hair to answer for him.

"You dishonour our guest, Alcalde," says the gentleman,

Carey. "She travels with us a while. She helps with the victuals."

I look at him in surprise. I had not imagined he had noticed me.

"I know what she helps you with," says the judge. "I know her. She has been before me."

Diego pushes the judge towards the General with the hilt of his sword. "And now," he says in a low voice, speaking Castilian, "you find you are called before her. And I caution you to mind how you speak to her."

The judge clasps and unclasps his hands, his fingers bulging like overstuffed tamales around his many rings. Putana di Dio, I will pay for this.

Laughing and roaring, the Englishmen climb aboard. They wear altar vestments and crucifixes around their necks. They call each other Padre. Vile Pyke takes a damask altar cloth from his neck to wipe the sweat from his brow. He spits on it and scrubs at a bloody cut on his forearm. The priest watches, one hand to his stomach, as if he might be sick.

The General breaks his silence. "Are these the only men in the town?" He inspects them like steers at market.

"The only ones who did not run fast enough," says Diego. "We found the vicar in his church worshipping his images and false idols. Naturally we have taken care of them for the sake of his soul."

"*Pyke* took care of 'em," laughs one of the men.

"The judge was in his seat at the courthouse," Diego goes on, "ordering fresh barbarities upon some poor man, who took the opportunity to run into the hills. The court officials ran likewise. As for the Alcalde – you can see for yourself he is not fit to run."

"How dare you interfere with the justice of New Spain!" shouts the judge. "That prisoner was a fugitive – a slave and an arsonist!"

The General turns, speaking in a low and even tone directly into the judge's face. "Do not talk to *me* of the justice of

New Spain. I have seen how your traitorous Viceroy keeps his word. I was at San Juan de Ulúa when he attacked my cousin Hawkins' fleet after assuring us we would not be harmed. Do you know how many of my countrymen were killed by his villainy? How many of those who survived his cowardly attack were dragged to the scaffold and burned? How much he stole from us? The goods and coin in the ships we were forced to abandon – and which he sunk?

"No!" the General shouts. "Your Viceroy has killed enough of my countrymen. And now, I learn in Valperizo, there are more in the cells at Lima waiting to be burned!"

"Heretics!" says the judge, but quieter now. His eyes flick from the deck to his burning courthouse on the shore.

"Good Christians," the General lowers his voice. "Captain Oxnam sailed with me. I know him well."

He smooths his jerkin and turns from the judge. "Now." He speaks louder for the sake of his men who crowd around him. "Unlike your Viceroy, there is no need to fear me, for I am a man of my word. On my ship your lives will be protected as well as my own. But you must do something for me first."

He strides off to go below. Catching at my eye as he passes, he motions me to follow.

"Come now and see your quarters," says Carey. The judge and the priest shuffle to keep ahead of the point of Diego's sword at their backs.

I am about to fall in behind them when I stop to see what the men are struggling to pull aboard. The plunder from the pinnace lies in three piles on the deck: of victuals, weaponry and treasure. Now a dozen of them heave on the ropes, straining with the effort.

"Pull!" Pyke shouts and here it comes. Something vast and shining that sends the sun flashing back into the sky, and a clang that echoes as it is hauled aboard. The men roar in their great delight.

Malhaya Dios, I shudder and cross myself. It is the church bell of Guatulco.

13

When I catch up with the General, they are heading to the hold, where he will show them the treasures he has stolen and the Cage where Pascual lingers.

I turn instead to the Great Cabin. The boys are there already, setting out dishes of fruits from the town. I take a guayaba and eat it at the window that looks to shore. The smoke from the burning ship at harbour has thinned, but still it can be seen high in the air. The sky is clear. It will be seen for many leagues in every direction.

In all my life here in New Spain I have not seen an official of the realm nor a man of religion used this way. These Englishmen have come from the Southern Straits, pillaging and assaulting all the while – and still the Spaniards cannot catch them. How much longer can their fortune hold? My fortune too, I do not forget. When the Inquisitors came for Master Symons in Ciudad de México, it was enough to have me thrown in the cells, to be examined for the taint of his heresy. Three months I passed with the rats in the darkness. I, a mere girl of his household, then not yet sixteen.

So if I am found here, with Luteranos who have committed such outrages. What is the punishment for that? I do not have enough necks to break nor bones to burn.

Footsteps approach the cabin door. The General speaks soft

and low. If I did not understand the words I might think him soothing a crying child, such is the sweetness of his voice. But he is saying: "He will send for you, your Viceroy, to obtain information about me. When he does, you must tell him that he is not to kill Oxnam and the Englishmen held in Lima, for if they are killed it will cost him two thousand Spaniards. I shall hang them myself and send him their heads."

He is smiling as he opens the door. In he comes, followed by the judge and the priest whose mouths are drawn open in horror. The judge finds fury afresh when he sees I am here.

The lion-haired officer Carey follows, sticking to the General like his shadow. Then others of the General's close circle: a tangle of four men pushing against each other to stand nearest him. Steward Legge and Bosun Winter come in, then the chaplain, Fletcher.

Diego comes last. The men part grudgingly for him to make his way to the side of the General.

I pour for each man a cup of wine and go to leave but the General puts a hand to my arm. "Stay."

He turns to the Spaniards: "Sit, please. We will dine shortly. But first," he addresses the judge: "You will write a letter giving me authority to enter the town."

"You have already entered the town!" the judge splutters.

"Indeed I have not. If my men were a little excitable at seeing land and disobeyed my orders, I cannot say. But I have not set foot in Guatulco."

"And if I do not write this letter?"

"Then it will go very badly for you."

"You will return our goods?"

The General leans back in his chair, joining his fingertips. "I will not. I came here to recover the sum that your Viceroy stole from my cousin Hawkins eleven years ago, and I carry authorisation from my Queen to commit whatever... unpleasantries... are necessary for this purpose. Thirty thousand pounds we lost! I doubt your sorry town has riches of that sort."

"But the grain," begs the judge, "the wine. You have taken everything. We will starve."

"It is bad wine." The General grimaces, setting his cup back on the table. "You may have a cask back. And some of these – whatever they are," he gestures to the untouched corncakes, "when you have written the authorisation."

"And then you will go?"

The General nods.

"Which way?" The judge's brow hangs low over his eyes.

"First, we stop at Acapulco," says the General, and I burn with fear. For if he does not set me down here, I cannot return to Acapulco! The Viceroy's soldiers are there. His gunships. I cannot be found with these men!

The General holds up a hand and without a word, up jumps Legge and passes him a chart rolled around a wooden pole. "This was made for me in Lisbon," he says, taking four cups from the men nearest him to weigh down each corner. "It cost me eight hundred cruzados, can you believe it?"

The malice is gone. He is like a boy. He points out special marks and features of the map – the island Seylan, the south side of Nova Guinney so newly navigated and charted – as if he is with a friend who shares a passion for such things.

The judge looks on in disbelief, clutching at the table edge. His rings are gone, fingers puffed and sore where they have been prised away.

"See here," the General gently strokes the chart to flatten it. "There are three ways for me to get home. The way I have come, by Chilley. Or this way, by Cathay and the Cape of Good Hope." He points to the southernmost tip of Affrica.

"And the third way?" asks the judge.

"Ah," says the General, taking up the cups. The chart rolls back in on itself like a porpentine. "A man who tells his secrets to his enemy is a fool!"

He passes the chart back to Legge.

"There is no third way," the judge blusters.

"There is indeed, and you will know it soon enough when

you find a fleet of Englishmen in these waters. I have lately discovered this route," he smiles at the judge. "It will no longer be necessary for us to come by Magellan's Strait and go to so much expense and trouble. All we desire is to trade. But we are turned away from every port. Prevented even from taking on water and other supplies."

The judge is stern-faced. "We do not trade with heretics."

"But you will," says the General. "Because this is just the start of it. Do you think I am alone? Do you think I am the only Englishman who will come here to relieve you of the jewels from your fingers, the grain in your granaries – the treasures in your holds? The Queen of England prepares a fleet as I speak. And if your King does not give us licences to trade, we will come through my new route and carry away all the silver. No longer can you think this ocean your own Spanish lake."

He leans back to reach the pouch at his waist and brings out the fire-opal.

"Pretty, is it not?" He holds up the stone to catch the light. "I took it from one of your countrymen. A prized gem of the Viceroy's collection. Mine now. See here, how the face of Our Lord shines from it! A wonder indeed – a miracle."

The judge stares at him with fury.

"An opal," the General goes on. "My favourite of all the jewels for it has the colours of them all." The gem sparkles and shines: orange and golden rays seem to shoot from his very fingers. "And I see New Spain has them in abundance."

"How fitting that you like them so well," spits the judge. "The opal is the stone of thieves."

"Is it?" the General laughs. "I did not know."

Carey coughs and intones looking upwards:
It gifts the bearer acutest sight
But clouds all other eyes with thickest night.
So that plunderers bold in open day
Secure from harm can bear their spoil away.

"Thank you for the recitation, Carey," the General snaps sideways. He sets the opal back on the table. "Now, do not be a fool. Write the letter. I must have it for the sake of my Queen. You can tell your Viceroy you were forced at the point of a knife, it matters not to me."

"I have such a knife," Diego, brings out a dagger from his hip. "If it should aid you in your writing."

The judge stares at him. Winter hands him parchment, a quill and ink. The judge writes furiously, looking up every now and then at Diego, who plays with the point of his blade across the table.

"There's a good fellow," the General nods.

The priest of Guatulco has not dared say a word. His eyes pass from the judge to the General to see when he might safely interject. "The church vestments," he pleads. "The reliquaries. The chalice! We must... May we... have them back?"

The General's triumphant smile disappears in the instant. He leans forward, hand raised as if he would strike the priest. Instead he snatches the rosary from his neck.

"Why do you wear this?" he spits, throwing it to the corner.

The Spaniards are horrified. I find I am too.

"Yes!" shouts the General. "You ought indeed be grieved. You are not Christians but idolaters! You call us heretics? You, who shut the light of the Gospell in darkness!"

The priest raises his eyes to the face roaring in fury above him. He rubs his neck where the snatched beads grazed the skin.

"You dare to talk to me of your vestments! Your reliquaries! Your chalice! You worship these things instead of the Saviour, our Christ!"

The Englishmen nod and bang the table. "Aye! Papistry! Monkery! Whores of Rome!"

Save for the chaplain. Fletcher stares at the broken crucifix. His hand shakes a little on the table, fingers squeezing into his palm over and again.

The General seems set to continue bellowing when a knock at the door stops him. The boys come in with more food. A fine haul from the kitchens and storehouses of Guatulco.

Roasted fowls and bacon, fresh pork, cornbread, beans and greens stewed with pepper and spices, cocoa-nuts, melons and plantains.

They set down the dishes and the General reorders the plates, lining each one exactly in the centre of the table. He is very careful to put the meat in front of the Spaniards.

I see it instantly, what he does. A wonder, this man's appetite for small victories. He waits for them to protest, like a cat with his mice. Which man will it be? Which will be the braver?

It is not the man I'd have wagered on. The trembling vicar of Guatulco speaks: "Forgive us. It is Lent. We cannot eat meat."

The General pauses for a heartbeat, then holds his arms to the heavens. He looks sorely grieved. "Forgive me. Some fish for our guests," he calls to a boy at the door. "Tis Holy Monday. The papists cannot eat meat."

He gestures to the stool beside him. "Maria. Sit with us." Never have I sat with him at the table. "Will you take the pork?"

Ten years now, since Fray Calvo baptised and confirmed me a Catholic. I trust in the Most Holy Trinity, three persons and only one true God. As for the rest, I confess much of it is a mystery to me. So why heretics eat meat in Lent and we cannot, I do not know.

But that is not the question for me now. Rather, which of these sparring cocks do I back?

I am in it to the neck with these devils. There will be no saving me if the Spaniards catch me now. My life is in his hands.

Also I am hungry and the honeyed meat smells good.

"Thank you. Yes, I will."

He beams at me as though I am a dog who has learned a new trick.

14

When first I saw Ciudad de México, coming through the mountain passes and valleys on the long walk from Veracruz, I thought I was dreaming. I had seen nothing like it before – nor will again, I do not doubt.

The roof of the cathedral shone as if it were solid gold. Sparkling canals wove through the city, little canoes bobbing in the water, like cacao pods on the breeze. Broad streets and airy piazzas so different from the diseased alleys of Veracruz. The whole spectacle reflected in the vast lake that surrounded it as if there were two cities: one on land and one in water.

It was beautiful. Different in many ways from the place my mother had warned me about. But she was right enough in the particulars that I saw it instantly. The moment I set foot on the causeway leading into the city, dust-covered and exhausted, I knew I was walking into the land of the dead.

I thought it a story when my mother first spoke of it. I can see her now: talking as she span in the evenings, her long fingers working the cotton with one hand and the spindle with the other. The firelight glows on her arms as she works. I wish I could remember her face. But there is only a haze where it should be.

All the women of my father's household: my grandmother, his other wives and the girls came to my mother's fireside when the work was done, for she was the first wife and had the best house.

Outside, in public, the women would laugh: *Women can't tell stories. Stories are lies, only men can weave lies.* But in their own houses, they would talk, telling the stories that came to us from our ancestors.

My mother's were the best. She came from the east to marry, so she spoke a different language. As she talked in her own tongue, a beautiful sound, like water trickling over rocks, she would translate for the other women – two, three, four languages. We spoke in many ways in my country, for most of the wives, and all of the slaves, came from elsewhere.

I would sit at her feet and hold the baby Fode, for I was the eldest, and he was the smallest. How beautiful he was – the loveliest of them all. Still can I feel the curl of his hand in mine, and the weight of his head resting on my shoulder.

My mother's words come back to me now. "There was a time," she said, "when a person died, that their soul went straight to Grace. But the people got into bad ways. They stopped respecting the ancestors. They lay sisters with brothers and fathers with daughters. They ate the flesh of their own people when the harvest was bad.

"And the Almighty was displeased. So now it is that when a person dies, their soul must go to the land of the dead."

The shadows from the fire played out behind her head on the plaster of the wall.

"At first, the soul lies in the grave. For one month, it rests. Then it rises and wanders the earth. The soul knows it must go to the land of the dead.

"The journey there is hard and wearisome. The soul must cross a great sea. When it reaches land, it must climb hills and mountains, travel through valleys and meadows, before it descends into the land of the dead.

"There, there are ghosts with white faces." She always circled her face with her long, delicate fingers when she said this.

"They eat food, as we do, and they drink and they sleep. There are animals and forests and trees. There are villages and markets and boats.

"But it is the land of the dead. There will be trials to overcome. Only when it has passed many tests, can the soul be reborn and join the Almighty in Grace."

This is what she said.

And this is what happened to me.

After the attack on my village I was taken. My grandmother and I, only we two left of all my family. We were put in a ship for many weeks. We lay in the darkness packed tight together. It was like the grave.

After six-and-a-half weeks we reached land and they started to sell us.

A slave is sold by the pieza. A healthy male is one piece. Women and the sick, the young and the elderly are less than a piece.

First, they sold the men and the strongest boys at Isla Margarita, where they dive for pearls. For such work, a whole piece is required, and many of them, for it is dangerous work and mighty short-lived.

Others were sold at Rio de la Hacha in Tierra Firme. I was taken off at Cartagena, where I was torn from my grandmother, the last of my family I ever saw.

I sailed on another ship to Veracruz, where I was sold, naked and trembling, in the marketplace. Fray Calvo bought me. I lived in the priory there for three years. When I was thirteen, an agent from the big city bought me. He said I must go with him to Ciudad de México. We walked there. Rather, I walked. He rode on a mule. In a caravan of Spaniards, slaves and mules. It took many days.

First we climbed mountains. There was snow. I had never seen it before. I thought it was salt till I felt it cold and blistering on my toes. I licked it. It tasted of air and fizzed to nothing on my tongue. We passed through sweet-smelling meadows and valleys. One night we stayed in a village of freed slaves. I do not know how or why they had such good fortune. The women bathed and wrapped my feet. They gave us fresh herbed corncakes to eat, and wept bitterly, embracing me when we left. We made the final descent into Ciudad de México, where I saw the land of the dead laid out before me as clear as glass.

Our stories are not for idleness. They come direct from the spirits, our ancestors. They knew this time was coming and they warned me. So I would know what to do when I found myself among the ghosts with white faces in the land of the dead. That I must keep going. I will not give up. I will survive my trials, and be reborn with the Grace of the Almighty. This was my mother's warning to me. I do not forget it.

15

I have not seen Diego since the midday meal and my one eventide candle is burned close to the stub by the time I hear footsteps at the door. I do not care to see his face so I go on as I am, taking the biters from my hair with a fine-toothed comb, leaning in close to the little light beside the bed.

"Are you come to taunt or preach at me?" I ask, when I hear the door close softly behind him.

"Neither. Or should I say – both."

I turn in dismay at the General's voice, leaning too far over the candle and setting light to my hair. The fizzing smell of sulphur fills the room as he comes over to put it out, his thumb rubbing roughly at my forehead.

"What have you against my preaching, Maria?"

"Pray, General, nothing. I thought you Diego." I keep my eyes down.

"Indeed. He is not a good preacher." He pats the bed beside him and I sit.

He puts out his hand for the comb and I give it to him. He pulls at my hair, not gently. "Rather, I came to ask you something."

I turn to look at him, but he tilts my chin firmly to keep me facing forward.

"Tomorrow, our guests will leave us. The no-good Spanish

pilot also. Will you join them? We can put you ashore upriver. Away from the town."

"No!" I go to stand, but he holds me down with firm hands on each shoulder. "Please, no," I stammer. "I would stay – with you."

He says nothing for a while and resumes the combing. Then – "We have a long and wearisome journey ahead of us, Maria. It will be bitterly cold. I think you not used, nor able, to bear it."

"I know cold well enough." I think about the snow in the high places above Ciudad de México. The crunch of it. The blinding reflection in the thin air.

"Not like this," he says, taking out a good knot of my hair with the comb. I close my eyes to master the pain. "And... there would be... difficulties. If you were to return with me. To England."

I take his hand from my hair and hold it, my thumb pressing into the soft part between his thumb and forefinger. "Please. I would not leave you." How loathsome to say these words, but I must, and I must stay.

So close are we on the bed, thighs touching. He takes out a louse from the teeth of the comb and slices it with thumb and forefinger, flicking it to the floor.

I put a hand to his cold cheek. His beard scratches as I caress him. His chest heaves. His breath carries the vinegar scent of Canary wine. I lean forward to kiss him. He suffers it for a moment, then stands, righteous and angry.

"Do not play me for a fool, Maria. I am no lust-filled Spaniard you can bend to your will with perverse desires."

Certainly, he bends less easy than Don Francisco.

I stand to press myself into him, and I feel the fast-beating drum of his heart. "Natural desires," I tell him. I lay my head on his chest, which is a mistake, because my hair still smells of burning and he turns and coughs.

"There is no discussion. You must leave with the Spaniards," he says. But he stays in my embrace.

I reach down to feel the part of him he cannot reason with. His body straightens, braced, as if for the hit of a high wave. There is nothing I can say to turn his mind. With his body, I fancy I may have some hope.

16

We wait on the poop deck for the boat to take the Spaniards ashore. Still I do not know what the General will do. His mood is mighty changeable and he will not meet my eye.

The judge stares at the town across the water, where smoke still rises from the church. No longer does he threaten the General with the might of the Viceroy of New Spain. Nor does the priest complain that the men use his altar vestments as waste cloths. That they ring his bell to summon sailors to the pumps.

I search out the river where it snakes, shining in the morning light, through the forest beyond the town. How far is it from Guatulco? How many hours is my start?

The General cannot resist one last game with his mice. "My friend," he says to the judge. "Here is your safe-conduct." He holds out an unsealed paper, his signature a spidery hand at the bottom.

"My safe-what?"

"Safe-conduct. I told you I have not come alone. There are two more ships behind me and they will ravage your town again without it."

The judge tears his eyes from smoking Guatulco. He stands in the full glare of the sun, the sweat dripping from his nose.

The General shelters under an awning. "They will obey

my order," he says. "But he is a very cruel man, the captain of my other ships. He would not leave one man alive. Take it, my friend, and go in safety."

The judge shuffles forward, puts out his hands for it and mutters his thanks.

"Tell me," the General starts, as if he passes the time of the day in the street. "How are the Cimarrones at Vallano?"

"Why ask me of the Cimarrones?"

"At Vallano," the General repeats. "By Nombre de Dios in Tierra Firme. Are they peaceable now? I know they have given you a great deal of trouble."

"They are criminals. Runaway slaves." The judge turns back to the town.

"We do not observe your law that makes us slaves," says Diego.

The judge looks at him sharply.

"Yes – my man Diego is of their number. A prince among them, no less." The General puts his hand to Diego's back. "He came to me, you know – at Nombre de Dios seven years ago. Paddled out to me, in his leaky canoe. Begged me to take him aboard! Though my men were shooting at him like he was a target for practice."

He laughs. Diego blinks very slowly.

"Dodged every shot!" the General slaps Diego on the back. "I knew then his worth. And what riches he brought me! The treasures at Nombre de Dios were merely the start. Afterwards, he and his men brought me through the mountains to show me this ocean for the first time."

"Then they are traitors as well as criminals," says the judge.

"We owe you no allegiance," Diego barks at him.

The General nods. "You cannot enforce loyalty, my friend. Better by far to inspire it. When they brought me – somewhere there, many leagues over to the east – am I right, Diego?" he gestures towards the forenoon sun.

Diego nods, very slightly, but keeps his eyes on the judge.

"We climbed a treetop in the mountains, and I saw the Mare Pacificum for the first time. I said then: 'I shall conquer that ocean.' And here I am! Conquering it well enough. To think! Had it not been for Diego and his brothers – I should not have conceived the fancy to sail here into your waters at all."

The judge coughs.

"You must tell your Viceroy, Alcalde, he has much to fear when we Englishmen return. With our ships and arms, and our friends the Cimarrones, who grow stronger all the time in the mountains. Do you think you can win such a war?"

I wonder – not for the first time since I met this man – when did the English become the friends of slaves?

"And here is the boat!" proclaims the General. "Ready for your return."

The judge and the priest cannot jump into it fast enough. Casks of wine and oatcake are already put into it. Pascual is brought from below, rubbing his wrists where the chains have chafed them. He spits on the planks in front of me before Diego pushes him to the steps.

"Why is he coming?" The judge looks at Pascual with disgust.

"He's done his job, brought me here," says the General. "I want no Spaniards spying on me now. Not where we're going." He winks.

"And her?" The judge nods at me. I close my eyes.

There is silence as he walks towards me. I feel his hand grip my shoulder.

"She is not Spanish, my friend. She stays with me."

Sweet Virgin in Heaven, I shame myself with my gratitude.

Diego loosens the rope and the oarsmen take to the water. From behind us, the bell of Guatulco peals out a mocking send-off for the Spaniards.

The General turns his back on the spoiled town. Black smoke spirals into the sky behind him. "Now, masters – friends," he grins, arms raised in good cheer. "Let us be gone from this place. We sail north!"

The men roar their adoration as he goes through them, towards the stair leading to the Great Cabin. All save the scowling man in the velvet cap, who stayed aboard when they raided Guatulco. He stands apart and alone, as he does always, an invisible barrier between him and the other men.

The General smiles at me as he passes.

"North?" I turn to Diego in my disbelief. "But England lies westwards!"

"Nothing goes the way you expect with the General," he says.

I have to shout to make myself heard above the noise of the men chanting as they bring up the anchors.

"Are there other English ships behind us?" I ask.

"Of course not," Diego laughs.

"And will the Spaniards follow?"

Diego watches the boat bobbing in the waves, the judge staring back at us in his fury.

"They will surely try."

APRIL, 1579

MARE PACIFICUM

22°30'N

17

A scheme grows, hardening, like the kernel of a nut within my breast.

The hatred they bear for each other, the Spaniards and the English. It saved me before. It can save me again. I wonder I did not think of it earlier.

The General leads eventide prayers. Fletcher stands by him, a smile on his lips. The skies deepen from pink to crimson then purple. Stars appear like pinholes, a needle pricking at the leather of the sky.

They call it prayers. More like it is a battle cry: a call to arms against the cruelties of the Spaniards. The men adore it. *Yea!* they call out, slapping palms against thighs. *Verily! Papist dogs!*

In the marketplace at Veracruz I shivered. With fear, and because night was coming, and I was naked. Just me, alone, left from all of us taken from my village. The men sold at Isla Margarita and Cartagena. Others at Rio de la Hacha. The young and the old, my grandmother among them, kept on the ship when I was taken off.

The other captives spoke strange tongues. The women wailed and wept over their own children, deep in their misery.

Their wild keening echoed off the thick walls of the priory. Circling overhead, vultures screeched it back at us.

When the cool of the evening set in, the priory's thick oak door opened and the friars came out in single line, faces hidden deep in their hoods.

From person to person they went and asked: *Are you a Christian?* I had some words of Spanish then, but not the Credo nor the Ave Maria. For those that did there were clothes to hide their nakedness. A blanket to cover them at night.

But I had heard the English sailors on the slaving ship recite their prayer.

Our Father, I started, when a full-lipped friar with rosy cheeks came to me. Which art in Heaven. The words fell heavily from my mouth, mangled and uneasy. He stared at me, eyes widening, his jaw dropping low and wide.

Our Father, I said again. Which art in Heaven. It was all I knew. It was enough.

"Where have you learned this?"

I looked at the ground.

"What else have they taught you? What damnable doctrines have you learned? What poisons have you supped from these devils?"

I had nothing else to say, so I said it again. "Our Father. Which art in Heaven."

He marched to the auction-master and demanded I be given up to him for only twenty pesos. I must go directly to the priory to be saved, he said, from the eternal hellfire to which the English dogs had damned me.

"You are lucky," said little Luisa, when he put me in her care at the priory. She found me a shift to wear, showed me where the girls slept and worked: in the dairy and the garden. "Hardly ever do they buy slaves now, and nowhere else in Veracruz would you see out the year."

She had been there five years herself. She was my age: ten, perhaps twelve years. Temne, she told me. I knew some few words in her tongue.

"The friars are kind. The work isn't hard. There is always food to eat. Barely do they touch a girl before she is of age."

"I have always been lucky," I told her.

The General closes the book on the low table in front of him, and stands, brushing the dirt from his knees. The men pass prayer books from one to the other and into rush baskets at the end of each line.

He ends with the ship's ordinances.

Serve God daily.

Love one another.

Preserve your victuals.

Beware of fire.

Keep good company.

As if there were choice over the company to keep.

Thomas makes his way to the front, face hidden in the long shadow cast by the gallery. Musicians take up an air and the boy dances. The men watch him. Too keenly. He keeps his eyes closed.

He finishes with a lacklustre kick and a hop and skirts his way around the men like a beaten dog, to sit on the step to the quarterdeck. An older man, Fludd, comes forward and takes up a low and mournful song in a fine voice.

When he is done, it is dark, and the men wander off: the starboard watch to their duties, the larboard men to their beds. I watch, as I always do, to see where Pyke goes, that I may keep well away. The lonesome man in the velvet cap starts for his solitary shift in the lookout.

Lit up by the dim lamplight, John's head floats around the gallery and disappears again: he is keeping watch for some mischief. Fishing during prayers, no doubt. He will be put in the bilges for it if he is caught, cousin or no.

I wait until the General sees me alone beside the foremast.

"Maria," he smiles coldly. "Did you enjoy the sermon?"

"Very much, General."

He is mighty pleased. "But I know what you are thinking!" He holds up his forefinger.

"You do?"

"You think me a devil! A man who robs by day and prays in public by night!"

"Nay!" I say, and my horror is real. Who in the rightness of their mind would say such a thing to him? "Rather, was I thinking – hoping. May I ask you something, General?"

"Of course." He puts out his arm. I take it.

Behind him, John's bobbing head appears again. He whispers something to the gunner Blackoller, who slips back with him into the shadows.

I steer the General from them. "I… wish to ask you something of the Christ."

He smiles at me like an indulgent father.

"Your Christ," I start. "He is the same as in the Spanish religion?"

"Yes Maria – and he is everyone's Christ. Yours too. Though the Spaniards and all papists do not extol Him as we do. They worship instead the Pope."

"But the Pope – he is the vicar of Christ, is he not?"

"Nay! He is an imposter! A tyrant. A man of great sin. Indeed, he is the Antichrist."

"Forgive me for asking, I have been raised in the Spanish ways. But how do you know?"

"Scripture, Maria! The Scripture is all. It tells us there are no Saviours but Christ. He is the only mediator between God and Man. The sacrifice of Mass, pardons and saints – all that the papists love. These are blasphemies! Monkery. Abominable doctrines. All that is good is in the Gospells."

"And I – I may read the Gospells?"

"You *must* read them." His merry air disappears like smoke. He takes my hands. "It is your duty."

He pulls me to the table by the mainmast. "You must read this too."

He opens the book he read from at prayers. So vast, the

lamp lights only part of each page at a time, so he moves it along, watching my eyes to be sure I am reading.

There are pictures as well as words. Penitents in hoods and robes in procession, with the scarlet mark of the cross on their bellies. These I know well from Ciudad de México. There are men and women in torture – chained with their feet roasting in an open fire and tied to stakes in flames, hands joined together in prayer. Some images in brown ink, others in bright colours, burning flesh in red and pink.

He stabs at the pictures, tearing one as he turns the page in haste. "See here, Maria. Here you see those martyred and burned by the Spaniards."

He points to an image of a man chained above a fire, upside down so his head is to the flames. His hair hangs down, flames lick at his face.

"And here!" He turns the page to show a dungeon of people in torture. A man hoisted from the ceiling by his arms tied behind his back so they are pulled up in mortal pain. Stretched both ways, his feet are pulled down by a heavy weight around his ankles. Another man tied upside down on a crucifix, his head in a fire. Yet another, in a coffin, his hands tied at his chest, while liquid is poured through a funnel into his helpless mouth.

"What have they done?" I ask in horror. "For what are they punished?"

"For preaching the Gospell. Denying the Pope. They say only what sense and reason teaches them. How can bread and wine be the body and blood of Christ? Naught but Romish superstition! His body is in Heaven. Can it be anywhere else?"

He looks at me earnestly. "How can a monk sell a Heavenly pardon? It is not his to give! Why does he preach in a tongue that his congregation cannot understand? These are things repugnant to the word of God!"

He grips my shoulders, eyes set on mine. "'Tis a great fortune for your soul that you met me, Maria. Do you feel it? The Almighty Hand that placed you in my path?"

I nod. Certainly I feel *his* hands pinching into my flesh.

He lifts the book into my arms. It is even heavier than it looks. "Take it. Read it. And my Bible in the cabin. They tell all."

He dismisses me with a wave of his arm.

I feel his eyes at my back as I walk the few steps to the cabin, stumbling under the weight of the book. I pass the men crowding around the catch that John and Blackoller have hauled aboard: a little porpus, which twists and turns on the deck.

I do believe I have it. That which I can barter for his protection instead of my sex. My soul. A great surprise to find it should prove of a purpose.

18

In the Great Cabin, the General calls council and at last I hear his policy as I pour the wine.

Diego sits at his left, as he always does. The General's close men – Carey, opposite him, and others to his right. They must be used to it by now, but still they scowl at Diego, who returns his own icy glare. Steward Legge is there and Bosun Winter. The chaplain Fletcher sits below the window, hands set upon his knees.

The General picks up his brass globe of the world and knocks it on the table to start. "Masters. Your attention."

He slams his open hand on the chart of many colours before him. The world an outstretched disc, fluffs of white cloud around the edges.

There is England. How small it is. How far they have come. Below Europe is Affrica: the edges coloured red and yellow and blue where the Europeans have made their investigations. The inner parts – where we came from long ago, before the Great Empress Mansarico led us to the land beside the river – are quite clear. Blank spaces that do not exist for the makers of this map. If only they had stayed there, the ancestors, far from the dangers of the coast.

Below Affrica and Chilley – across the whole of the bottom of the chart is the huge continent marked Terra Australis

Nondum Cognita. The Southern Land Not Yet Known. Not known by these men maybe. But I know it. I was in Valperizo when Juan Fernandez, the Wizard of the Pacific, returned, proclaiming his discovery.

"Gentlemen, masters," the General repeats. "We know America to be an island."

His thumb taps like the beat of a drum on the chart, over where we are now: an empty white land, the edges of it tinged with pink: *America*, it reads, *or India Nova*.

There is a thump on the table. I look up. Carey's hand hovers, still balled in a fist. "But *how* do you know America is an island?"

No one else talks to the General like this. The other men look down or out the window. Fletcher's eyes are set firmly on the fingers clasped together on his knees.

"See here: it is clear on this chart," the General gestures to it with an open palm.

"But no one has been there!" says Carey.

"Nay," says the General, reasonably. "But it is known. Twas known to the Ancients," he says, one brow arched high. "Did you not read Plato, Carey? You, who talks so often and so loudly of your learning?"

"Yea," Carey flicks a lock of his fine hair from his eyes. "But—"

The General does not permit him to finish. "As you remind me so often my friend, I did *not* go to the university. I learned my trade at sea as boy and man – while you were laying in your feather-bed, with a cup of Canary wine and a warming fire in your hearth. But even *I* have read Plato's *Critias* – of the great island of Atlantis, west from Gibraltar and navigable all around."

He reaches to a chest behind him and brings out a book with a page marked by a cord of red leather. He reads: "Atlantis was swallowed up with water by reason of a mighty earthquake. By which accident America grew to be unknown to us and was lately discovered again by Christopherus Columbus in the year of our Lord 1492."

He looks up at Carey who frowns. "So that in our days, there can be no other mainland or island judged to be this Atlantis than those western islands which bear now the name America."

"I *have* read Plato," says Carey. "And Plato said Atlantis was sunk below the water and lost entirely."

"Most of it," says the General. "But not all."

Carey gives a long drawn-out sigh. "You would risk eighty lives – eighty men and boys – on the fancies of a heathen who died two thousand years since!"

Eighty men and boys. Por amor de Dios. I stand next to this man. Only just now did I brush his arm when I poured his wine, and still he does not see me.

"Not just the heathens," says the General. "Look in your Scripture. Atlantis is the land of Atlas, son of Japheth, son of Noah."

Here I think he is mistaken because now I have read the Genesis in his Bible, and I think Fletcher has something to say of it also, because he is squirming in his seat. But no. He says nothing, though he has the look of a man troubled greatly by wind.

But still Carey will not stop. He taps his fingers on the table. Diego watches them, his fury unhidden, as they tap tap tap against the oak.

"Plato was never here. Atlas was never here," Carey says. "There is no proof of a passage. Even if there were, we do not know how far north it may be. For all that we know, it may be perpetually frozen and impossible to pass."

"Frozen in winter," the General says, as he returns the book to the chest. When he faces the men again he is frowning. "But not in summer. We know from the travels of Frobisher that the seas and straits of Labrador are free from ice to the 75th line in June."

Carey goes to speak but the General stops him, raising the forefingers of both his hands.

"Remember – I do not say this on my own account. It is

the view of the Queen and her counsellors too. You would not wish me to report you gainsaid Walsingham." He raises his eyebrows. "Would you?"

Carey opens his mouth, but the General has had enough.

He lifts up the brass globe and slams it onto the table. Every man stiffens.

"This globe was given to me by the Queen of England! She sent me to seek the passage and encompass the world. This is my commission. I am sovereign here, and my will is law!"

The General examines the bottom of the globe to be sure he has not cracked it. In a soft voice, without looking up, he says: "Remember Doughty, Carey."

Carey stops still, his eyes widen. The other men watch him nervously.

But now the General smiles. "Have courage, my friend. And faith! When was I ever wrong in my navigation?"

The General smooths out the chart before him. "Good." By which he means the council is over. "Here on the north side is where the sea severs the *island* America from Groynland, where Frobisher informs us there is a westward-leading passage. And here," he says, making a circle with his finger over the word *Anian* on the north-west coast of America. "Here is the other side of that passage. Which we will now discover."

On the poop deck before prayers I scan the horizon, as I do daily, for Spanish sails. I find myself here often, when the men are eating. I cannot bear to watch them like wild animals upon their meat. They squabble over the upturned barrels that serve as tables, growl and blaspheme, as they fight for a share of the stewed salt-pork on platters before them. They bellow as they eat, spittle flying from their mouths and seeping into their beards. Their knives spear each other as much as the meat in their gluttonous rivalry.

Diego comes to see to the hawsers. Nor will he eat with

the men, taking his meat earlier with the General or alone below deck.

"Will we put in at Acapulco?" I ask, still looking southward to the blurred horizon.

"He is daring, but not mad," says Diego. "That was merely his sport with the Alcalde. He would send the Spaniards to look for us there and leave us unmolested on the ocean."

"Will it work?"

"With luck and fair winds."

"I thought you scorned luck?"

He bends over a great hawser, pulling it into a coil. He stops. I cannot see his face, but it seems to me his shoulders shake.

"Then we must trust in the winds."

He is in good humour. Can I ask what I have not yet dared? I wait till he stops to catch his breath.

"Is it true, what the General said? About how you met him?"

He heaves the heavy rope into place, sweat shining on his clenched jaw.

"True enough. The gunfire is his invention. The man cannot tell a tale without some adornment. But I did row out and entreat to join him." He raises his brows. "I told you. A man sails his own ship."

He turns to go, and the words tumble from my mouth before I even think.

"Who's Doughty?"

He looks back sharply.

"Doughty. Whom the General warned Carey—"

"A mutineer," he cuts me short. "A gentleman. He set out with us from Plymouth."

"What happened to him?"

"What happens to all traitors," Diego says evenly, drawing his finger across his throat.

19

In the forenoon, the men gather before the bowsprit. The waves are high and angry, the air is close and stifling.

Thomas was found filching from the store again. Now he hangs by the feet from the spritsail yard, arms tied behind his back. He kicks and bucks to keep his head from the water. His ribs look ready to burst from his skin for the lack of flesh. His face is purple. From the effort of keeping his head above the water or the bruises from the beating he took earlier, I do not know.

"He ought hold still," John says, head to one side. "He'll tire before he's even dropped."

"Then what happens?"

"They'll drag him in the sea awhile."

"He deserves it," says Diego, frowning at the pity on my face. "That was the last of the biscuit and cheese from Guatulco. He must be punished."

The men have no pity either. They lean over the gunwale, spitting at him as he bobs and turns in front of them. The man in the velvet cap watches the boy with such a face I cannot tell if it is because he would halt Thomas' punishment or willingly execute it himself twice over.

I am struck by guilt as if pierced by a real knife. I left him to this.

The chaplain Fletcher struggles to be heard above the noise. "Let him down! Let the boy down!"

But he can barely be heard. The men shout and jeer, *Filthy thief! Nasty muckworm! Fucking filcher!* They cheer when they land their phlegm upon the boy.

Fletcher pushes himself to the front of the mob. He raises his hands to the heavens. "How can this boy know the right path? What has he seen on this ship but felony?"

The men push Fletcher to the side. Pyke turns from Thomas, spits into a cloth and hurls it at the chaplain instead. It lands on his shoulder with a dull smack.

Fletcher throws it to the deck without a pause. "We have stolen from the Spaniard! We are all guilty! Is it any wonder God sends felons among us?"

The General is in the waist, where he makes a show of inspecting the ropes and the sails. He has so far taken little notice of the commotion of the mob and the misery of the boy. But now he looks up sharply.

Fletcher continues blindly: "Wickedness is all about us!"

Bosun, who sits on the yard above Thomas, starts to loosen the rope. The boy screams as he lurches downwards.

"Do something!" I beg Diego. "He's exhausted already. He'll drown."

"No one's died of it yet."

A high wave rears and submerges the boy to his waist. It falls away, the water pouring from his head, his mouth open in shock, chest heaving as he gulps at the air before going under again.

The men roar their approval. Pyke leads the mocking laughter. The man in the velvet cap storms away.

"Here comes another, filcher!" Blackoller calls out gleefully as a second mountainous wave rolls towards the boy.

I cannot bear to watch it. I come away with my guilt, pushing my way through the mob. Only when I reach the stair to the gallery do I hear voices raised in anger and fury.

Diego is on the bowsprit, hauling Thomas up. He bucks and twists, not realising he has been saved, till he is bent over the yard, coughing and spluttering. Trails of snot run from his nose, which he rubs away with his shoulder while Diego unties the cords at his wrists.

Fletcher has not noticed the boy has been taken up. Still he prays. "Have pity on us Lord, according to your great compassion and abundance of your mercy!" The General, his body fair shaking with fury, watches Fletcher.

The men jeer and howl at Diego. All but Pyke, who makes the foul and obscene gesture of the fig at me with his right hand.

At the end of the day, when the sun quickens its final drop to the sea, Thomas comes to me on the poop deck. "He said *you* had me taken down," he sobs. He leans against the bulwark, eyes red from crying, still rubbing at his wrists and ankles that burn raw from the cords.

"I wish I'd not left you there alone."

He shrugs his thin shoulders.

"We are all alone," he says. "You save yourself, as best you can."

I squeeze his hand. "We are not alone."

I kneel to put in place the mortar-stone Diego brought from the store for me. "Do they take from you your ration?" I ask him. "Is that why you steal?"

"That too," he wails.

"Then you must make yourself a friend of the cook. Put yourself in sight when he wants a boy to prepare the beans or to stir the pot. Then you will never go hungry."

"Can't eat this though, can I?" he kicks at the mortar and scowls at the pain in his toes. He sniffs.

"Not yet."

Diego brought up the pestles too, and I put one in his hands now. It towers above him. "These are the husking and winnowing things. So we can eat the rice."

"Englishmen don't eat rice," he looks at me down his nose. "We took it. From your man, Don Fancybreeches. But we don't *eat* it."

The mention of that man makes my heart sicken. I think of him less and less now. Hardly ever do I remember it is a part of him growing in my belly.

"And we got the big sticks and the bowl," he kicks the mortar again, "from the Portingales in Verde."

Voto a Dios, do Englishmen ever make or do anything for themselves?

"Lucky you did," I tell him. "Rice is better than corn – ay, and the biscuit you were so hungry for this morning."

He does not care to be reminded of this. He grasps the pestle like a musket.

"Stand up," I tell him. "Straighter!" I tap his thin legs with the clubbed end of my pestle. "Let it fall – but gently. Tap and roll the rice, like this. Twist at the end. It is a great skill to husk the rice, yet not break it."

"Can I sit?"

"No, you need the weight of the fall. Stand."

I take the other pestle and we grind in silence, first one and then the other dropping the pestle into the stone. The boy puts out his lower lip and settles his eyes angrily out to sea.

"Faster, Thomas! Unless you wish me to return you to Bosun."

He mutters under his breath, but picks up speed.

The tap of the pestle on rice is like a balm. It is the sound of home. Of dawn breaking, and every house preparing its rice. Of children yawning and asking if they can stop yet to eat. Women calling out across the galleries of their houses. It settles Thomas too. His face softens. His brow is smooth, the fury gone from his lip.

Above us, gulls circle in their leisure. Trails of cotton-tree clouds fly past. The wind roaring in the sails masks the din of the ship – the men shouting and cursing, the hammering and the mending that never stops.

This was my job too, when I was the age Thomas is now. On the first ship.

I husked the rice then, for my grandmother to cook. A great fortune for us both. It brought us up from the hold like an oven, where men were chained to each other, no room to turn. Children screaming. Women moaning. The smell down there. Madre de Dios, the smell. The necessary tubs overflowed and swilled up and down the people crammed upon the boards. The stench of the dead, who rotted so quickly in the heat. We were plucked from this hell, my grandmother and I, to prepare the food.

Because I am lucky, she said. *Chosen by the snake.*

Such good fortune brought us food and air to breathe. Water to keep off the madness of thirst. You cannot know this madness till you have felt it. The dreaming, though you are awake. The heaviness. Of every limb and finger. Each lash of your eye. Your very tongue swells in your mouth, choking you.

It brought us pity too, from the sailors at whose feet we slept. Pieces of pickled-pork and dried fish they would summon from their smocks, a tin-whistle for me to play with. Strange, for they had no pity for those just like us in the hold.

It was a small ship. *Angel*, she was called. I asked what was an angel, and they told me. Like a spirit, I thought. Come to carry us away. She was the smallest of the fleet – and that was my luck too, for the holds of the larger ships, whose sails we saw only as specks on the horizon, were more closely packed, the sailors far crueller for being under the eye of the Admiral. So they told us.

But every day, before they would suffer to go down themselves, the sailors would send me below, with a pot of burning pitch to clean the air. My grandmother tied scraps of sailcloth tight to my mouth and nose to keep out the smell and the disease. I stepped between people packed like animals, feeling my way so I could keep my eyes closed, singing songs in my head to shut my ears to the pitiful moaning, to keep from feeling the hands on my ankles, begging for water.

I made pretence I did not know these people. This man lying here was not Bala, who taught me to catch catfish with a basket. This aged hag was not dear Saba. As I returned to the light and the air, I did not stop to think of what the sailors, pushing past me on the stair in their haste, came to do to the girls down there, no older than me, mere children.

Much harder to pretend I did not know these wretches when they were brought up, at the edge of death, eyes rolling back in their heads, to be whipped at the capstan for refusing to eat, or thrown to the sharks. I took a spoonful of water to Saba as they dragged her to the gunwale, parting the nets put up to stop us from jumping overboard. But she was beyond the need for water then.

I stop, and still Thomas' pestle to feel the rice. Is it ready yet for winnowing?

It runs through my fingers, each life-giving grain. Each one a gift from the ancestors, my grandmother said. Each one has within it all it needs to grow and thrive.

"How'm I doing?" Thomas looks down at me.

"Well," I say. "But try a little softer."

"Course – you should be doing this, not me," he says. "This is women's work."

It pleases me to see the Devil returned to his cheek. "Ay, Thomas," I smile. "We are all women here."

He says nothing, but he continues to grind. Not fast. Enough to keep me from complaining. He looks up at the gulls sweeping across the sky, following one as it soars higher to drop down, plummeting like a stone for a fish we cannot see.

I still his pestle and pour the husks and grains from the mortar into the winnowing basket and flip it into the air with a flick of my wrist. The husks take to the wind where they catch the setting sun like grains of gold before scattering into the sea behind us. Thomas leans against the pestle, mouth wide in delight as he watches the flakes of gold settle into the frothy wake of the ship.

Is it slow-falling husks or something else that hovers in the haze between sky and sea? I cannot tell. I pour the grains into a deeper basket for Thomas to take to the steward's store and show Cook what use he can be.

I will make the rice later. The best bit, the crust at the bottom of the pot, I will save for Thomas to eat. As my grandmother used to do for me. On the other ship.

20

The wind is low. The sails hang limp at the yards. There is little to do. The men are forbidden from playing cards or other devilish games as the General calls them. But I have heard them whisper when I pass by that he broke the rules himself when he brought a woman aboard, and they will do as they please. Though they keep where they think themselves unseen – behind barrels of powder in the gun deck. In the manger, with the last of the hens pecking at their feet.

Fishing though, the General permits, for it saves the ration, and today is a fine day indeed for it. A little cloud for cover, a good stretch of sea-grass on the ocean many leagues long to draw the fish. All over the ship, men sit in the shade of the sails, holding a line or bent over a bucket, up to elbows in fish guts. The boys sit in the waist salting and packing the catch tight into barrels.

Pyke has caught a baby tiburón, what these men call a shark. An evil-looking thing. They slice off its fins and gouge out its glassy black eyes, dropping it back into the water, still living, a bloody mess. They lean over the gunwale, laughing as it sinks, unable to turn for the want of fins, till it is torn to shreds by its own kind. Thomas laughs with them, but turns away, coughing at the smell of the blood.

I creep past them, unseeing in their gruesome sport, to

the gallery behind the General's cabin. None will come here because of the smell of the privies, but it is tolerable for the peace.

Today, the little wind takes the stench out to sea. Someone is here already. Diego sits with his back against the cabin, knees drawn up, trailing a line into the sea. I turn to go.

"Nay, Maria. Come. Help me."

Never can I tell if he is in the mood to befriend or torment me.

He pushes aside a basket of slapping, twisting fish to make room. Mostly, they are what the Spaniards call cabálla, slim things of blue-green, a splash of white on the belly.

I stretch my legs out on the sun-warmed boards and settle my head in the shade of the bulwark. It is fine here, the business of the ship behind us. The sea and the Spaniards slipping ever further to the south.

"Thank you," I nod. Diego looks at me. "For setting Thomas down."

"I didn't care for the cheese in any case."

From a little bag at his side he brings out an oatcake. He breaks it in two, the worms and weevils in the newly broken edge flailing in the sun.

"Tell me," he says. "How came you to know the Alcalde?"

He hooks the oatcake to the line and throws it far into the sea.

"He said you came before him," he pushes, when I don't answer.

"What concern is it of yours?"

"I would know what sort of woman we have on board."

There is only one sort of woman on board a ship. She who is there against her will – or running from something worse. But the sun is too warming on my legs, the breeze against my cheek too pleasant, and I still too glad he saved Thomas to annoy him.

"The usual sin. For living in a mal estado."

There is a pull on the line that jerks Diego forward, till he masters it, and falls back to the shade.

"Who was the man? Who brought you to this bad estate?"

"No one." I allow myself one image of Miguel from the storehouse of my memory: his long limbs, and he still ungainly with them. His eyes, soft and loving on me as the morning light floods into the washroom of Master Symons' house in México.

"And how did you escape your punishment? Did you whore yourself to the Alcalde too?"

"I had no need. Though if I did, I would, without a second thought."

He looks alongside at me. "Why no need?"

"I denounced myself. I told him I renounced God. If you do this in public, they cannot punish you for you must be sent to the Holy Office to be corrected. Do the slaves in Santiago not do this?"

"I was young when I left," he frowns. "What the slaves in Cuba do to save themselves, I do not know. Save that they run – fast – when the hunting dogs are set after them."

"How did you come to leave?"

He will not answer. "What happens at the Holy Office?"

"There you say that the Devil had your tongue, that He blinded you, you were out of your mind. That you are an ignorant woman with no judgement. And if you have the right prayers, you can escape the whipping. You say the Pater Noster, the Ave Maria, Salve Regina, the Credo. And the Commandments."

"In Latin?"

"The friars taught me."

I lean forward to watch the fish on the line. He is a dorado. More beautiful than cabálla and better on the eating too. They shine like jewels underwater: emeralds, sapphires, rubies and gold, dazzling even brighter when you bring them in.

"Then you say that if they whip you, you are afraid you

will blaspheme again and lose your soul, and they will bear the guilt."

"And they believe this devil's piss?"

"It is what the girls do in México. But they ordered, the judges, that I must be sold to stop me returning to sin."

That is how Gonzalo came to buy me for his own sinful ends, putting me to a life on the Manila galleons. He, a balding man of fifty years, and I, a girl of sixteen. It is not a mal estado, understand, if the man owns the woman, and she has no choice in the matter.

I do not want to think about Gonzalo. "Is it cold in England?"

"So cold in winter the rivers freeze and you can walk on water as if it were land. Sometimes the birds drop dead out of the sky and kill a man as he walks in the street."

He takes me for a fool.

"And you are sure: I cannot be a slave there?"

He pulls the fish in and unhooks him with a flick of the finger in his mouth. I watch him for a while, in the basket on my lap, twisting, still flashing like a jewel.

Diego scratches lazily at a bite on his wrist. "You cannot be a slave on English soil. But you will be... different. An oddity. You will be free – but at the mercy of their good will. Or ill will – if it should suit them better. Never will you forget you are not the same as them."

He looks at me. "If you take their religion, it will go easier on you. You can keep a little of yourself here," he presses his palm to the bone of my breast.

He keeps it there – one heartbeat too long, fingertips pressing like hot coals into my skin.

In the basket the fish flaps and flails as he searches for water. He shimmers from silver to deep blue, then a beautiful lake-green, as if he would live every colour remaining to him before he dies. He fades through yellow to a deathly grey as the life leaves him. One final kick of his tail and he is gone.

Diego recasts into the sea. I follow the line out to the horizon, where there is no denying now, the three square sails white and solid against the sky. We watch them, both of us, without remark.

I find myself thinking of Mansarico. The warrior queen, the Great Empress – my ancestor, if my mother is to be believed, on her own mother's side. I think of her striding towards her new dominions beside the sea. Never would she have been satisfied with just a little of herself.

MAY, 1579

MARE PACIFICUM

42°20'N

21

I will never forget the basket of hands. Huge, it was. High as a man's waist and filled to the brim with severed hands. Men's hands, marked with burns from the forge. Women's hands, still blue with gara dye from the steeping pot. The tiny hands of children, fingers curling inwards, as if they were taken still holding onto their mothers. Blood collected at the bottom of the basket, dropping thickly onto the forest trail with every few steps.

He was a Portingale, the man who carried the basket. I know this now because of his wide breeches in the style of that country, and the cut of his hat made from wool. I did not know it then. The basket was heavy and he stopped every now and then to offload it from his back and rest it on the forest floor. This is why he was so far behind his companions, and why I did not understand for a long time what he did.

From the slow-going boat on the river I watched him with growing horror. What did he want with these hands? Are they for eating – a delicacy among the Portingales, as the wing of a fowl is to us? I looked over the Englishmen sailing our boat. They were busy, all on deck, the young captain as well as his mariners, poling the broad hull from the thick mud of the riverbed.

Was this why they had taken us, these men? To eat only of our hands? What would they do with the rest of us?

I asked my grandmother. She did not know.

Saba was still talking then. She squeezed me tight to her. The hands were for sorcery, she said, and not to fear. Most likely they were taken after death, not from the living. It did not soothe me.

After the rapids, the river deepens, and the boat made faster progress. The captain called his men away from the poles, and put them to pushing and hacking at the vines that trailed into the water, entangling the rudder. From the distance we saw ahead of us – ahead of the man with the basket of hands – the train of people walking in one line. Three or four dozen. Men, women and children, stumbling forward at the points of swords. Closer, and we saw coffles of iron round the men's necks. Red-faced Portingales drove them faster.

The rains had started, and they fell on us now, fat drops falling so thickly they made a wall of water. The riverside path churned with clay. The people fell often. They struggled to get up in the thickness of the mud and when they could not, the Portingales fell upon them with a stick or the flat of a sword. Sometimes those who fell did not get up. They lay lifeless, not moving even when they were stamped on the head or kicked in the belly.

Then I discovered why the man carried a basket of hands. Coming from the rear after the train had moved on: at every unmoving body in his path, he aimed one blow with his gleaming sword. From each person fallen, he severed one hand. He stooped to pick it up, and threw it by curling fingers into the basket at his back.

I turned and saw the English captain watching too. His sea-cap of blue so sodden, the water ran straight through it, and down his face, dripping from his lip curled in disgust and horror.

Beside me, my grandmother muttered an oath. "He's counting them," she said.

I looked at her. She sat, as she always did, like a girl: legs out before her, hands laid upon her knees.

"His way of counting for the overseer the people lost on the march. By the number of hands in his basket at journey's end."

22

How cold it is. It creeps round the ship like a spirit, chasing out the heat that felt thick as wool below deck. The timbers creak as the warmth leaves them. The cold smothers the foul smells of the ship: the sourness of the sweat, the bitter tar and the stench of the rotting things rising from the bilges.

So cold it can be seen, in breath hot from the lips. When first I saw it, as Diego sat up and yawned in the cold dawn light, I thought an evil spirit was leaving his body. He breathed harder. "Tis only the cold!" and he blew into my hands to warm them.

The mists that came and went as we sailed north are bolder. Thick, stinking fogs they are now. They smell evil, of something sweeping in from the very gates of Hell. Never have I seen the like of them before – or not seen, rather, for it is a whiteness that doesn't blink. Truly we sail into the very blank spaces of the charts that occupy the General so, hunched over them in the Great Cabin all his waking hours.

He sleeps there too now, more and more. I am becoming a Christian woman, he says, and shall be baptised when we reach England. It is not fit to continue our former intimacy. As if I sorrow over it. And in good time too. My belly remains flat and girlish. I have only eight weeks of life in it or thereabouts, but it will give me away soon enough, abed. And to be free of his clammy, poking hands – ay, I am blessed indeed by his absence.

Spite the cold, the men toil in busyness all about the ship. Carpenters fix and mend. Boys follow them with buckets of pitch, daubing it on the freshly-mended boards and yards.

In the cabin I turn the pages of the book the General bid me read: his *Book of Martyrs*. The paper is thick and weighty, with ridges like veins. Ink brown as dried blood. By my faith, a book *is* a living thing, as I fancied as a child.

The work outside is deafening: hammer on nail, metal against wood, the crackle of fires. A backdrop fit for the horrors in these pages.

Beside each picture of a martyr in torment are words on their life and death. Some burned in Spain, as the General said, but most in England in the days of their Catholic Queen.

Laurence Saunders, reads one. Burned for the defence of the Gospell at Coventry, Anno 1555. He cheerfully took his death with wonderful patience in the defence of Christ's Gospell.

He was a Lutheran. But now they burn Catholics in England and the Spaniards burn Lutherans. All because they cannot agree on what their God wants. Whether He wishes us to adore His saints or not. If a holy man may give a pardon. If the bread is truly the body of Christ and if the wine is verily His blood.

Yet it is the same God the world over, Fray Calvo told me. The Almighty we worshipped – whom we did not name – is also the same. But He was angry with us, Fray Calvo said. Angry we did not give Him prayers the right way, so He bid our Fall.

My grandmother said every blessing comes from the Almighty and every sorrow too. But you would no more give thanks for them than beseech favours. Montas! You should not talk to the Almighty at all. The Creator is above such things.

Ancestors – spirits. They you can pray to. Their souls walk the earth as we do. They concern themselves with the living.

The friars talked to the Holy Mother and the saints, so I thought they would understand. But they said our spirits were not saints like theirs, but devils who must be cast aside.

I think about Master Symons in his yellow penitent's vest, the blood-red cross stitched on it front and back to mark him in his shame, shuffling in shackled feet on the scaffold. Reported to the Inquisitors for taking down an image of the Virgin to hang his coat upon the nail.

He would have seen us married, Miguel and I. By the Spaniards' own law, then we could not have been parted. But Master Symons is burned to dust. Miguel is in the mines. And I am here.

The hammering has moved from the foredeck to the waist, and there are shouts above the relentless din.

At the door I see John and Thomas standing beside the hatches. The carpenters Eyot and Collyns nail them shut in preparation for the north. Beyond the ship, fog masks everything. The boys' buckets of pitch are at their feet, brushes laid across them.

"You lie!" Thomas shouts.

Eyot, his beard wild as an overgrown vine, shakes his head, waving his hammer about. "God's own truth! Great islands of ice there are. Rising from the sea half a league wide and more. They crash about upon the ocean like a giant's anvil, gashing and breaking a ship."

John looks about to search out these ice mountains, though the blankness beyond the ship is complete.

Foul-tempered Collyns breaks in. A big man, he wipes his tar-stained hands on his leather apron. "Nor can you see where you are sailing for the fogs. Only when they clear can you see that you sail midst two great mountains of ice that will grind you to dust."

I have heard these tales before. Both these men sailed with Frobisher and they delight in scaring the boys with their tales of frozen lands. I do not care to hear more, but I will whether I choose it or no. So I go nearer.

"I saw," Eyot leans forward and lowers his voice, "a bark of our fleet – one hundred men on board – take such a blow from the ice she sunk before our eyes, each man flailing and shrieking as he fell into the frozen depths."

"Frozen," Collyns fixes John's eye. "And unmerciful. A man will die in an instant should he fall in, so great and piercing is the cold. There is no hope of rescue."

Thomas opens his mouth but Collyns stops him with a raised finger. "Nor needs you fall into the sea to freeze! A man's nose or ear may rot with the cold, blacken and fall off his body while yet he breathes!"

The wind whistles across the open deck as I reach the hatches.

"Ho," says Thomas, who cannot be held off with a mere finger. "So why'd you come on this voyage then? If it's so bad as all that?"

Eyot draws himself up. "So *you* was consulted on the General's plans, were you boy?" he roars, waving his hammer before him. "We are not so high as you. I'm done with the north! I wanted none of it! That's why I joined him!" He swings the hammer towards the stair to the Great Cabin. "For a jaunt to Alexandria. To take on a cargo of *currants* – as I was told!"

"We thought to be home by midsummer," barks Collyns. "Last midsummer!" He looks about to see if he has spoken too loudly, and continues, quieter. "Even after we crossed the Ocean – not a word of the north passed his prick-mouthed lips till we got through the Strait."

"Anyhow," Eyot brings his hammer back to point at Thomas, "you think we don't know how you was dragged in kicking and screaming from *The Boar* in Plymouth? So don't be asking why we're here, as if any of us have a choice."

"You did. Squealing like a pig for the chop," laughs John. He turns to Eyot. "Do men live there – in the north?"

"No one save savages," says Eyot, hammering at the hatch again. "For there is no food. No grain, no crops will grow in the ice. They eat flesh – fish and foul – raw, howsoever they find it. Men's flesh too if they find no meat."

"Men's flesh!" Thomas' eyes widen.

"Nor is there fresh water," says Collyns. "They suck on ice. They use no horses but wolves. Fierce white wolves that will kill you as soon as look at you, yoked together as we do with oxen."

"How do they live?" I ask. "Do they have dwellings?"

Collyns looks to the side of me. He won't answer or own I have spoken. He thinks, as most sailors do, it is bad luck to sail with a woman. That we anger the sea with our womanly forms.

Instead he turns to John, as if it were he who asked. "They live in tents of sealskin, for there are no trees to cut for timber."

"It sounds fearful," says John, his voice unnaturally high. "But we shall be through it soon enough. General says we will pass over the top of America and into the warmer zone in some few weeks."

Eyot snorts his disbelief.

"Aye – if we don't end up like Willoughby," mutters Collyns.

"Who's Willoughby?" asks Thomas.

Eyot hammers in the last of the nails. "He went to find the North-East Passage twenty years past."

"Where's that?" I ask.

Eyot will own me. He is older than Collyns. Not so superstitious. "North of Muscovy. Willoughby got severed from his fleet in a tempest. The other ships came home without him. They were thought lost at sea."

"And were they?" asks Thomas. "All drowned?"

"Worse. Every man who sails prepares to die in the sea. It's not a bad death. It's quick. No pain. But this," he lets out a low whistle. "Twas another year before word came from the court in Muscovy."

Collyns waits, enjoying us watching, willing him to go on.

"When spring came, the merchants sailed north again. They found Willoughby's ship – stuck hard in a sea of ice. Every man aboard frozen where he died: sitting, lying, or at table. One man with the logbook before him, stopped in the midst of a word. All of them, statues of ice, eyes open and unseeing till the Judgement Day."

I am reading when Diego comes to the cabin later. Not the Book of Martyrs, it is too horrible. A book of navigation, from the General's collection.

"Why north?" I look up from the book on my lap. "Why go there if it's so inhospitable?"

"To find the passage to England," he frowns. "I told you. Then he can come and harry the Spaniard whenever he likes. Never will we get through the Southern Straits again, the Spaniards will fortify them."

He opens the General's sea-chest and takes out a linen undershirt. Crouching low on the floor he takes off his jerkin and shirt to put it on underneath. Even Diego is feeling the cold.

"But why not south-west?" As he stands, I see how low are his breeches, the curls of hair rising to his stomach.

"Nothing there."

"There's the unknown land." My eyes run along the lines of the book, reading nothing. "Terra Australis."

"Empty land," he scoffs. "No spoil. No silver, no spices."

"That's not what Juan Fernandez said. He said it was a fine country."

"Juan Fernandez?"

"El brujo del Pacífico. He is a hero in Chilley. He found it."

Diego stands and pulls his breeches higher. He ties them with the rope at his waist, a fine mariners' knot. "Then why do the Spaniards not have it known as their land?"

"He's not allowed back. Because he went without the Viceroy's leave. And no one else knows where it is."

"You know a lot about it," he comes over to me. "Did you read it? In a book?"

He slams the book on my lap shut, but the tip of my finger holds my place.

"It's on the charts," I shrug. "You've seen it. Why not go to England that way? Find the unknown land. Claim it for the English. Avoid the frozen zone altogether."

Diego nods.

"Do you know," he asks slowly, the corners of his mouth twitching, as he stops himself from smiling, "what happened to the last person who suggested to the General he give up his search for the passage?"

"I do not," I tell him curtly. My finger pains from the crushing weight of the book.

"He took off his head. Rather, he had Bosun take it off."

Diego gives in to the smile now.

"Don't look like that! The thing was done correctly. A jury of forty men judged his guilt."

By the Virgin in Heaven, a fine jury forty of these men would make.

"The mutineer Doughty," he goes on. "That was his treason. When we reached the Southern Straits, he argued for sailing direct to the East Indies. He thought himself above the General on account of his breeding. But he found a man's name can be washed away by the sea. The General bid him choose: stay ashore with the savages – or lose his head."

"He *chose* death?"

"Oh yes." Diego ties the shirt-strings at his wrists. "We were by the River Plate. Savages in those parts are mighty fearsome. He and the General dined together like gentlemen. Then Doughty willingly put his head on the block." He smiles broadly now. "And *they* were friends. So I wouldn't mention Terra Australis to the General if I were you."

He pulls his own shirt back over the undershirt, laces his jerkin and leaves, whistling.

I open the book again and shake my finger to bring back the blood.

What a choice! I'd sooner take my chances with the savages ashore than these ashipboard. I return to the book where I kept my place.

What is the use of Navigation? it asks.

"The use thereof is this: how to direct a course in the Sea, and to consider what dangers are by the way, as Rocks and Sands and such other like impediments. How to attain a port, if the wind does shift or change; and if any storms do happen to consider how to preserve the Ship and bring her safe unto the port assigned."

Malhaya Dios, I like that! How fine it would be to have a port assigned to me.

23

The cold and fog bring on the seamen's sickness. One man, Stokes, has already died of it. Another lies in the gun deck, his groans echoing up through the closed hatches. Old Godfrey, they call him, since he is of a very great age for a seaman – some fifty years and counting.

Stokes was a favourite of the General, thuggish brute that he was, so he was put into the sea with a piece fired from the cannon to send him on his way. We sang prayers and psalms on deck – led by the General. Fletcher is banned from services since his foolish words at Thomas' hanging.

In its shroud of sailcloth the body met the sea. It turned and twisted in the waves, then rose sharply as if he thought better of it at the final moment. Then he sank below the waves, the water claiming his mortal remains.

As the cold fog closes over his resting place, Collyns lets out a long, high whistle. "This was the end of poor Foster, too," he says. "He died from the scarby in the north seas. By God on his throne, I hope Stokes don't come back like he did."

"What do you mean?" asks Carey. "He's dead. How can he come back?"

"You may mock and disbelieve," Collyns nods his head. "But I have seen it done. Foster came back and there was no denying it."

"Where?" asks Carey. "When was this?"

"New-found Land. Or thereabouts," says Collyns. "When I was—" and the men join in with the words they know are coming: "*with Frobisher.*"

"Come now. Since you has 'eard the story, you may tell it yourselves," he sniffs.

"Nay Collyns. We don't know this one," grins Carey. "Tell us."

Collyns turns his back to the sea and leans against the gunwale. "After Foster died and was put into the sea, the ice packed around us hard. Gripped the ship like a vice. Looked set to snap her clean in half. Lucky we was near the shore, so we abandoned her – anchored and left to her fate. We stopped and made shelter on the land. A terrible winter it was. I have not the words to describe it." He looks down at the boards.

"Then pray, Collyns, do not," puts in Diego. "Just tell us: What happened to Foster?"

Collyns eyes Diego darkly. "The ship did not snap. Six months later, when the ice started to thaw, we went back to her. Those of us who lived, that is, for many died from the cold and the hardship. And there he was – Foster. In the gun room where he spent his living days."

"What do you mean?" roars Carey. "How could he be in the gun room?"

Collyns smirks. "The ice had broken into the ship and let in water. He must have come in then, after he was put into the sea. And then the water froze hard in the ship. So that's how we found him. Frozen in the ice from the waist down, waiting for us to return."

I shiver. To be preserved in death and not buried: a fate deserved only by the worst of enemies.

"What did he… look like?" asks Thomas. "His face I mean. Six months in the water and ice is a goodly time."

"Well," Collyns crosses his arms and thinks it over. "Not bad, when you consider it. A touch grey. But not so bad as you might think." Then he grins as he remembers something.

"The worst of it was his flesh. Cold and slippery as a dead fish. When you touched it, it flip-flopped on his bones like it was a glove." He flaps his own hands in Thomas' face in mimicry of poor Foster.

I get a moment's warning of it and then I am sick on the boards. Three times, barely able to catch my breath between each retching.

John has finished his picture. He has painted me on the poop deck, my hair loose, a thickly-forested land falling away behind me. I am holding a sprig of a dark-green-leafed plant, a mystery to me when first I see it.

"What's that in my hands, John? Why do you have me gathering herbs for the pot?"

"It's myrtle, you goose. It means new lands. A likeness-painter from Napolis told me that's what you draw in the hands of an explorer."

I laugh. "Am I an explorer now?"

"We all are," he says, gravely. "We're all going somewhere no one's ever been before."

"Why myrtle?"

He shrugs. "It signifies… new things. New places. New life. Brides carry it when they marry, to get a baby quickly."

My hand flies to my belly in horror. Has he seen? But I see from his face he has not.

"I see," I turn from him. "A charm."

"Like a coney's foot."

"A coney's *what*?"

"Foot," he sighs. "It's a charm to bring good luck. Sailors wear them to save from drowning."

My heart slows. I peer closer at the picture. John has softened the lines in my brow. I do not look so very angry now.

"Do you carry one? A coney's foot?"

"Course," he grins, and pulls out the mangled, no-longer

furry paw of some sorry animal from where it hangs at a cord around his neck. "Ma gave it me when I left."

He puts the painting with the others in the sea-chest and scurries out the door. So there I lie, flat on parchment, between the pengwyns and the camel-sheep, the Indios with their canoes, the fire-shooting volcanoes and the fish that fly through the air.

Whatever becomes of me, wherever I end, I will be in this picture always. Perhaps John is right: the Queen of England will look upon it one day. What will she think of me then? A wild-haired woman, in a place she does not belong and should not be. Carrying new life inside her, the myrtle in her hands screams it plainly. I am glad this picture exists. That she may see it. Perhaps she will show it, for all to see and know that I was here.

MAY, 1579

MARE PACIFICUM

44°10'N

24

Now comes the sickness to Master Fletcher.

His legs swell up like a baby elephant's. The blood drips from the blackened mess of his gums down his cheek. His teeth are loose and bloody in the root when they come out. In all, it is a ghastly sight, and one that occupies me greatly, for the General has put aside his fury with the chaplain for his treasonous words at Thomas' hanging and had Fletcher brought to his own cabin.

So here he lies grizzling, while I pick out the dead and rotten flesh of his gums with the point of a knife, wipe the sweat and blood from his face with sea-soaked cloths and help him use pots under the bedclothes to discharge his waste.

The surgion's boy comes – the surgion himself lost long before I came to this ship – and Fletcher's face fills with horror. "Let him not near me!" he hisses. "He will take my blood. It does not help."

"He is much improved," I tell the boy – clear to see a falsehood. "No need to let his blood today. I will prepare him a salve." The surgion-boy leaves, muttering that the sorcery of savages will save no one.

In faith, I can make a salve, for I have seen the disease many times. On the Manila galleons, the sailors drink the juice of lemons and limes to ward it away. I still dare not go to the steward's store myself, but I have John fetch what I need.

I rub lemon-juice on Fletcher's gums and pour it in his throat, stroking his neck like a baby to make him swallow. I mix the juice with oil to make a sticky salve to rub on his aching joints, and a broth of rosemary and thyme and saffron for him to sup. I wash his sorry legs and exercise them like he is walking in the air. He groans with each movement, but slowly becomes more agreeable to my ministry.

Why I go to these lengths for him I do not know. But it is good to have a purpose.

The General sleeps in the Great Cabin, away from the stench and bother of sickness. But he comes to visit, sweeping into the cabin in all his vigour and lusty health. He springs one leg upon the stool to rest his elbow on it. "And what is all this, Master Fletcher? They tell me you have something of the scarby. What did I tell you about keeping busy? Idleness breeds the disease. Would that I had put you to the ropes, ha!"

His manner does not cheer the chaplain, and even the General sees mercy is in order. He prays with him, and very prettily too. But when he has finished he takes out paper, quill and ink and asks such things as fill Fletcher with terror anew.

"Tell me, my friend. What words shall I record for your family?"

"For my family?" Fletcher splutters, bloody drool dripping onto the linen.

"What do you wish to say of them for your will and testament?"

"You think I will die?"

"Nay, Master Fletcher," the General smiles. "But we must all prepare ourselves, for death is ever with us and all around. We will all face the judgement of Almighty God sooner or later, and tis better to have done our duty by those we leave behind."

He seems little concerned whether it is sooner or later for

poor Fletcher. "Are you owed any monies? Do you owe any to others?"

"No!" says Master Fletcher. His palms rub the bedlinen, smearing into them the stain of his blood.

"And to whom do you wish to leave your possessions?" The General picks up Fletcher's fine Geneva Bible, and opens it at the Psalms, nodding at the rightness of the book. Fletcher leans forward and takes it roughly back.

The General looks at him in surprise. "Well, Master Fletcher. Think upon it. I shall see you again in the eventide."

He is out of the door without a farewell. Indeed he cannot get out fast enough, his steps echoing around the silent cabin as he runs down the steps to the maindeck.

The chaplain holds his Bible with both hands, staring at the cross etched into the front cover. His thumbs gently stroke the lines of gold that mark the edges of the book.

"If I die Maria, you shall have it," he says quietly. "There is not one villain on this ship who would profit by it."

After this, the chaplain starts to recover. Mayhap to spite the General – or is it my savage sorcery that works its magic?

In time his moaning wanes. Now, instead of turning from them, he asks for my broths and the salve I make from oil and herbs and lemons to rub on his aching limbs.

He teaches me the Lord's Prayer, to prepare for my baptism when we reach England. *Our Father*, he prompts me, and I go on:

Which art in heaven, hallowed be thy name.
Thy kingdom come, thy will be fulfilled
As well in Earth as it is in heaven.
Give us this day our daily bread
And forgive us our…

"Trespasses," he smiles.

Forgive us our… trespasses, even as we forgive our…
trespassers.

And lead us not into temptation, but deliver us from evil.

For thine is the kingdom and the power and the glory for ever.

He grips my hands and looks fearfully into my eyes.

Amen.

But I know he is truly mending when he gets out of bed and starts to walk about the cabin. I watch him from the table, where I mix lemons and oil. The sticky juice drips down my forearms to the crease of my elbow. The scent hangs sharp in the air.

He inspects the General's belongings on the shelf, taking each one down, turning it about, and he nods, or grimaces at the item, according to his approval. He takes down the astrolabe, and plays with it, moving the peg around the disc while holding it to his ear, to hear the mechanism.

"How does it work?" I ask him.

"Come," he says. "I'll show you."

I wipe the juice from my hands with my skirt.

"Hold this," he says, placing around my middle finger a cord. The disc-like device hangs from it, heavy. It spins, wrapping the cord even tighter around my finger.

"Hold it up," he lifts my elbow with two fingers, and holds my wrist steady when the disc reaches level with my eyes.

He stands beside me, careful to keep his body from touching mine.

"Then turn this peg to line up with the sun at midday –"

"Only at midday?"

He nods, gravely.

"And note here the number the peg points to on the disc."

He goes to the shelf, and looks through the books, bringing one out to lay open on the table. The pages are filled with lists and rows of numbers, written small in brown ink. He follows one line with his forefinger.

"So when you know how high is the sun at noon, this chart tells you how far you are from the line."

"From the equinoctial?"

"Indeed."

"And how do you tell how far east or west?"

He laughs. It is good to see his shoulders shake. "We guess! Not everything can be known, Maria! We must leave to the Almighty some of His secrets."

When the sun has gone, and the chill of the day sharpens into ice-cold night, Fletcher and I, sitting in the cabin, hear the last Amen from the men gathered in prayer in the waist. Fletcher asks me for his journal, pen and ink, and I help him to the table where the candle flickers.

A full and weighty book, he has kept up the writing of it since they left England. He writes in a small script, yet readable, and many line drawings in his own hand to show the wonders of the voyage. They are fine. Some rival John's in skill and he is pleased to have me tell him as much.

He writes, frowning, then takes out a sheaf of bound pages from the inside of his shirt. He writes in that too, passing from the book to the papers, but in a scrawl. Not in Latin letters; in curious shapes and figures, circles and dots. "What is that?"

He looks up, as if he is trying to read me.

"Cipher," he says darkly. "*He* bade me write the journal. That when we return I shall write the history of his glorious voyage. But I would have my own record too, for there is much I would keep from his eyes."

"What will you do with it?"

"I don't know. But he who has the pen writes the story, Maria!" He holds up his pen before him as if it were a knife. He goes back to his writing. "It is my surety."

"To be sure of what?"

He clasps and unclasps his hands. "My honour. Which I do not wish to be mingled as one with his."

I straighten the bedcovers and put a blanket around his thin shoulders.

"Because of what he did to Doughty?" I ask, lightly.

"You have heard that shameful tale," he nods. "Yes, that. And – other things."

"You think the General dishonourable?"

He dabs with a handkercher at a blot of ink on the palm of his hand. "Shall I say – that I do not think it safe to return to England enriched with the Spaniard's treasure – and I *know* it is not honest."

"But your Queen will be pleased with such riches, surely?"

He looks at the portrait of her. A manly-looking woman, she stares across the cabin to the picture of her envoy, the General. A piercing gaze. She seems to hold him to account already.

"That falls on how things go with the King of Spain," says Fletcher. "He is her brother still, for he was her sister's husband. And we cannot know how things stand between them till we return.

"And do not forget," he turns to me, "that the Queen is not our highest authority." His finger is raised to the heavens to be sure I understand. "And if he does not bring upon him the fury of the Queen for provoking the Spaniard, he will not escape the vengeance of Heaven."

I look out the window. For the first time in many nights – weeks even – the stars are starting to show. Like so many eyes waking from a long sleep. The fog must be lifting. "But he thinks himself owed, the General? For the money lost at San Juan de Ulúa? That is what he told the Alcalde at Guatulco."

"He may think it," Fletcher's voice shakes. I turn in surprise. "But it was not his money! Nor his cousin Hawkins' neither! It was not gained through honest trade but through brutality and violence."

He turns a page of his journal, smoothing the pages flat. "In any case, they brought out most of the silver from the ships before the Spaniards sunk them."

He puts the pen down and rests his head in his hands. "Do you know what they did not bring out? What was lost in those ships, when our General and Hawkins escaped?"

Of course I do not know. I shake my head.

"Or I should say rather: whom. For as the ships burned and sank, they saved themselves and their silver, and left chained in the holds fifty-seven slaves. Each valued at four hundred pesos of gold in the accounts Hawkins submitted to the Admiralty Court in demand for recompense from the Spanish crown."

My throat feels as if it could close up and choke me entirely.

"Fifty-seven men, women and children, Maria! Drowned before they could be baptised."

Baptised? Drowned before they could live!

"Then he was on a slaving voyage, the General?"

Fletcher nods, still holding his head in his hands.

"Why did you sail with him?"

"I was put forward for it – by the sort of man who cannot be refused. To be his eyes and ears for the sake of his investment in this voyage."

"Then you are a spy?"

He grimaces. "Not a spy. An interested... observer."

He opens another pot of ink. A little cord of leather links the cap to the pot like a lifeline.

"And they said we would bring heathens to Christ." He looks up to the heavens.

"Have you?"

"Have I – what?"

"Brought heathens to Christ?"

He sighs. "We have not."

He scratches at the blot again, which marks his skin.

"Nor do I doubt now," he says quietly. "That they are better left where they are in their ignorance, with Christ looking out for them from Heaven, than to be put in the earthly hands of such men."

He labours for some time more, turning from the large book, where he writes in plain English, to his cipher-journal, where he makes his unreadable symbols and marks. When he is done, he asks for my arm, and I help him to bed. I rub his legs with the salve. They improve daily. He will return to sleep in the armoury soon and I shall miss him.

He reads his Bible in silence by the dim candlelight, says a prayer in a low voice where he lies in the bed, and then signals me to put out the light.

On the floor, I lie on the mat where Diego usually sleeps. It smells of him. Of animal grease from the ropes. Of his sweat and the ship's tar. Of the cigarros he smokes when the General, who disapproves of the habit, cannot see him. Musty and rich. He could be in the room he has so strongly left his mark.

I am thinking of him, of where he lies now, just below these boards in the Great Cabin with the General. I am thinking of the way he sleeps: on his side, with one arm cushioning his head, and the other thrown over it – the only time he is ever careless about anything – when I hear the chaplain murmur: "Only you, Maria."

I rise up in confusion. "What is only me?"

"You are the only heathen we have brought to God."

25

I saw the battle at San Juan de Ulúa. Where those slaves were burned and drowned. I had not been at Veracruz long.

From the tower of the priory you can see the fortress island, not far out to sea. It is where the slaving ships come in.

They unload the miserable people there on the rocks, blinking and shuffling in irons. They can walk, though they have been lying head to toe in the darkness for so long, because those who cannot walk have been thrown in the sea, and those who remain have been danced on the deck for hours on end in the days before they arrive to make their muscles strong.

San Juan de Ulúa is also where the flota comes in twice in every year, bringing from Old Spain wine, olive oil and almonds, weapons and soldiers, officials. Very rarely come the wives and the families of officials and they are careful to leave Veracruz very quickly because of the bad air. Not a single baby has been born there to a Spanish woman and survived.

In the weeks before the flota goes back to Sevilla, trains of mules arrive, snaking down the hillside paths, bringing pearls from Tierra Firme, cochinilla dye from Antequera, silver from Perou, and the treasures of Cathay brought to Acapulco on the Manila galleons.

One morning, some weeks after I myself arrived in Veracruz, there came some unexpected visitors. There was a terrible storm. I remember, because I was still scared of them. Later, I got used to them, so I would say to newcomers, as did the friars, that you cannot sleep unless you hear the wind trying to tear down the walls around you and lift the tiles from the roof.

This storm was bad and it had raged for a week already. I held tight to Luisa in bed alongside me. If we were to be blown away, I did not want to be alone.

The next morning, the wind died. After my work in the dairy was done, I went up the bell-tower to see the damage. Instead I saw six ships, listing and torn, sail into San Juan de Ulúa. One had lost its mainmast. Others had great gashes in their broadsides, lost fighting-tops and yards. All were sail-torn, flags and ensigns damaged or gone.

This was why, the Spaniards said later, that the soldiers guarding this most defended port in all the New World, let them in without a shot. They thought this bedraggled fleet was the flota bringing the new Viceroy of New Spain, whom they expected at any moment.

Then I understood that there was something wrong, because all of a sudden, men poured from the ships to take the cannons and culverins on the island. Merchants ran out the warehouses to race back to Veracruz. The water was filled with their little boats, people swimming even, in their haste to get away.

They arrived in the town screaming: *Luteranos! The Lutherans are upon us!* It echoed down every street in Veracruz. The merchants rolled up the great sails that shaded the marketplace, put away their stalls, packed what they could onto mules, locked their warehouses, barred their doors and left for the mountains.

"Should we leave?" I asked Fray Calvo.

"Nay, child, we are safe. God will preserve us."

The people thought so too, because they streamed down every street carrying what they could, pleading for sanctuary from the English pirates.

For six days, the city stopped still. Every day I climbed the belfry to watch.

From the roofs and steeples, the vultures of Veracruz watched with me. They were used to death, living in such a place. They could smell it coming. And it did – but not yet. First came the real Spanish fleet, which brought Don Martín Enríquez, the new Viceroy of New Spain.

He will send them away, the merchants thought, and they came back to the city.

But the English ships did not go.

Now there were two fleets packed tight into the harbour, barely an inch between them, broadside to broadside, the full length of the harbour wall.

In the pitch of the night, I lay sleepless in bed holding Luisa's hand.

The only Englishmen I had ever known were those who took me in Guinney. I had no desire to meet any again.

There was the crunch of soldiers' boots on the cobblestones outside: tens of them, more: hundreds. It took many minutes for them all to pass. They were silent, whispering, but could not mask the clank of their weapons against armour. They rowed with muffled oars to the English ships at the fortress island.

At dawn, a trumpet sounded long and urgent. The battle began.

26

The sun is at its midday peak, softer now, less fierce than in the south. The air is cold. The fog has lifted. Without the heat smudging the horizon it is clearer and sharper. The sea is darker, bottomless.

Each day the helmsman puts pegs in the traverse board so even those who cannot read can see how far we have travelled. That is not enough for me. The sails to the south gain on us every day. I must know when we pass the 44th line above the equinoctial.

I beg of the General his astrolabe and he indulges me.

"See, Carey." He pulls him to where I stand on the foredeck, taking the declination, as Fletcher showed me, one eye shut against the sun. "A wonder is she not?"

Carey sniffs. "I wonder at you, for what is the purpose? You may as well teach a dog to sound the depths."

"I warrant I could teach a dog my shipcraft," says the General. "The meanest mutt would have a finer sense for it than you!"

He laughs with his head high and back, as he does when he is pleased to remind a man of his place. Carey punches him – gently – in the shoulder, and smiles, as well he ought.

They may have their jokes. It matters not to me. Because now I know that somewhere over there, where the waves glisten like glass in the morning sun, is the 44th line: the northernmost limit of Spanish exploration on this ocean. They can follow us as they wish, the Spaniards' warships. Past this line they have no claim to me.

I am free.

It makes my heart sing.

Eleven years of slavery. Four masters. Once taken, once given up, once bought, once won. Each time passed from one man to another as if I were a side of beef. Oceans crossed against my will – many times. A life at sea with lustful, violent men. Two babies in my belly by a man I loathe.

Eleven years – and now I am free. This is why I jumped into the unknown. This child, I will not lose. This one will not be taken from me.

Ten weeks, Diego says. Ten weeks till we pass through the passage. That is all I need. With binding, I can hide the swelling for three months more. By the time I am discovered, it will be too far to turn back. Even he, surely, would not set down a baby in the wilderness.

I watch, mighty content, as the bow cleaves the foamy waves, nothing before me but the sparkling sea. A little blackbird, lost from the coast, alights on the foremast yard. I watch her, plucking at her feathers, lifting her beak into the air, to scent the land. I could watch her all day. But when she is rested, she takes off, lifted by the winds rising from the sea, riding on the current landwards to the north-east.

As I watch her go, I find – already – that my freedom is not enough. I make pretence. That the ship itself is my own. That she takes me where I command her to go, and not where I am taken. That I go, like the Empress Mansarico, where I will, and these men, bickering and cursing behind me, follow.

Why not? There, on the horizon, where the sea darkens into indigo and the sky fades into a haze: that is a new place. A different world, again.

Anian, I say it to myself, rolling the word about my tongue like a sweetmeat. All things are possible there.

Book Two

ANIAN

June – July, 1579

JUNE, 1579

MARE PACIFICUM

52°40'N

27

Land is all we think of. So when the sailors report the signs that we will soon fetch the coast, I do not know if they are real.

I discern nothing. No shadow nor shape in the gloom before us. Merely shades of grey of the steel-coloured sea before it melts into the fog.

"Can you smell them?" asks John, coming up behind me on the foredeck.

"Smell what?"

"Flowers. The men say you can smell them when the wind comes from the east."

We breathe in lungfuls of the biting cold air. Naught in it I can smell, save the rot of the fog and the salt of the ocean.

Later Eyot comes up to see to repairs. "There it comes!" he grins. "The roll of the ship has changed."

Thomas mimics Eyot's stance. Legs apart, knees bent, his arms held out to the sides. "I can't feel it!"

"Nay lad, and nor will you for many years," says Eyot. "You can't learn it. The roll comes up from the sea-bed direct to your bones. As sure as the beat of a drum to a mariner."

Eyot goes to his business with his hammer. For the rest of the day, I find Thomas standing in the same manner, frowning with disappointment.

But for all the tales of the old sailors, John is the first to sight land. He drops down from the lookout like a wildcat, the fur of his winter-cape standing up around his neck. He pants so hard I can barely hear what he is saying. But at last I understand.

"That's what I *said*. I saw *land*. And it's not all white with snow – there's green. Trees – big ones. Lofty mountains. It is the main – no island."

Diego comes. "How can you see anything in this fog, boy?"

"It's clearing up there," says John. "See for yourself."

The men peer up, where the foremast disappears into the mist. No one moves.

Yet. There is a patch of sky above us, beyond the sails, that billow, full with wind. I have never been in the lookout – nor the rigging. I never thought to climb it. Before they stop me I am up – flying faster as I rise, falling into the rhythm: hand, foot, foot, hand. Like climbing a tree. The men disappear into the mist below.

Freezing water in the air, but I warm as I climb. I stop, clinging with my legs and one arm, to tear the mantle from my chest and tie it around my waist. Past the roaring sails. The higher I go, the greater the pitch. The mast drops one way and then the other, so violent, I fear I will fall into the sea. The sickness rises. I stop once, twice, gripping on for my life, until it passes.

For the first time I understand what John told me about the lookout. The lonesomeness, the feeling that you are utterly abandoned. That all life and industry below was just a dream. And he was right. There is land. The first I – nor anyone on this ship has seen – in fifty-five days.

Here, above the mist, the world stretches out as far as I can see. To the south, rugged grey cliffs appear through the fog like floating islands. To the north, hills rise into snow-covered mountains. There are meadows in the foothills, dressed with yellow and purple flowers. Everywhere, a carpet of deep green. Each giant tree become a mere stalk swaying with the wind. I want to weep I am so glad to see it. How I have missed the colour *green*.

How vast it is, how different to anything I have seen before. Is this Anian? Certainly, it is a new world. Empty and unspoiled. Where are the limits to this land? What lies beyond the mountains? I cannot believe the freedom! There is nothing higher than me here – nothing!

But in the vastness of the blue sky, there is something. A bird – far greater than a hawk. She soars above me on the wind, her feet tucked underneath, her eyes on her aim. So rightful in her place she need not move her wings. The wind carries her as if she is no weight at all.

She sees beyond the mountains. What is in the forests, among those thick and close-grown branches. She can follow the sparkling rivers back from the sea, through meadows and hills, rocks and cliffs, narrowing to trickling streams at their sources.

She turns – the merest tilt of a wing downwards, and soars towards the land.

I watch her, mighty content. That is freedom. To go where you will, with all you need to get there the right and proper parts of yourself. I watch until she is long out of sight, towards the peaks. To her nest, I picture it: perched on the ledge of an unreachable mountain crag.

"Now what?" I ask Diego when I am down.

"We follow the coast." He points where it sweeps to the north, the green line of trees as it meets the rocky coast. The fog has lifted below now too, and he gestures to the gaps between the mountains. "There will be inlets, rivers. We search every one for the passage."

"I thought the General had found it?"

"'Tis only a matter of time. He never fails in anything he sets his mind to."

"But it will take months!"

"It cannot." His eyes sparkle like the snow on the mountains. "We must be through before winter."

He thinks as does the General. He desires it, then it will be so.

Already he has moved on. "We will eat well tonight!" He calls to Lawney the cook, in the throng of men at the gunwale, jostling for a sight of the land. "Slaughter the hens!"

Lawney turns, his little eyes full of venom. But he answers with a nod. "All of them?"

"Aye. The men have had no meat for weeks. There will be game in the forest to fill the stores."

Diego takes the mantle from my waist and wraps it around my shoulders as icy rain begins to fall. "And tomorrow, muñeca, we seek safe anchorage. We need water and firewood as well as meat."

"Muñeca?" I ask. He looks at the boards.

Thomas comes up from below, rising to meet the excitement.

"Any sign of savages?" he asks.

28

On land at last! Steady land that does not move, or creak nor pitch. It does not grumble nor reek of saltpetre and tar.

The earth is frozen solid. It is hard to walk, for Diego has given me his land-going boots. Stuffed to the toes with cloths around my feet, the great leather cuffs reach over my knees.

The air is clean. The smell of the trees is everywhere: heavy and sweet, like fruit ready to drop. The trunks are vast: as wide as a shop-front. They soar to the heavens, higher than a ship's mast.

Diego did not want me to come. There is no sign of savages, but a strange land seems empty enough, he says, till the first arrow comes whistling out of the shadows and thuds into a man's back. But I had to come ashore. How could I stay aboard when here is *land*?

I was in the Great Cabin, reading the Gospell with the General when Fletcher came in and begged to come ashore with the watering party. He would make drawings of the trees and plants, he said, to record God's magnificent bounty in this new Eden. I saw the chance directly. "And I would collect herbs and flowers as are useful against the scarby." For they are quite in demand now, my salves and broths, after my success with the chaplain. Not one man has died after taking them.

So here we are, following the creek inland. We are thirteen. Collyns leads. Pyke puts himself behind me so he can tread on my skirts to keep me mindful he is there. Fludd, Blackoller and others carry barrels for fresh water. Fletcher dallies at the rear, where he can stop and wonder at every drooping leaf or crouching frog. Thomas carries the chaplain's pens and inks at his heels.

The water babbles beside us like a talkative child. Fish swim against the stream, the colour of new silver. I dip my hand to feel how cold. It bites.

Pyke stops with me, his knee hard in my rear. He shifts the musket at his shoulder, to remind me he carries a weapon – the only weapon we have between us. Collyns refused to come without it – and the surest gunner on the ship to fire it. Indeed, at first, Collyns would not come at all, till the General pulled him from the mob. "Come, Collyns. You know the north. Show us your worth."

He does not look so proud now. In faith he looks nervous as a sparrow, darting his eyes into the dark forest as we climb the snow-patched boulders beside the creek.

Here on dry land, where I cannot anger the sea, Collyns will own me. "Keep up, wench!" he barks when he spies me stooped by the water. "We stay together. I'll not get myself killed waiting for you."

They do not even agree on what it is called, this land. Fletcher said it is the island of California. Eyot said the west side of Labrador. It took three times of asking Diego. He shrugged his shoulders as though nothing could be of smaller consequence, and said only: *America*.

The roar of a waterfall gets louder, and soon we see it – water like glass, dropping down the rockface. Something flashes in the wide pool at the bottom and as we near, we see it is the fish. They leap – fly even – into the air. Most drop back again and again. But one in every dozen or so attempts lands in a little pool on a higher level of rock, from where he tries to go higher.

"God's blood!" cries Thomas. "They're trying to climb the fall!"

"Easy takings," nods Collyns. "They'll catch themselves if we put a basket under them. We stop here."

He orders the men into the ice-cold water to fill the empty barrels. "You too!" He hands Thomas a bag of nails. "Hammer the barrels shut."

Thomas watches the men shivering in the water and shudders himself. He turns sharply towards the top of the fall. "What's that?" he points.

All eyes follow his finger. Fludd starts to wade back to the bank.

"Stay!" roars Collyns. "There's nothing there." His eyes run along the ridge at the top of the fall.

"There," Thomas narrows his eyes. "Something black and – I might say – furlike."

"Yea," I say. "I see something," though I do not.

"I'll climb up," says Thomas. "If it's a dead thing, it will foul the water. An' *I'm* not having the shittin' sickness again. Not after what happened to Jenkyns."

He starts to climb the rocks beside the fall.

"I'll go too," I say.

"As you like," says Collyns.

"And I," says Pyke, starting behind me.

"Not you," says Collyns, and I breathe again. "You and the weapon stay with us."

"Then I shall go," says Fletcher, rolling up his shirtsleeves.

Collyns shrugs his shoulders. "No need for a weapon, Fletcher – your God will look out for you!" He laughs. "And hurry mind, else we turn back without you."

Above me, Thomas climbs swiftly as a goat. It is even harder to climb than walk in these boots and my feet slip on the icy rock. I pull at roots that come out in my numbed and frozen hands, spraying loose earth down on Fletcher below.

But it is not so very high, and soon I am at the top, where Thomas lies on the moss by the stream. The water churns as it flows from one pool into another before tumbling down the levels of the fall, to where Collyns and the other men wait in the icy water below.

Here, I am amazed to see, are fish that have climbed the

fall. Stronger and fatter than those below. Long and fast, they make their way through the rolling water and onwards, against the current, into the darkening forest.

Nowhere is there anything black nor the least furlike in the water.

Fletcher's white fingers and then his face appear above the rocks at the fall's edge. He pulls himself up. "How gratifying," he smiles, "to be free from that loathsome man."

He calls down to Collyns. "Nothing here. Merely leaves in the water. But we will go on a while and check upstream."

There is no answer from below.

"Shall we go on?" he beams.

We continue, following the water. It starts to snow – cold pricks like a pin on my cheek. It is dry, not bothersome, till it turns to freezing water on my brow and on my ears. I pull up my mantle to cover my head. Thunder rolls in the distance.

How different it is from forests in the south. No monkeys screeching, nor the crash of big animals in the undergrowth. Only the sound of the water, babbling away, the rustle of the tall trees swaying in the wind and birdsong: a two-note call that sounds like a greeting.

From the underbrush, long-eared conies stop to watch us, then run for cover under blackberry bushes. On the bank of the creek, sharp eyes in wet-furred heads follow us keenly. In the water, the fish swim on, so certain of wherever it is they are going.

"Witness, Maria," Fletcher sighs happily. "The providence of our Creator; the bounty of His creatures. All that He has made for our service."

"Who was Jenkyns?" I ask Thomas.

"Ship boy. Died before we got to the Canaries. After lying in his own beshitten filth for three days."

Fletcher walks slowly, sweeping before him a big stick to clear the trailing ferns and low branches. He stops often to look at a leaf or animal droppings. He feels everything. On his heels to rub the stem of a flower, or squash and smell the berries of a low bush.

"Here, boy," he calls to Thomas. "My things if you please." And he takes his journal and a quill while Thomas holds the ink, and he draws against his knees, his eyes moving from the trunk of a vast tree to the page of his journal to capture the pattern of its bark in perfect detail.

I leave them to it. The snow settles on the ground. My feet are numbed, even in the great boots. But I get used to it, and barely do I feel the cold for the wonder of being in this place.

There are a thousand shades of green. The light itself seems to glow, like coloured glass in a cathedral. Vast columns of trees, branches holding up the roof of the sky.

I realise with a start that here, ahead of Fletcher and Thomas – and far ahead of the other men – I am the first to see this new land. John was right, I am an explorer.

So many times did I cross the South Ocean but I never once set foot in a virgin place. In Manila, when the galleons were stuffed to the waterline with the treasures of the east, the marineros would talk of it. Of taking off, with a sack full of precious gems from the hold, out of the hands of the Viceroy. To the islands in the south: the famed jewel markets of the rajas of Sumatera, Java and Gelgel. And further: to the unknown land Juan Fernandez boasted of: empty, unspoiled, ungoverned Terra Australis.

More than once Gonzalo threatened to do it. He never dared. Not one of them ever did.

But I! They should see me now. For here I am further than they ever travelled. Beyond the charted world – beyond all imagining. Truly do I merit the adventurer's myrtle. John will be glad to be correct in his painting. He must paint me for his Queen holding a thousand bunches of myrtle!

The snow thins. I stop to listen. As I pull down the mantle

from my head, the better to hear, something whistles past my nose from the treetops. It comes to a thud in the dusting of snow at my feet.

A bird. A tiny fluff of a thing, soft and white on his belly. Fallen frozen from the sky, just as Diego said.

Behold the fowls of the air! Master Fletcher would say if he were here and not idling so far behind. *For they sow not, neither reap, nor yet carry into barns, and yet your Heavenly Father feedeth them.*

Yea, and He stills them too, in the midst of flight, to crash upon the earth.

But the bird is not stilled. It breathes. Its heart beats faintly, so very fast. I scoop him into my hands, his tiny body so light and soft, and I whisper to him. I peel back my mantle to warm him at my breast.

The beat of his heart slows. His beak opens and he breathes sharply. He blinks at me, and I talk to him, like a fool. When he is calmed, I set him on the ground under a bush. He stops, twists his head to look at me. He hops – once, twice – then soars into the air. He trills, a little whistle of three notes. It is because I am watching my little bird take to the treetops that I do not see them till it is too late.

The savages, who watch me from above, standing on rocks overlooking the stream.

I stop, rooted to the earth. At the moment I see them I remember: *I am all alone.*

There are six of them. So strange, so different to my eyes it takes me some moments to comprehend. They carry spears taller than themselves. They wear capes of feathers and animal hair, which cover their shoulders and fall to their knees. Their undershirts are woody, like bark. Their legs and feet are bare, despite the snow.

Their faces are daubed with red and black powder in different shapes. They wear cone-shaped hats, hair pulled back under them. All carry bulging baskets and bags. One, standing apart from the others, drops something. Red berries pour down the bank to settle in a pool at my feet.

So still are they. So frozen am I. Each berry crackles as it rolls down the frosty ground into new snow. The stream babbles beside me. The wind lifts the branches of the great trees, the smell of their leaves sharper and sweeter to me in my fear.

I hold out my hands to show they are empty.

He standing foremost points his spear at me, and turns to the others, speaking quickly.

The tongue is hard, otherworldly. The others raise their spears and answer, using the same words. High in pitch.

I should run. But I am frozen.

As they pour down the bank towards me, calling the same sounds over and over again, their spears raised aloft and their feather capes lifted by the rushing air, I see it at last – they are women.

When Fletcher and Thomas arrive I am alone again. On my knees, surrounded by baskets of berries, roots and fish.

"What happened? Who was here? Are you harmed?" Fletcher runs the last paces to me.

"Nothing. No one. I... found the baskets. Here. By the stream."

He crouches, searching to see what they carry. "There is good food here. Why would anyone abandon it?"

"Maybe they heard us and ran." Why do I lie? I do not know. Save that this is my thing, this business. It is not for anyone else.

The way they called to me, over and again – not Maria, as I said to them, my hand on my breast to show I meant myself. They called me – I do swear it. It sounded so much like it, though different in their tongues – Macaia.

How can that be?

They came in close to me. They took each basket from

where it hung at their arms, or lashed to their backs, put them at my feet and walked away, backwards. They sang. It was calm and peaceful. The melody gentle as a hymn.

Then they kneeled before me, picked up rocks and stones from the earth and dashed them against their limbs and faces, tearing great gashes in their skin. I tried to take the rocks from their hands. But when they had no rocks, they used the nails of their fingers, blood streaming from their wounds.

Till Fletcher and Thomas came near. Branches snapped. Fletcher's stick cracked. The women ran into the forest, spears aloft, noiseless and fast.

I cannot think what to make of it.

Fletcher is looking at me. "Maria!" Maybe he has said it several times because he is shouting and his face is full of fear.

"I do not know," I stand, brushing the snow from my skirt. "I don't know why they were left here, but here they are all the same."

"We must go." He takes my arm to lead me away. "At once."

Thomas picks through a basket. "What do they want with all this *bark*?"

"We should take these things," I say to Fletcher. "We are lucky to find them." I pull my hand from his to take up the baskets and bags.

"Take these," I say to Thomas. I do not want him to see the bloodied rocks on the ground, though surely he can smell as I do, the scent of blood in the air. I load them into his arms. He looks at me as if I am a stranger, and I crouch to scoop the spilled berries into the bag that was dropped on top of the bank.

Back at the waterfall, the barrels are filled and nailed shut. Two wide baskets lie next to them, filled with silvery fish.

The men idle on the bank. But they jump up when they see us running, the worry and fear on Fletcher's face.

Pyke, with his weapon, is the only man not running as we

race, stumbling back to the shore, the men bearing the barrels as well as they are able.

We row to the ship in the pinnace. I am quiet, my arms folded into my mantle, watching the fish, slapping their tails against each other, dreaming that they are still climbing the fall on their way to the heart of the forest.

Pyke stares at me. "What have you there, wench?" He picks out roots and berries from the basket in my lap and throws them into the sea. "Stuffs for your witchcraft?"

I turn away. "And what have you on your face?" He cups my jaw, hard, with his hand, to force my face back to his. He wipes my cheek, hard, with his thumb, and dips his hand in the water to wash away the red and black powder from his fingertips.

JUNE, 1579

ANIAN

58°00'N

29

Still, we go north, keeping to the coast to observe the waterways.

Such slow work, sailing into the wind. We beat against it to and fro. It is even colder, if such a thing is possible. The air is insufferable, the decks slippery with frost. The mist comes and it goes, and with it the vile and rotting stench.

What would I not give to breathe freely again? To feel the living sun on my arms. Who would come willingly to this place not fit for man nor beast?

I pull the bed furs tighter to my chin.

It is morning, I think. The sky brightens, though the sun has yet to show itself over the frozen hills to the east.

My hand goes idly to the basket beside the bed, made by the women in the forest. So fine and clever, woven so tight. The colours are the same as the powder on their faces – blood-red with black lines, a pattern that runs down and across the basket all the way around it.

We were fine weavers in my country, though of cloth, rather than the rushes of these baskets. People came from far away to buy our blue-dyed garments. Even the Portingales came. At first, through their agents, the Susu traders to the north. Then on their own account – before coming, at last, to understand how to take it without the burden of paying for it.

So I can tell this is fine work. Even the Englishmen – when they were safe on the ship and not in terror for their lives – marvelled at it and wondered at the people who made them.

"These are no savages," Fletcher told the General, when we came aboard. "It is our duty to bring them to their Saviour, Christ."

"We cannot stop here, man! Would you have me leave my mission – the Queen's mission! – to go looking for heathens to preach at?" He softened, putting his hand to Fletcher's shoulder. "There will be time enough to bring them to God when we have found the passage and made our colony."

A colony! I shivered.

They knew me, these women. They knew my name. Do I imagine it? The company of women has been denied me so long. Not a single woman has touched me since the midwife in Lima.

It makes me ask of myself anew: what am I doing here with these men?

From outside, I hear a whistle, and a low voice. "Putana di Dio!"

When did Diego leave the cabin, I wonder. I did not hear him rise. The General was gone while it was still dark. Never does he linger beside me now.

"Look at that!"

I go out to see for myself, taking the bed furs, wrapped tight and trailing at my feet.

The mist is low. Mere wisps float above the water, which is flat and calm. The stench not so suffocating as usual, though still I must bury my nose in the fur at my neck.

Just off the headland is what has caught Diego's eye – a pillar of rock rising from the sea. Taller than a steeple and grey as dull metal. Flocks of sea-birds sit on its flat top, screeching and squawking.

"Well, muñeca, you are about." He smiles, and it is like the sun burning away fog.

"What *is* it?" I come to stand beside him.

"I fancy that would rest upon who saw it," he says. "*You*, I would wager, think it some giant from an old wives' story. Master Fletcher with his Scripture in hand would say it is a miserable woman, turned to stone for disobeying her God. And the General—"

"Aye," I frown, that he mocks me. "What would the General say?"

He looks about and lowers his voice to make the words come softly, in stops and starts, like the man himself. "He would say: tis a sign – placed there by God – for his own especial notice – to direct him – towards the passage – that he is destined to discover."

"For the glory of England," I go on, "and for his sovereign lady, Queen Elizabeth – in due return – for his industry – travail – and the rightness of his endeavour."

Diego laughs then his arms stiffen, and he pulls his jerkin closed at his breast.

"And what does Diego say?" I ask. Still he frowns from his own want of caution.

"Diego says: tis a pillar of rock." He brightens some, returning to good humour. "With some birds atop it."

I return to the cabin to find on the floor an altar cloth that was not here when I left. I have seen it before. Black damask. One of those stolen from the church of Guatulco. No accident. It is a message for me. I pick it up and put it in John's sea-chest to put it out of my mind.

Every morning after prayers, I climb into the lookout. Now that I have felt it solid beneath my feet I cannot bear to lose sight of land again. Not that it can always be seen – many times have I climbed, only to find myself swaying in the clouds, even my hand before me impossible to discern. A nothingness, a lonesomeness like no other. Then, even the scent of the so-close land, the sweetness of the meadows and the musk of the trees, is masked by the smell of the fog when it falls upon us so fast and thick.

But today, the sky is clear. The clouds too high to cloak us. As soon as Fletcher closes his final *Amen*, I break from the congregation and run to the foremast.

The rigging is frozen to the touch. Rope so cold it burns. I pull the sleeves of my linen over my icy hands to keep going.

They fall away from me: the men and the ship, their chatter dropping to a hum below the thunder of the wind in the sails. My mind clears as I climb. All thoughts of today's ration and the baby fall away. My head, clear and fresh as the air around me. The sails snap tight, the mast creaks. The icy wind drives into my face. My eyes stream with the cold.

I reach the nest and climb into it. Malhaya Dios, I am too late, he is here already, the lookout. He must have climbed up before prayers, the heathen.

Muffled against the cold, a blanket around his head and ears, I do not see at first who he is. It is only from the scowl on his face and his refusal to meet my eye that I understand it is the gentleman in the velvet cap.

Scarce is there room for us both. How he continues to pretend he cannot see me, I do not know. He shuffles back against the rail to keep from touching my arm.

"Pray, forgive me," I start. "I will not stay long."

He grunts.

I look to the land slipping past. So empty, so green. To the far distance in the north, great mountains rise, covered in snow. Forests cover the foothills. Midway between the trees and the mountain-tops sits a thin layer of mist, like a barrier between two worlds. Along the rocky shore, sea-wolves bask in the weak sun.

The cold air and fresh winds make me bold. "Who are you?" I ask.

He stares directly ahead, at the sea, not the land. But he speaks. "I might ask the same."

He cannot very well not know. I can hardly be mistaken among the men. But I tell him anyway.

"What are you doing here?"

"It pleases me to see the land."

"I mean to say," he says, slowly, still staring ahead, "what are you doing on this ship?"

I rest my head on my arms on the rail and watch the sea-wolves on the shore. There must be hundreds of them. A great noise they make. I owe this man no explanation, but I am weary of guarding myself. "Escaping."

He seems to drop his guard too. He loosens his hold on the blanket wrapped so tightly around him.

"How is this escape?" he shivers.

"It is freedom," I tell him. "Look at the mountains – such majesty. The emptiness. You can smell it!"

"You won't find freedom on this ship," he sneers. "Only tyranny." He folds himself back into the blanket.

I watch the sea-wolves for a while. It is good to see them – so many of them – left to their lives. Unhunted, unpursued. Set apart from the multitude, on a lone rock leading into the sea, is a mother with a little pup.

"My name is Doughty," he offers, suddenly.

My arm slips on the rail. I turn to him. "I thought—"

"His brother," he says.

He leans closer when he sees I shrink from him. "Has no one warned you to keep from me?" he asks, breath hot in my face.

I shake my head. "And – you are still here?"

"Where else would I be?"

I turn to the land. On the rocks the pup, white-furred and fat, follows his mother to the sea, but cannot bring himself to slip from the rocks into the water. He heaves himself up, searching for her in the grey sea.

"Could you not... desert?" I ask him. "Run away at port?"

"I am not permitted ashore," he says. "As you have

observed. Nor do I desire to work the Spanish galleys or be burned as a heretic."

"There are no Spaniards here," I gesture to the vast landscape, to the soaring mountains and dense forests.

He winces. "Nor do I wish to be captured by heathens and made their slave. Nay. This is as far from him as I can be," Doughty gestures to the narrow width of the nest. "Till we are home, I must abide here, alongside the man who murdered my brother."

The nest sways sharp to starboard and I fall against the rail. He puts out a frozen hand out to steady me. I see how young he is, his beard not yet grown. The fair wisps on his cheeks and lip are thin and new. His face is unlined when he is not frowning.

"Then we are both stuck," I smile. "You till you fetch home, and I till –" I look back to the little pup. I missed the moment he found his courage, but there he is now, in the water beside his mother. He dives and leaps in dizzying circles around her.

I should get down to the ship. I climb over the rail and blow on my hands to warm them for the ice-cold rigging.

"Don't trust him," calls Doughty, the brother, over his shoulder. "A fresh, pretty face like yours. You can do no wrong now, I'll warrant. You won't see the danger till he turns against you."

He turns back to the grey sea and pulls the blanket tighter around his chest.

30

The mountains of ice come without warning: not a sound, till they show themselves out of the fog, high as a house. They creak, a great unnatural sound as menacing as gunfire.

The men take up oars and push at the ice in our path but it is too heavy. The General gives the order to bring up furniture – chairs, sea-chests, stools. The men smash them with hammers and fasten the broken wood to the broadsides to soften the blow.

I watch them, bent over their work in the shadow of the wall of ice. Mere planks, the broken legs of chairs! What can they do against such a foe?

They complain bitterly. They rail against the biting cold. The meat, which freezes on its way to their bowls from the fire. That all the liquids are frozen solid and they must hack off pieces of ale with a saw. That it is midsummer at home: the season of fruits and fat cream. Soon their brothers and neighbours will be at harvest. They bemoan God who has brought them to this pass, and the General whose fancy to find the passage will kill them all. They wail about the want of shoes: that they must work with cloth wrapped around their feet that do nothing to stop blisters rising, big as plums. And as they work, breaking up the furnishings, drying the gunpowder, preparing the pottage, they whisper it is all in vain for we will die here, frozen to the boards, like Willoughby.

I fear they are right. Never will we reach England by this route.

Before the ice and the endless fog, the General's words lit up the men's faces. They listened to him. They repeated his fine words to each other as they worked. They talked often of the glory that would be theirs when they return to England for their part in this great venture. "Witness the strength of the current," one mariner would say to another. "A sure sign we are close by another sea. The passage cannot be far."

But lately when he speaks to the men, the General's words fall flat, fizzling out like a torch in the rain.

I watch him, speaking to the men at evening prayers. His beard is frozen, spears of ice drop from it, as though he is freezing solid before our eyes.

"My faithful companions," he pleads. "Be not dismayed! These... troubles... are merely some short extremity. I call upon you, to remember – for my sake! – that all that is good is given by God. All in creation is made by God! Look around you!"

Few of the men look around for the blankness of the fog to greet them. The lamps light up nothing but the swirl of the mist as it sweeps across the ship.

"There is nothing here that God has not decreed. This is all made for us to endure. Divine providence, and God's loving care will preserve us all!"

The men shuffle from foot to foot to keep the blood moving. They know as I do that God's loving care comes and it goes, and it is nothing to set your life upon.

"So great an enterprise has never been sent out of England. You must have courage and acquit yourselves like men! That we may attain speedier comfort and greater glory. If we succeed, the humblest sailor will return home a gentleman!"

Ay, there is glory in this venture for one man, I know that. For Carey and Fletcher too, and the other gentlemen if they are lucky. Perhaps for Diego, who shares in the General's good fortune. The rest of us will take the hardship and none of the reward. The men know it. It is clear in the fury and the fear in their faces.

One day, there comes through the bitter northerly wind a new sound. It echoes off the walls of ice, booming across the deck, up high from yard to yard, and slipping down the stairs to the cramped places below. A low rising moan that seems to enter a body and stay there, waxing and waning in the chest.

It comes from the water, lasting some minutes. "Devils!" the men whisper, lifting the woollen caps from their ears. "Daemons. Come to carry us to Hell!"

But it is a sorrowful sound, not evil. The sound of longing and searching. For that is what it is: creatures calling to each other across the rise and fall of the waves.

Every November, the galleons return to Acapulco from Manila. Once, we fetched the coast too far north, hard by California. We heard this sound then – long before we saw them. Whales, that is – for it is they who make this mournful cry. Great beasts longer than a ship and twice the bigness. I have seen them crush and splinter a vessel with one hammer blow of the tail.

But when finally we see them I find I am wrong.

First, we see only the fins. Slicing through the water like blades, rising and falling. They come from the south. Ten, fifteen – twenty of them, heading for the ship, out of the fog. First one, and then another rises full out of the water and we see they are whales like no other. Patched white and black, they play like dolphyns in the foamy wake.

One leaps and blows water high into the air. Icy spray falls back on us watching from the deck. As thoroughly drenched as if we were in the sea ourselves, it chills to the marrow of our bones.

The men curse and bellow. John squeals in delight, going

nearer. Another whale leaps and slams the water with his belly, sending such a torrent across the deck it knocks John from his feet, near washing him off to starboard. Still he laughs.

The men fall back into the ship, below to the gun deck, up high to the rigging. But John cannot keep from watching them. I go as close as I dare, not leaving for fear he will fall in.

For an hour they follow us. They dive below the boat, knocking it – a quake that shakes us all from our feet. They spiral and leap, slap the water with their tails. All at once, and all together, they bob half out of the sea, as if they stand upon their tails, heads uppermost like men. John's eyes flick from one to the other, nailing each image to his mind to put to paper later.

As quickly as they arrived, they are off, keeping in a herd, calling to each other long and low, as they go. We watch them, John and I, as long as we can, till the last heart-shaped tail slaps against the grey sea and melts back into the fog.

Mayhap it was the whales that led the way. For the next morning, we rise to see land on both sides of the ship.

To the west, towering mountains running north. To the east, hills riven by creeks running into a wide bay.

"Call the leadsman!" shouts the General. "Take the soundings!"

"This is it," he whispers to Diego, as they stand together on the prow. "It is the passage. I feel it." A smile curls at the edge of his lips.

Diego scouts the land with an eyeglass.

"Have John brought up to draw the coast," the General calls back to Diego as he strides away, to pore over his charts in the Great Cabin.

John comes, walking stiffly in his many layers of salt-dried clothes. He sits on a barrel in the waist and sets up paper against a board on his knees. He draws in short bursts, gripping a lump of coal in one thinly-wrapped hand, stopping to stretch his stiffening fingers, drumming them against his thigh, warming them under his linen. He takes a pen to make stronger lines with ink, then returns to the coal to shade the forested hills.

I watch over his shoulder, my own freezing hands wrapped tight against my breast. How I love to watch him draw. I can see the mountains there, to the west. But as he makes them appear on the page, it makes me look again, and I see for the first time the snowy peaks are lit a holy pink glow as the early sunlight reaches them. The same with the blue ice floating before us in the bay, and the sea-fowl with their feathers fluffed around their short necks.

He draws faster now, warming his hands less often as the page fills.

When he pauses, I point to the little duck he has drawn, faithfully from those that are before us.

"This fowl –"

"What of it?" he grunts.

"Is it made of stone? Will it stay there long enough to be a mark of the land?"

He sighs.

"That is the aim, is it not? To mark the coast for those who will follow?"

"It is little trouble," says John, eyes fixed on the mountains in the far distance, "to give a sea-chart some life as well as direction."

"And they show your talent – these pretty birds you draw so well."

He wrinkles his nose. "The Queen will see these charts, Maria. They say she likes little creatures."

His forehead creases in annoyance, but it soon passes as he falls into his drawing again – eyes narrowing and closing, first one and then the other, to check the distances. With one swift move, he draws a curling line rising up from the valley. I look up to the real valley and back again to his page.

"What's that?"

"What's what?"

"That line you drew. There."

He draws unthinking, like an instrument, not the artist. We both examine the land in front of us. It is not possible to mistake: a thin column of smoke rises from the trees beside the river leading inland from the strait.

"Savages!" John squeezes the coal so hard it crumbles onto the paper. The effect on the men around us is instant. The few that are on deck call down the hatches to the men sleeping below. To the men clinging to the yards and ratlines. Up to the lookout, where Fludd, who should have seen it, is asleep on his watch.

Diego comes, still holding the eyeglass. "Stay!" he laughs. "You, who have faced the Spanish guns so many times. Will you fear the pitiful wretches who live in such a wilderness?"

He pushes men out of the way to where we stand in the waist, and takes up the eyeglass.

"What do you see?"

"Dwellings. Made of timber. Something tall – the bare trunk of a tree." He trains the eyeglass on the edge of the forest beside the wide river that runs down to the bay. "And boats. Many boats."

He stops suddenly, lowering the eyeglass, strains his eyes, and then takes up the glass again before turning and striding towards the Great Cabin.

"He saw something," says John. "Did you see the thunder in his eyes?"

We look to the land beside the river, but it cannot be made out at this distance.

"Will we turn back now, do you think?"

"No chance." John blows into his hands. "We haven't met the heathens yet who can match our firepower. And the General won't turn from this strait. See how it runs directly north – straight to the sea of the pole star."

He is right. The General gives the order to head to the

mouth of the river emptying into the strait. Wide, but shallow, the waters roil and tumble where they meet the sea.

As we get closer I see what startled Diego. The dwellings are not simple huts, like those on the coast of New Spain or Perou. Vast houses – ten or fifteen of them, thirty or forty feet long apiece. Each has before it a huge tree, cleared of branches and leaves, and carved into faces. Man and bird, fish and beast, one atop the other. The faces threaten, with bared teeth or beaks, hands or claws raised. All painted in bright colours that scream in warning – *Get away!*

On the water, a fleet. Twenty boats, thirty maybe. Wide vessels, to carry threescore men apiece. With sails and oars, outriggers. Painted red, black and yellow in the same warlike manner as the faces carved in the trunks.

On the shore of the wide river men call to each other, pointing at us. They run into the cover of the forest, into their dwellings and out bearing weapons.

Every man on the ship looks to the General. His eyes narrow. "Hold steady. Take your arms." He gestures to the guns, muskets and pikestaffs already hauled from the armoury and laid out on deck. "No one fires till my command."

"And if they offer us violence?" Collyns' voice shakes.

"The Spaniards have never been here," says Diego. "They know no evil-doing from Christians. No reason to bear us malice."

"What if they attack?" asks Pyke.

"Then they will see the power of our guns," says the General softly.

We wait and watch.

The boats set off from the shore paddling towards us in one line. Over the wind, above the sound of the gulls, comes the singing of many voices, all together in different parts, in time with the splash of the oars.

They wear capes trimmed with fur over their shoulders, bare arms beneath. In the first canoe, a figure in richer furs holds something fixed in outstretched arm before him.

They all look directly ahead, as if they do not see our ship, and all of us staring at them in wonder. They paddle and they sing, eyes forward.

As they get nearer, we see their weapons. Bows and arrows. Long spears. Daggers at every hip. Faces and hairlines powdered bright red. Their hair is white.

"See!" says Thomas. "They are nothing but old men."

But they are not. They are young and strong. Their hair is white from the down of ducks, fastened to their scalps.

The Englishmen are different. Not so certain and strutting as they were at Guatulco. Their fingers white where they hold weapons tight to their sides. They mutter under their breath.

As the boats get closer, the men gasp in horror. For among them, every tenth person or thereabouts has the head not of a man – but an animal. Fearsome wolves, beaked birds and sharp-toothed beasts.

Christ Jesus and all that is holy, what is this devilry?

Witches!

A wolf!

"A mask," says Diego.

A wolf! A wer-wolf!

"Merely the mask of a wolf. And there – a bear, and beyond, a great bird. You can see the heads of men clear enough behind them."

"Likely, they's all wer-wolves. They will leap aboard in the guise of men and tear out our throats as wolves."

"Hold your tongue, Collyns!" the General barks. "Man is created by the Almighty God. He cannot turn himself into a beast. It cannot be done!"

Many of them have scars – old, deep wounds. The man with outstretched arm in the first boat has pulped flesh in place of an ear. He is close enough now to see what is in his hands. A dead fowl. He holds it by the legs, head and body dropping down, wings falling back.

They are so close they could touch the ship's side with one of their long, carved paddles. Instead the first canoe turns sharply, with not a word between the oarsmen, and heads to our bow. The others follow.

Bonner has forgot himself so entirely he is reciting the Pater Noster in Latin not five paces from the General.

Fletcher, staring at Bonner from aside, intones over him:

O our Father, which art in heaven, hallowed be thy name.

The men fall in with him. *Thy kingdom come, thy will be fulfilled.*

Bonner too, when he realises his mistake: *As well in Earth as it is in heaven.*

Some of the men step towards the gallery, to follow the boats, then to larboard, as they continue around the ship. I go too, searching their faces. Are these the same people I met in the forest? I should have told them. The General. Or Diego at least.

But though I search in every canoe these people are different. Their garments are made of fur, not woven hair. On their heads they wear feathers instead of conical hats.

From the waist of the ship comes the low hum of prayer.

Give us this day our daily bread, and forgive us our trespasses, even as we forgive our trespassers.

And lead us not into temptation, but deliver us from evil.

Even I am praying with the men now. It softens the fear.

For thine is the kingdom and the power and the glory for ever. Amen.

When I return, Pyke is close to the General's shoulder, talking in his ear. "You see it do you not?"

"See what?" the General frowns.

"They're going widdershins."

"What does that mean?" I ask Diego.

"Against the sundial," he says, not taking his eyes from the canoes. "They think it unnatural. Against the right order of things."

"What of it?" the General spits. "What matter, which way they go?"

"You know it. Taking the widdershins path means calling the Devil. These are witches."

"There is no such thing anywhere in the Bible." He looks at Pyke with fury.

The Indios surround the ship. Twenty canoes, bow to aft entirely encircling the ship. Still they paddle, high in song.

I have not seen the General uneasy before. He blinks, as if he wishes the scene before him might disappear each time he re-opens his eyes. Spaniards, gunfire – even ice: these things he knows. But the sight of these people, clear in their purpose and unafraid, has unmanned him.

The Indios stop paddling. The man with no ear raises his voice to the wind. It rings across the water in long stretched-out sounds.

On the ship we are deathly silent. He holds the dead fowl higher in the air and plucks the feathers from its body. The breeze takes them up and back to fall on the canoes behind him, the people giving no notice, letting them fall where they may. He sings as he plucks. The people behind him chant back his words.

"You know as well as I do," Pyke urges, louder now, "that the cockrel is a holy bird. They desecrate Christ before us. It is witchcraft. We must fire."

Witchcraft, devilry. What they call all they do not understand. They would rain firepower on these people, who have none.

"Use your eyes!" I say it too loudly. "That is no cockrel, tis a waterfowl. And when you recall your reason, look at their boats –"

I am pleading to the wrong man. I turn to the General. "Look at them. They are strong and sturdy, built for crossing oceans. Their weapons – that is a harpoon! They hunt the creatures of the open sea – whales even."

"What of it?"

"If there is a passage, these people will know it. You should beseech their help, not raise violence against them."

He says nothing, staring, as if through me.

My voice has reached the Indios on the wind. The man with no ear stops plucking. He too stares at me. He says something that carries back with the onshore wind to the people behind him.

All is quiet on the maindeck. A gull caws from above.

The Englishmen look alongside at me. One, and then another, mutter that I am a savage, like them. "Harken the witch," Pyke spits. "We should give her up to them. Then fire at the lot of them."

Diego steps closer to me, hand on his dagger.

A blur of movement from the canoes, and we turn to see a figure stand, holding aloft a long pole. A garment tied to it dances in the wind. Shells on the cloth tinkle and clamour as the breeze stirs. She says something and it ripples through the canoes. It is visible: the transformation of the word. Like magic – or the blessed sacrament. The people change. They soften. One by one, they say something we cannot hear. They hold still their oars and stare at me.

The air hums with chatter. The canoes rock as people take to their knees to see better. They turn to those behind them. The same word carries through the little fleet. What was in order and unity is now chaos. The Englishmen mutter and curse. They hold tight to the weapons at their sides. Only the General looks on without fear or fury. He is no longer vexed. His lip curls. He puts out his hand to my arm and pulls me to him.

"Courage, Maria," he whispers. "They think you a heathen goddess or some such nonsense." He grins widely. "Stay close to me. I always knew you for a charm."

31

The pinnace rocks from side to side as we gain entrance to the inlet. The oarsmen struggle to keep it facing forward in the rolling, roiling waves.

Ahead of us, the Indios fly over the tempestuous waters. Already they have reached the beach. They land with a turn, driving into the midst of the river, then gliding backwards astern. They leap out and pull their canoes onto stones at the water's edge.

Eventually we too pass through the turmoil where the waters meet and come to the beach where they wait. Vast trees tower over the water on both sides, so the sky itself closes in on us. The entrance of the inlet, a mere thumb's width to my eye, is far away.

We are few – the General, Diego, John, Carey, Eyot, Fletcher and myself – and ten men to row us ashore. Too few to resist if they do us harm – though I see from the glint of an arquebus hidden in the pinnace that the General proceeds with caution. Pyke remains on the ship, a mercy indeed.

Come, the old woman with the pole signals. We look to the General.

"Too late to turn back," he smiles, and jumps into the water.

I follow, holding up my skirts, and sinking into the icy water to my waist. So sharp it takes my breath away. Underfoot, the stones sink and shift. I struggle to wade through the current to the shore.

The richly-furred man leads us up a path through meadow grasses into a grove of sweet-smelling trees. The General's hands are behind his back. His head moves sharply, like a bird looking for an insect. He bends low of a sudden to pick up a stick from the path.

As we come out of the trees into the clearing of the village, we see crowds of men, women and children outside the dwellings, many dozens of them, all clad in furs and skins, watching us in silence.

Up close, the houses are even more fantastical than they seemed from the ship. Each one as big as a church, made of flat timbers and painted in bright colours, with shallow, sloping roofs.

The carved trunks that tower over us mark the entrance of each house. This is where the Indios lead us now, up the steps of the biggest dwelling, through a gateway carved in the base of the pole – towards complete and total blackness.

It is like walking into the depths of hell itself. The smoke-filled air is thick with heat. At first, all I see is the fire raging in the midst of the room. When my eyes bend to the darkness, I see a sunken pit around it. People sit on rush mats, straining their necks this way and that as we enter. Baskets line the walls and hang from the beams in the roof. Pots too, and spoons. Cooking tools of wood and bone hang from the rafters.

Around the edge of the dwelling are beds on raised platforms. Women sit there holding babies or rocking them in cradles they work with their feet. Children play with wooden toys and little furred animals.

Other parts of the dwelling are kept privy, with boards making chambers. Small and grubby fingers clasp the edges, hinting at the infants behind them, who will peer out when we look away.

The air is choked with sweet-perfumed smoke and the smell of the fish hanging above the fire, open-mouthed, swallowing the smoke.

My heart beats like a drum. It echoes in my ears, over the sound of children squealing and laughing, animals mewling, and the crackle and spit of the fire.

The king shows us where to sit, on mats by the fire. Hands reach out to touch my skirt and my feet. The General pulls me roughly to sit beside him. Diego, Fletcher and the others go to his far side.

We sit on our knees like children. I blink. The smoke scratches my eyes. Still do I feel the hands on me from behind – butterfly touches. They brush against my elbow, my shoulder, pull at the wrap of my hair, as if by accident.

I lean towards the fire to dry my skirts and warm my frozen fingers.

Then he sits, the king: on the skin of a great beast of brown fur. Its head looks up from the ground in fury with teeth bared and yellow eyes.

So quiet. So still and so hot. A child laughs behind me. Smoke stings. Everywhere I look people stare at me, unblinking.

More footsteps – people coming in from outside. Between them, two women carry a great dish carved from wood. They set it down on a stone by the fire. It is filled with a thick liquid like oil.

More people come, bringing smaller carved bowls, and spoons they carry reverently, each server bearing only one, on uplifted palms.

They ladle the thick substance into a bowl, and set one on the floor before me. It smells of rotting fish. Sickness rises in my belly. A woman comes, bearing a spoon she hands to me on her knees, and still kneeling, moves away backwards.

The spoon is long-handled, of bone. Faces and images are carved up the handle, a version in miniature of the giant poles outside the dwellings.

The servers bring more dishes, more spoons, then fish, pink in flesh, on a platter. It smells of the earth and the trees in the grove. The sweat runs behind my ears and into my neck.

The woman who sets it down shows me with her hands that I must dip the fish into the oil. The king and some of the people sitting with him eat too. Everyone else stands or sits and watches in silence.

"Eat," whispers the General.

The oil smells fierce and foul. They watch me. I dip the fish in it and swallow. It is soft and falls apart, like rotting flesh.

The General is well practised in this art. He makes a play of enjoying the food and the men follow his lead.

Outside through the open doorway there is light and the rustle of the giant branches. I want to run from the room into clean air.

Other platters are brought in – berries and fruits, fish mixed with leaves, seaweed and fish eggs. This, I can stomach, and we eat while they watch us in the flickering firelight.

No one speaks. Time passes.

The king has stopped eating and watches us intently. The General looks around, eyes sharp, tilting his head by small degrees. He makes some sign to John.

With great relief, John lays down his bowl and searches inside his doublet. He brings out his drawing of the coast, unrolls the paper, and lays it on the floor before the king, placing stones on the corners to keep it flat.

The king stares at it in wonder. The pillar rock is so artful, it is impossible to mistake. He leans forward and traces his finger from it to the smaller rocks in the sea near the headland before his village, then to the hills and streams running down to the bay and the wide passage. With his forefinger he strokes the line of smoke rising from the village where we sit now. "Yaa," he says.

Others come forward on hand and knee to see it and they too gasp in wonder.

The king looks up at John. He touches John's hands and

then opens and closes his own fists quickly. John nods, looking back to the General to see if he is doing right.

The General nods curtly and comes forward too, on his knees in the dirt. He points at the strait on John's chart and clears his throat. Taking up the stick he brought from the path, he taps at it. "Can we pass here?"

The king looks at him blankly.

The General taps again on the image of the waterway. "Does this passage lead north? Can our ship pass this way?"

The king looks around to see if anyone can make sense of him.

I was skilled at this when I was a girl – talking to those with no common language. Seven different tongues were spoken in my father's house alone, between the wives who came from elsewhere, and the slaves from other places. Not a month went by when we were not visited by traders from foreign lands.

Later I had cause to speak to those from further away. To the Portingales who came looking for our cloth. To the English, who destroyed our homes and carried us across the ocean. To the Spanish in the New World, who spoke and preached in two different languages. To the Affricans of many different nations: the Lukumi, the Brans, the Wolofs, stumbling off the ships in Veracruz, and to the Aztecas who brought in fish and corn and fruits to the markets in Ciudad de México.

Talking to strangers is more than the words. First, you must find what you have in common.

I come forward and ask the General for his stick. I draw in the dust of the floor the ship – a crude picture indeed. But the bowsprit and masts and sails mark it well enough from the boats of the Indios for the king to understand.

I tap at the ship and draw a line through the dust to the strait on the chart. I tap at the strait, looking at the chief. He says something in his tongue, puzzled still.

To the north of the strait, beyond the edges of the chart, I draw the pole star, and the six other stars that make up the sign of the little bear. I point to the roof of the dwelling to signify the heavens beyond.

He peers at the shape of the constellation and he understands. He points to the north, behind him. I nod and tap again on the ship and draw through the straits towards the pole star.

He stops me. He leans forward, takes the stick and draws a line across the strait at the top of John's chart. Then he rubs away the ship drawn in the dust and crosses his hands at the wrists.

"What says he?" hisses the General. "That the ship cannot pass through this strait?"

A fool could understand that. I nod, watching the king.

"Ask him – can we sail around the coast to the north?" the General urges.

I put out my hand for the stick with my head bowed, and the chief passes it to me.

I draw on from where John's chart of the coast ends at the edge of the paper. I tap at the mess of the scrubbed-over image of the ship, and I trace a line around this new coastline, towards the north, looking up to the chief in question.

He frowns and takes the stick back from me.

He scrubs out my coastline and draws a new one, stretching out far to the west.

He draws circles every now and then along the coast, starting at the strait, where we sit, below the line of smoke curling upwards. He taps at this circle with the stick and brings both hands to his chest, gesturing around the room. He points to other circles, and brings both hands together, the fingers of each hand curled to grip each other like hooks. At other circles, further away on the coast to the north and west, he points and raises his weapon-hand in play of violence.

"The coast stretches to the west, not the north," I tell the General. "These circles are other villages. Enemies. Dangerous people."

The General's face falls instantly. He seems to sink into the dust.

The king nods sharply at me. He hands me the stick and takes up John's chart. He looks at him – asking if he can keep it.

John looks at me and then to the General, who nods, and the king takes it up with care and hands it to an attendant. He says something and claps his hands. In come more people.

They bring gifts – finely woven baskets, decorated with pearls around the brims. Bags of fine-smelling herbs that smell of the forest. Capes of fur, skins of beasts, and they lay these gifts before us – before me – in a great pile.

The attendant who took John's chart comes back holding a board made of timber with something painted on it brightly in red, yellow and black. He lays it before John and walks away backwards. It is an animal of some kind. A fantastical bird, with great talons and a beady warlike eye.

The General has brought gifts too, and he calls Carey, who carries them in a rough sack. He brings out good Devon cloth, which he unfolds now to show the king its worth, showing him how to feel its warp and its weft between finger and thumb. There are whistles and glass-mirrors, hawk-bells and other little trinkets that are worthless to the Englishmen, but the king delights to see.

Then one by one the Indios take up a song and they dance. Some of them wear the masks we saw on the boats. The men join their voices in different parts to the dance, the women silent, but dancing.

The dance is a thing of such beauty. The masks are so skilful and lifelike it is as though they are in the room, these eagles and ravens and bears and wolves, dancing together in the smoky darkness, to the beat of a drum, which started I know not when, and to their voices all raised together.

A man wearing the mask of a bird pulls a cord, and the wings rise high into the air. I could almost think him about to take flight.

Around the edges of the house, the children dance too, copying the grown people. It holds me, draws me in. The smell of the smoke, the herbs and the fish, the beat of the song and the dance. The movements, all different, but as one. I feel tired of a sudden, my eyes starting to close. The heat and drowsiness of the room. It melts around me – something so entirely strange and at the same time so familiar.

I feel I am falling. Backwards in the darkness. Back on the ship, through Lima, and Acapulco, Manila, Ciudad de México and Veracruz, back on the first ship in Cartagena and Rio de la Hacha, Isla Margarita, then Guinney, to the bay where the English ships were anchored. Back on the pinnace that brought us there from the river beside my village. Before the siege, when we too danced and sang and musicians played, on slit-log drum and ivory horn, and no one told us it angered their God. Back with my mother, her hand on my head like a blessing, and my sisters at my feet. Our sweet baby Fode kicking his fat legs and clenching his fists in time to the music. I am lost in it.

I cannot say how much time has passed when the General brings me to myself. He stands, coughs for attention, and says we must leave.

Outside, I am shocked to see sunlight. I thought it was night. It starts to rain – soft drops on my face, so welcome after the heat of the fire.

As I stand there blinking, breathing in the fresh clean air of the forest, the woman with the pole of shells comes to me, her head bowed.

She talks to me, the sounds not like any words I have heard. I know not what she says, but she does not stop. I do not know how she breathes, so continually does she talk. She touches my hands with hers. She puts her hands to my sides, my head, and she puts something in my hand. It is the spoon I ate with.

I smile to show her my thanks.

She raises my hand with the spoon in it and she points to a figure near the top of the handle. Below a stag, a woman's face, hair loose on the brow and falling to her shoulders.

She points to me and then to the figure on the spoon, and she says a word I could not even begin to fix to letters, so strange and alien is the sound.

She points to the river, which can just be seen sparkling beyond the thick trunks of the forest. She points to the silvery fish drying on cords hung between poles all about the village – hundreds of them, everywhere – that I never noticed when we arrived. She opens wide her arms and looks up to take in the vastness of the trees themselves and the cloud-filled sky above them. She puts her hands on my shoulders, and says something else, looking fearfully into my eyes.

Mayhap the General is right: they think me a spirit or some such thing. I am no wiser – and the Englishmen, already clamouring to get back to the ship, pay us no heed. Only Diego looks on.

But whatever the old woman thinks, it is something mighty strong and powerful to her – and to the others standing around. To the women most of all, for they have come to the front of the crowd, some kneeling, giving no notice at all to the soft, cold rain that is falling quite heavily now, flattening out the feathers and the hair on their heads and collecting in little pools upon the earth.

The General is silent on the pinnace. He stares towards the sky in the north, where the pole star is starting to show itself, so very high up, in the sky. He does not notice nor call out to the little children who follow us back to the ship, some no more than five years of age, yet so very skilled with their child-sized paddles and canoes that they master themselves, even over the roiling waters of the channel.

Back on board the ship he paces. He leaves Fletcher to lead

evening prayers alone and unobserved for the first time since Thomas' punishment, and he goes below.

At the stair, John asks where to put the wooden image of the great bird.

"Throw it overboard for all I care," he spits. "Tis their heathen god, a false idol."

Fletcher is overjoyed to be leading prayers again.

He gives thanks to God for the peaceable communion with the heathens. In time, he says, they will be brought to know the true and ever-living God and the Christ Jesus, sent for the salvation of all men.

I lean against the mainmast. Even with my eyes closed, I can tell how mighty pleased he is to find a passage so fit.

"Many kinds of voices are there in the world, and none of them are without signification. If I know not what the voice means, I shall be unto him that speaks an alien, and he that speaks shall be an alien unto me."

I open one eye to see what is the shuffling all about me. The men move away already, though Fletcher preaches still.

"I will pray with my spirit and pray with my mind. I will sing with my spirit and sing with my mind."

Poor Fletcher. They would not dare leave prayers if the General were here.

Yet – I am so hungry. Diego catches my eye. He jerks his head to the stair, where I see the peak of John's cap disappearing below, Carey and Eyot at his heels.

I run to go with them, to the steward's store, for whatever is left of the day's ration of biscuit and pickled-pork.

In the armoury, beside the Great Cabin, we gulp it down. "I swear food has never tasted so good," says Eyot, holding up a hard, tasteless biscuit as if it were a fresh, white loaf.

Through the crack of the door I see the General, head in his hands, tracing his finger over the chart that covers the table.

I chip off a mouthful of frozen ale to wash away the fish oil that still assaults my tongue. I am blinking away the sharpness and coldness of it, when the door opens.

He seems a different man. Hunched, his chin is down. He coughs, then addresses himself to Diego with a hand to his shoulder. "Many plans are there in the heart of a man, but the will of the Lord shall prevail. We cannot but follow Divine Providence. Give the order, Diego."

Diego nods, and the General retreats into the Great Cabin, closing the door behind him.

"Almighty Christ Jesus," says Eyot. "What does he mean now?"

"He means," says Diego, turning about, "that you, Master Carey, shall get your way." He slaps Carey on the back, who stops deathly still, frozen as the chipped pieces of ale we hold in our cloth-wrapped hands.

"He concedes it," says Diego. "There is no passage. We turn south!"

JULY, 1579

NOVA ALBION

48°40'N

32

I felt it this morning for the first time: a fluttering in my belly, like mayflies on the wing. The quickening. Then it is here: my baby's soul.

A real thing, a tiny person, no longer inanimate flesh.

I must think. For what will I do now? We will never reach England in time.

Nine months it will take, across the South Ocean, to the East Indies, Cathay, and below Affrica. I do not have nine months. The baby will come in five. Where will I birth this child? Who will help me? I have no midwife to guide me, no herbs for healing. Not even a kindly hand to hold.

And we sail back south: towards the Spaniards and Don Francisco who can claim me still. I fret and I pace, but there is nothing I can do.

As I despair, the men's spirits soar. They are merry again. Their talk turns from the cold and hardship towards their homeland. To the wives that wait for them, their children, grown three years in their absence, to mothers and fathers, if they are living still. My mind runs to my own family and the image comes to me of the bones of my mother, my sisters and Fode, as they must now be: stripped clean and sunk into the mud.

***

We sail the way we came. Through the straits, past the pillar of rock, the mountains, forests and the many rivers. The islands of ice are long behind us. The snow retreats, so now it is seen only on the mountain-tops in the far east. The fog clears, sometimes for days at a time.

As the air warms, we pass richer, more verdant country. Villages too, we see now the air is clearer. Houses like the great hall in the north – long dwellings of timber, brightly painted, with the same carved posts at their entrances. Canoes on the water, keeping to the shore.

With the warmer climate, the men's trust in the General returns. They have no fear at all about the voyage we must make now the passage above America is denied us.

They talk of this coming trial as if it were a river crossing. But they should be frit. This ocean is twice the other in bigness and fury. Mare Pacificum, they call it. Mare Furiosum, more like.

I am the only body on this ship who has crossed it. And *I* will not be the one to tell them how many Spanish galleons have been lost between Acapulco and Manila. Nor will I tell them of the tedium of the voyage. How if by misdealing you should sail into the windless zone, how you will watch your water and victuals dwindle, day by day, until there is naught but shoe-leather and salt-water to live on.

I will not make them uneasy for there is no other way to England, with the Spaniards waiting with their warships in the Southern Straits, and the ice packed hard in the north.

"Thomas, what will you do when you get home?" I ask the little devil, as we scrub the boards one morning.

He answers without pause. "Keep from the inns near the shore for the first thing. I shan't be pressed to sea again. I shall take my earnings to the very midst of England. Up a mountain, if I should find one. I'll 'prentice myself as far from the coast as may be."

"To what trade?"

"Rice-husker," he says with a grin.

Eventide, and the viol plays fast and joyful from below, when I hear a shout from the deck. I open the door to a crack. Such a clear night, the like of which we have barely seen since we left New Spain on our journey north.

The moon shines bright and yellow, not quite full, and the sign of the dog's tail is clear as writing in the sky. The night air is cold. I wrap my mantle tighter around me.

"There!" shouts Collyns. "You see it?"

"See what?" Steward Legge, head rolled back, scans the night sky.

Collyns points at a bright star. "The comet!"

"That's no comet!" says Legge. "It's Venus. A touch hazy, but tis Venus surely as I breathe."

"A comet," says Collyns, sullenly. "A sure sign from God we go the right way."

Legge grunts and goes below, pushing past Diego at the stair.

"How can you be so sure, Collyns," he teases, "tis not a sign from the Almighty that we go the *wrong* way?" Diego smiles at Collyns' discomfort.

"Well, muñequita!" he grins when he sees me at the door. "I wonder that you open doors to look through them like a mortal woman."

I step aside to let him in.

The cold air comes in with him as he brushes past me. He smells of land, of forests. The smoky, musky scent of his cigarros.

"They think you a god or some such in these parts, do they not?"

I go back to the bed, where I was sitting before Collyns distracted me with his comet talk, looking at the picture of the bird-god the Indios gave John. I would not have the

General throw it into the sea. I saved it. I look upon it when he is not here.

Diego pours water from the ewer and washes the grease and tar from his hands at the bowl on the table. "And are you?" he calls over his shoulder. "For now I come to think on it, you seemed like a fantastical being from the other world when first I saw you. A winsome djinni in that cabin, surrounded by jewels and treasures strewn at your feet."

The picture of the bird is beautiful. Striking and powerful. The creature is painted in bold lines of black, coloured in with red and yellow. It fills the board as if it is not enough to hold it in, wings raised to take flight. In its claw it clutches something. A fish, maybe. Its eyes are alert, fixed on me.

"What do you think it is?" I ask Diego. "Is this a god, too?"

He comes to the bed, drying his hands on his breeches.

I do not think it a god. I think they see the Almighty all around them. As we did. Before the Spaniards told us it was a very great sin. I do not know what they think I am. But when the woman with the shells looked at me, she saw to the heart of me. I was charmed again, lucky. *Chosen by the snake*.

We both look at the image in the light of the sole flickering candle. It seems to live, pulsing with the breath of the flame.

"It recalls to me something," Diego says, head to one side.

He goes to the shelf by the door and looks among the books, papers and instruments. He picks up the General's brass globe and turns it over. Carved into the bottom of the pedestal are the arms of the Queen of England. He points to the figure on the right – a dragon. He is right. How like it is to this beast of the Indios.

"What does it say?" he points to the banner across the bottom. "You are the reader of Latin."

I sit up to take it from his hands. "*Semper Eadem*. It means: Always the same."

He is very close, standing over me. The earthy scent of him is overpowering. Still does he smell of animal fat from the rope grease and his own dried sweat. There is only so much cold sea-water will do. On him, somehow, it is not a bad smell.

"Do you think we are?" I ask him. "However so much we all differ. In such far and distant parts of the world. Still somehow – the same?"

His eyes hold me. He takes the globe from my hands and puts it back on the shelf. "I think you seek meaning too much."

"What is wrong with that?"

He is too close. I shift further down the bed. He follows. "Nothing. Save that – there isn't always meaning to find."

He comes onto me, pushing me down into the mattress, and I do not move away, because he is warm, and the cabin is so very cold.

"Where is there meaning?" I ask, very low, because he is so close.

"In real things," he says, hot breath against my cheek. "In things you see and feel."

He works his thumb around the bone of my hip through the cloth of my skirt. So close am I pressed into him, rich in his scent and the workings of the ship. He stifles me.

"These are real things." His beard scratches the tender skin of my neck below my ear. "More important than things we can never know nor understand."

I cleave to him, feeling the full length of his body against mine. I breathe him in, all around me. Enclosing me. I barely knew it till now. How he has become so necessary. How I look for him alone among the men at toil, on deck and in the rigging. How he makes this ship tolerable – in faith, the only place I would be.

He draws me to him, like metal to the lodestone. Certainly, I feel him now. A real thing indeed.

The pull of him: Christ alive in his heaven, the very pull of this man.

33

One morning, we round a headland and see a rare sight. The men put down their work and stop where they are. They whistle and cheer at the vast white cliffs that stretch out to the south.

"Hail!" they laugh. "The cliffs of Albion! We are home already!"

Even the General cheers. He orders extra rations – of Canary sack, not ale – that the men may raise a cup to the cliffs that remind them of home.

After noon, we round the last of the cliffheads to find a wide bay of sand, sheltered from the northerly wind. Behind it, hills thick with trees, broken by a gorge, which must bring running water. Smoke curls skyward from the trees in the east. The air is sweet-smelling, of the fragrant leaves of the trees in this land and of meadow flowers.

"We will stop here awhile," says the General. "Caulk the ship and furnish ourselves for the voyage ahead."

The men take their orders and run in all directions – into the rigging to furl the sails, to the poop deck to sound the depths, to the hatches to ready them for unloading. The General is watchful, striding about the ship, eyes darting here and there to see all is as it should be, his back to the ribbons of smoke curling out of the forest and into the sky, where they disappear among the clouds like drops of water in the sea.

In the Hospital del Marqués in México is a painting of the conquistador Cortés looking haughtily on the natural people of the land he took for his own. They bow to him as if to a god or king. I fancy the Aztecas have a different recollection of the event.

It comes to me now because Carey has the very look of Cortés as we row to the shore. He sits straight-backed, his arms crossed, one foot resting on the bench in front of him as he surveys this new land. He wears a ruff that gives him the look of a white peacock.

Behind him sits Doughty the younger. I asked – begged the General – that he might come ashore this time. *For when a strong man armed keepeth his palace, the things that he possesseth are in peace,* I told him. He smiled to see me learn my Scripture. And where could he go anyhow, in this wilderness? The General assented, but sits at the prow, watching Doughty with hawked eye.

The waves are high and the going is hard. The men row, straining with the effort of the oars.

"Of course," Carey says, as if he were in the middle of a conversation, though no one has spoken, "the chronicles tell us that *Old* Albion was founded by thirty-three princesses. Banished from their homeland and set adrift in a rudderless boat."

He pauses, as if he expects a response, but the men are put to the effort of rowing. He raises his voice above the splash of the oars in the water: "And here are we, we eighty men," (and one woman, I say it in my head) "to take possession of this virgin land for ourselves – this New Albion."

This stirs Eyot. "It rather looks like it is taken already, Master Carey." He raises his oar towards the smoke midst the trees to the east.

"Why were they banished?" asks Thomas.

"Hmm?" Carey's eyes are on the distant mountains of his new land.

"The princesses?" asks Thomas.

"Oh, lad," Carey turns back to him. "Twas the usual tale of female treachery. They had plotted to murder their royal husbands."

"With good reason?" I ask.

I think Carey has never made a jest in his life. He looks at me with horror, and seems about to preach at me, when Thomas interrupts him again.

"And how did the people of Old Albion come about," he wants to know, "if there were princesses but no princes?"

Carey frowns as he tries to remember. He mutters:

So were they tempted with inward meditation
And vain glory within their hearts implied
To have comfort of men's consolation
And knew nothing how of them to provide.

"I recall," he says at last. "The chronicles tell that the princesses mated with the spirits of the land, to bring forth their offspring. These then were the first Britons."

I laugh, loudly. Such earnestness. From Carey the scholar, who scorns ignorance. Spirits cannot mate, for they have no bodies.

He shoots me a look of fury, but reddens as he hears how his history sounds to foreign ears. The boat is stilled and we pour into the thigh-deep waters of the shore.

Doughty, who has not set foot on land for above a year, falls on all fours. He digs his hands and feet in the sand as if to plant them, his forehead resting on the ground, weeping gently.

34

It is almost a town what we have created. A little fort of our own making.

The men cut vast trunks from the forest – so big are the trees here that ten men cannot encircle them with their arms – and laid them one atop the other to make an enclosure barricaded on three sides. The fourth opens to the sea, where the pinnace is roped to a post.

The ship is anchored out to sea – after it was beached and cleaned, heaved up on one side and then the other to take off the barnacles and weeds that cling to it, its timbers repaired and caulked and greased.

All about the enclosure are the big guns – eighteen of them, hauled ashore, with much sweat and blasphemy, to protect us from the savages.

Sailcloths cover half the open space to make a canopy where we sleep and eat, and where is also stacked the treasure, brought out of the hold of the ship, though there is no one within thousands of leagues to sail away with it.

It is quite something to see it piled high: chests of silver coin and bars, precious porcelain and bags of jewels. Somewhere in there is the Glory of Cortés. A treasure house to rival any in New Spain. It draws the covetous eye of every man here, but all is recorded and accounted for: the bulk of it to be delivered to their Queen, paid out to the investors in the voyage, and the rest for the General who will divide it into shares for those who carry it back to England, according to their rank and office.

Every day there is much to do. On the beach, the carpenters are at work, transforming one huge tree into planks to mend the boards that took the hit of the ice in the north. The smith has set up a forge. He and his boy boil the pitch to mend the leaking barrels and caulk the fresh timberwork.

By the shore, men wash the grime and tar from their winter clothes – not that we can put them away yet, so cold and nipping is the air when the sun goes down.

I sit beside them, on the sand where the grass comes through like tufts of hair, sewing and patching the sails that were torn in the icy wastes. Heavy work with needles big as knives to pierce the canvas, and my arms ache.

By and by, the men hunting in the forests come back, with hares and conies and fat little deer, feet tied on posts carried between them, necks lolling back. Everywhere there is linen hanging on sticks to dry in the wind. Bedmats lie unrolled, open to the sun to drive out the bugs and the biters.

In faith, it is a pleasant country. I am easy, because we are far from New Spain. It is warm when the sun drives away the fog. The game in the forests is plentiful and the rivers are full of silver fish that taste fine roasted on a fire and dressed with seaweed and vinegar.

There are fruits and herbs in abundance. The men soften. They grow fatter with the nourishment and cleaner with the sea-bathing. They are kinder.

The General is mild and makes merry with the men. He asks me often of the things I have read in the Gospells, and how goes my learning. He tests me on those prayers I shall say in a church when we reach England, to become a Lutheran, like him. He is mighty pleased with my progress.

The fort is open, with no dark corners or low spaces, so there is nowhere for the men to conceal themselves or lie in wait for me. Pyke can stare and linger as much he likes, he cannot lay a finger upon me.

The want of privacy drives us away, Diego and I, creeping into the forest to find ourselves alone: first one, with a backward glance to be sure of being followed, and then the other. We do not talk until we are far from the fort. In a damp and mossy hollow, or beneath an overhanging rock. Indeed, barely do we talk at all, until we are done, and lying back breathless, my cheek in the dip between his chest and arm and our fingers entwined.

The baby thrives. I feel potent and alive. If I can put from me the thought of the birth – and I can, most days, for there is nothing to be done about it – I would be mighty content.

There is only one thing.

It may not be a big thing. We do not know yet.

Only that we are not alone.

There they sit, the people of this land: on the hill overlooking our fort. They came on the day we arrived, and they have come, more of them, every day since. An army, watching us, and waiting, from the hillside. They are not frit nor wary, which comforts me because it means no Spaniards have been here. They are not afraid of the guns because they know not what they do, and I hope indeed the General does not show them.

They wear little to cover themselves: a fur or skin around their middles, or a covering made of hemp for the women. They go barefoot. As for weapons, they carry bows and arrows and knives. Nothing to trouble the English guns.

There they sit. By day that is. At night, they return to their village beyond the hills to the east where we hear them sing, sometimes the whole night. Until the morning light appears, which is long before the sun itself rises above the grey mountains beyond the forest.

In time, they creep closer. At first, just one, a man, speaking continually as he progresses towards the fort. The General bids us watch him with care. He puts men near the guns, and motions others to pick up muskets and stay hidden.

I climb with the men onto the timbers of the enclosure to watch.

When he is close enough he takes something from a pouch around his waist. He ties it to a rod he carries on his back and hangs it over the barricade.

The General regards it as if it were a bundle of gunpowder, but it is merely a bunch of feathers. From a crow or blackbird, gathered together on a cord, all cut to the same length to make a ball of exact roundness.

"Take it!" orders the General, and Diego reaches for the bundle of feathers.

Presently there comes another offering on the rod: a basket filled with a dried brown herb, fragrant, like the leaves of a cigarro. It smells of the forest and field warmed by the sun. The smell a person dreams of in the long weeks at sea, but cannot quite catch at when she wakes.

"We must make them some show of friendship." The General looks about the fort: at the treasure piled high, the game and the fish, and comes to rest on the washing drying in the wind.

"Take up the linen and we will show them to cover themselves like good Christians."

The men are aghast. "We need them!"

The General looks at them sternly. "I was naked and ye clothed me. And the king shall say unto them: as much as ye have done it unto one of the least of these my brethren, ye have done it to me."

There is no answer to him when he takes out his Scripture. So we collect together shirts and smocks, and leave the fort, one by one, holding them high on our heads to clear the water as we wade through the waves.

At the foot of the hillock beside bushes of red berries and little thorns we lay the clothes on the ground. The man who brought us the feather-ball comes first: slowly, eyes on us all the time. He picks up a garment and feels it, smells it. For all the washing they still smell none too good. Still looking at us, he motions to his fellows. They lay down their bows and their arrows and come down the hill to where we stand.

The General steps forward and touches the man of the feathered-ball on his shoulder. He takes off his own shirt to his undershirt beneath, and puts it back on again, slowly and with a great show. He hands a shirt to the man of the feathers and helps him to do the same. There is murmuring and chattering, then the other Englishmen do likewise, helping the men with the clothes.

The women and children have held back on the hillock, and I approach them now. A young woman steps to her feet as I get close and puts out her hands to me. She has fine, even skin and black hair pulled into bundles at the back of her head, dressed with beads and feathers. Her eyes are dark and smiling.

I give her a shirt that reaches to her knees, and others come too, surrounding me, laughing, the little children pulling at my skirts.

The first young woman, the boldest, takes up my skirt too, and pulls at it, nodding at me. We are not short of cloth, I can make another, and in any case I have let it out at the waist so many times. So I take off my skirt, pull it over her head and chest, and tuck into it the shirt at her waist. She takes handfuls of the cloth at each side and turns to see it move with her.

It is not cold now, with the mid-morning sun already high in the sky, but I shiver some in my thin under-clothes. She looks at me as if she sees me for the first time. She says something in her tongue. The women look at me up and down, at my belly, which I see now is quite round.

At the bottom of the hill, the men are singing a hymn. One they sing often at evening prayers, some of them singing the words low, and others high, like women.

The world is wrought right wondrously
Whose parts exceed men's phantasies

His maker yet most marv'lously
Surmounteth more all men devise.

The bold young woman takes my hand and sits me on the soft and springy grass of the hillock. Purple flowers tickle my bare legs. The women crowd around me, shutting out the light and all sight of the men down the slope. I hear them still:

No eye hath sense, no ear hath heard
The least sparks of his Majesty:
All thoughts of hearts are fully barred
To comprehend his Deity.

The women chatter in their tongue. I understand nothing, but I am not frit, their talk is soft, they speak so low. Though the sounds are foreign, it is comforting, like a lullaby.

A silvered old woman lays my head and shoulders in her lap. She smooths back the hair from my face, and runs her fingers from my forehead to temple, along the bones of my cheeks.

It is a long time since a woman has handled me like this. This is how it was before: to be enveloped always by women's care, by my mother, my sisters, the elder females too, who led the women and trained the girls. I have lived among men for so long I had forgot it.

The other women kneel around me. All I can see is the sky, and their heads bent over me, laying out my hands and feet on the soft grass of the meadow, as they chant words in time with each other.

The bold woman at my side says something and smiles. She speaks softly and without violence. She reaches inside the waist of her skirt – *my* skirt – and takes up a leather pouch. She takes something from it.

A cord. Long and thin, made from a twisted vine.

For the first time, my heart leaps. I move to get up, but the women hold my arms and legs to the ground. I am closed in.

She takes up the cord and moves it about her fingers and knuckles. Is it a garrotte? I saw it done once in México. They said it was a mercy to the man on the pyre, due to his rank.

Will they choke me here in the grass and flowers? Not fifty paces from the men. Do they think it a kindness?

I call out for Diego. The old woman covers my mouth.

More hands reach out to still my shaking arms and legs. They crowd over me. She leans forward, the bold woman. I feel her breath on my face. With her knotted string about her fingers, she hovers over my belly.

She makes quick movements, fingers dipping into the string between the fingers of each hand, and pulling back, sharply, bringing loops of string with it. Her hands turn inside and around. She uses her teeth to pick at the string when hands will not do. With each movement, the pattern of the string shifts between her hands.

It is like the game the boys play on the ship, making shapes with string: the cat in his cradle. But this has meaning, for the women push and jostle to see what is happening. The bold woman chants with each movement, and pauses, for everyone to see how the pattern of the string falls out. This she does four, five, six times. Is it the telling of a story? A prayer or spell?

The woman with the string makes one final shape and gives her last utterance.

She looks at me and her face breaks into a wide grin. The women whoop and cheer. They hold up their hands and sing.

Har dow e chuk, says the bold woman.

I lean up on my elbows. I do not understand. She pulls a child to her – a little boy of about four years of age. *Wik we ak*, she says, with her hand on his head. Then she calls something. A dimpled arm pushes its way between the women, then a full-cheeked face appears between them – a girl of two or three years. The woman pulls the little girl to her knee and holds her tight to her breast with one arm, like she would squeeze her into her own body. The child squirms and laughs.

Har dow e chuk, says the bold woman, with her hands on the girl's shoulders.

Wik we ak, she repeats, pointing at the boy. *Har dow e chuk* to the girl.

Then it is divination. Not a story, nor a prayer, nor a spell, nor sorcery.

Some way of determining that the child I carry is a girl.

Below us the final verse of the hymn comes with the breeze:

Behold his power in the sky,
His wisdom eachwhere doth appear:
His goodness doth grace multiply
In heaven in earth both far and near.

This is why she called to me, my ancestor, Mansarico. It was she, I am sure of it, who called to me through the stone. A woman's estate passes in the female line. She saved me. That this child, in whose veins runs her blood, as well as mine, will not be born a slave.

35

The man of the feathers is no king. He is an emissary. This we learn when the true king arrives the next day with much ceremony and fanfare. The man of the feathers leads the procession: hundreds of men and women, all dancing and singing. A guard of the tallest and strongest men follows, protecting in their midst the king. He wears a crown, high in its feathers, great long chains fashioned from animal bones in double-strings about his neck and a fine coat of snow-white fur, reaching his knees. He holds a sceptre of black wood a yard long.

The common sort of people wear feathers in their hair, and their faces are painted, each a different colour: white, black, some red. Each one carries something: a bag of herbs or roots, an animal skin, or a woven blanket.

Inside the fort, the men are watchful. The General bids them put on a warlike show, at the ready with guns and swords. He goes out with a guard of four men, more on the barricades, muskets primed and aimed. But the guns are not needed. Our friend the emissary speaks, given his words by another man, who takes them from the king. This oration by relay lasts nearly an hour, and when it ends the crowd gives word of agreement, *Ayayay!* Hundreds of people, all giving voice as one, the word rises into the air like a flock of birds.

Then they dance as they come towards us, in slow roundabout movements. The General nods to Legge at the gatepost to signal him to open the fort. In they come, as if there were not the smallest possibility of being denied entrance. They dance around and among us, coming so close their arms brush mine.

In the midst of them comes the bold woman who picked out the strings over my belly. She dances with grace, sending forth her new skirt – my skirt – this way and that. I have already stitched myself another from the blue-and-white shipcloth to match hers. Alone among the women, she raises her eye, holding a man's gaze. Her eyes are sharp and black, her cheekbones high.

The Englishmen eye her with unhidden lust. I watch them, watching her. She sees none of it. The dance dies. The people lay their gifts at our feet. They fall back on the ground, exhausted.

The king comes forward, walking through them towards the General. Two paces from him, he stops. He raises his arms to the skies, and in a great and booming voice he calls out *Hy-oh*. Again and again: *Hy-oh Hy-oh Hy-oh!*

The breeze rolls in from the sea, the great trees sway as if they bow to him. High above us a great bird glides towards the mountains. On the barricades, the barrels of the guns aimed at the king's head glint in the sun.

Complete silence. All eyes are on the General.

In faith, I do not know what he will do. He has seen by now these people are of little threat. Is it worth much to him, their friendship? Their lives rest on it: how useful they are. Do they have more to offer than roots and leaves? His eyes flick from one to the other of them as if he counts their value in his head.

He puts an arm to the shoulder of the king and calls loudly: "I thank you, my friend, for the welcome. You esteem us greatly. But –" and he looks around to be sure he is heard by his own men, "I am a man and not a god!"

Not, I think, that the king thought him so. But he continues, pointing skyward. "Above us is the living God whom you must serve!"

He takes the black rod from the king, who looks at it in confusion. "In the name and to the use of her most excellent Majesty, Queen Elizabeth. I take this sceptre, crown and the dignity of this country as Her proper own. Your willing obedience to Her will profit you! And by Her means, as mother of the Church of Christ, and by the preaching of the Gospell – will bring you to the right knowledge and obedience of the true and ever-living God."

He holds his hands skyward to show where resides the true and ever-living God. They do not look up.

The king looks at him, unsmiling. He sees his sceptre in the hands of this strange man, who came with many other men who do his bidding without question, on a floating house of timber, more vast and high than any vessel they have seen. I know before he does himself that he will decide such a man is a better friend than enemy.

The man with the feathers makes a movement, a blur at the edge of my sight. But the king puts out a hand to him and makes a tiny gesture with his head.

The General takes this as assent, and applauds, his men following his lead, and cheering, until the people, after some confusion and dismay, seeing the sceptre in the hands of the strangers, shout *Ayayay* again, and all are in agreement and there is great joy at what has occurred.

I catch the eye of my friend, the bold woman, dressed as me, in my own skirt. She smiles. I feel shame enough to look away.

After this, the people come every day and the General admits them freely into the fort. They watch every least thing we do. The metalwork fascinates them. One man cannot leave the smith alone. He is of middling age, his face lined, fingers covered in scars and burns. He watches the smith at work close to the fire till the heat forces him back.

Looking-glasses, pipes and whistles – above all, the little hawk-bells the Englishmen have in multitudes – they adore. The men make gifts of them, thinking themselves as rich as kings giving out jewels and coin.

For their part, they bring us gifts every time they come: the blankets they weave from animal hair and bird-feathers, baskets of the smoking leaf they call tabah, or the skin of the fat deer that live hereabouts.

They are skilled on the water, their canoes carved from one vast trunk of a tree with billowing sails of hemp. When they return from hunting at sea, they bring us the carcasses of sea-wolves, which yield a great store of meat and oil, baskets overflowing with fish and the fish eggs they find on the seaweed and esteem a great delicacy.

The General has stopped his attempt to make them understand he is no god, for they laugh when he points upwards. But oftentimes they ask the men to sing, by way of calling out with their palms upwards and looking towards Heaven in mimicry of the Englishmen singing hymns. The men are happy to stop their work and sing for them.

The General watches this with delight, for he thinks it shows their willingness to come to the knowledge of the one true God. I think mayhap they like singing.

As for Fletcher, he has found his purpose. This is what he has waited for for so long. The reason he has endured the misery and danger of this voyage. A friendly people, tractable and willing: heathens for him to bring to his God.

He holds back, he will not fly in. He hovers beside groups of them, smiling, as if he would step in and preach – yet something stops him. I see him, at the little table under the shade of the sailcloth in the fort, writing feverishly, then sitting back and looking into the distance.

He bides his time. No need to rush. His God wills it. It will be.

***

So they watch us and we watch them.

We are all wary and guarded. But of all these people, I am the only one who goes about with dread in my heart. Of what is to come here. For the Englishmen know they need have no fear, and the native people do not know yet that they should.

36

One day, the emissary comes and bids us follow to their village.

The General leaves men to guard the fort and all its treasures, and we go. Up the trail over the hill where first they watched us, through the forest of vast trees and thick brush, the twigs cracking underfoot. Till the sun shines through a clearing, and we come to their village beside a clear brook that trickles over grey-white boulders down to a wide sandy bay on the shore.

The houses are round, dug partway into the earth, but there is one long hall like that in the north. They have ruder huts for storing the great quantities of fish that are everywhere. They catch them in shallow baskets at the mouth of the stream, dry them on the flat roofs of the houses and smoke them over fragrant fires. Outside the huts, women sit in a line packing the smoked fish into leaf-lined baskets.

Here, we see the reason for their fascination with metalwork. It is not that they have not seen it before, as the men supposed. It is because it is a particular skill of theirs. Outside the houses are great plates of copper moulded into different designs.

The man with burned hands is a metal-worker. He melts the copper on a furnace and pours it into a finely-crafted mould. When it cools, he takes it out: a patterned plate, like those outside the houses.

From where do you take the copper, the General asks by signs. The metal-worker gestures to the mountains beyond the forest.

Take me, he signs. And off they go: the General, with a bodyguard of four armed men led by two of the king's fleetest guardsmen – and Diego, who comes to take his leave of me with soft and tender words.

With the General gone, they ask us to stay in the village.

For much of the night, they stay up around the fire, singing and dancing. This is the season of their rest, the king gives us to understand. When the fish are smoked and packed, they will return to the uplands to their winter homes.

The bold woman leads me by the hand to a small group of other women before the fire. She motions I am to sit here and when she retreats, backwards, I see with leaping heart why she does not sit with me. The women I sit among, in this favoured spot before the fire, have bulging bellies: all the pregnant women of the village.

I scan the Englishmen's faces. Have they noticed? I have bound my belly since the day the women made their charm over me, unwrapping my hair and binding the calico about my stomach instead. With that, and the folds of my skirts, I am well concealed.

But the General's sharp eyes would not miss this. I waver and wrangle, for what will he do when he discovers me? On the ship, in the midst of the ocean, he cannot take the baby from me. But here?

I hum, to mask my thudding heart. I keep my eyes moving. On the Englishmen sitting on the other side of the fire. On the women who bring us food: fish roasted on flat stones in the fire, mussels cooked in their shells, berries and leaves mixed with fish eggs.

The Englishmen watch the women too, eyes lingering on

their bare legs as they serve them, the swing of their arms honeyed by firelight as they walk away.

They watch the women, and I watch them. My heart slows and I breathe easier.

Drummers start. They beat out a rhythm that is taken up as a chant. A man is pulled into the cleared ground beside the fire. He stares into the darkness with such a look upon his face, my heart leaps again with fear. He seems to see something though I alone turn to see where he stares. Nothing there, but the slope of the beach to the shore. When I turn back, he cries with great emotion. He starts to circle the fire, singing and dancing in jerked movements. Across from me, the Englishmen are absorbed in the spectacle, following his every move.

After he has finished, others dance. The same thing each time: a wild look, a fright. Shaking, a mournful song. One man rattles a staff with the horns of deer fastened to it, others wear masks. All around the fire, the people keep up a continual hum, and their own songs – some wildly different to the dancer's.

The moon emerges from the mountains and starts to drop towards the sea. It seems as though the dancing will never end. Children sleep in their mothers' arms. Childless couples steal closer together. The bold woman sits beside the king with a man who lays his head in her lap. She picks the lice from his hair with tenderness and he touches her arm as she works. He whispers something to her and she laughs.

Fletcher's face is fixed in a smile. The flames colour his pale cheeks. John is watchful, as always. My eye passes over them all: Collyns, who drinks in the form of a woman dancing. Carey, whose golden curls shake as he nods his head in time to the music. Thomas, who has fallen asleep on the shoulder of Eyot.

Doughty hums. Fludd takes off his camel-haired cap and plays with its rim, tapping out the beat of the drum. Bonner's lips move as he watches the dance. And Pyke.

Pyke, who I see with a start, is watching me. He has a one-sided grin on his ugly face. He mimics the movement I make unthinking with my hand. I jerk it, with a guilty start from my belly, where I realise only now it has been resting.

A howl pierces the sky, and I think for one moment it has come from him.

But all eyes turn to the beach, where there is a wolf, calling to the moon, beside the canoes hauled onto the sand. The dancing stops, the drummers cease. A man is sent, torch held aloft to frighten him off, while the men and women around the fire huddle into each other.

The wolf stares at us for some moments, then picks up the broken-necked coney he had laid down. He pads upstream with it hanging limply from his mouth. Along the bank of the trickling brook into the dark cover of the forest, lopsided all the way, as if he is injured.

The dancing and the drumming start up again, but when I look beyond the fire, Pyke is gone.

The moon is dropping into the ocean when the bold woman takes my arm, motioning me to go with her. I am weary, yet so full of fear at Pyke's sudden departure.

She takes me to her dwelling. It is richly furnished: fine furs everywhere, polished copper plates hanging from the walls, a low platform, a bed dressed with furs and skins.

Where is her family I do not know. She cannot live here all alone. Where is the man from beside the fire?

She talks to me. Of what she says, I cannot guess, but she continues, chattering and motioning with her hands. My fear of Pyke slips away. What harm can he do me here?

She puts a hand to her breast and says *Eldokwila*.

Macaia, I tell her.

In the morning she wakes me early, before the sun has risen, and bids me follow. The village is silent, no one about. We walk through the houses, past the fire, embers still burning.

On a path leading to the beach we meet other young women, eight of them, waiting for us. One is not happy to see me, and she frowns and grumbles, till she is pushed and chided by Eldokwila.

The women and girls chatter, yawning. Birds sing to welcome the morning. Presently, the sea lightens from black to slate-grey as the early sunlight reaches it.

The tide retreats. With each step on the sodden sands, the water fans out around my feet. When we reach the water's edge I see why we are here. With the going out of the tide, the new-revealed rocks are spotted with mussels, huge and black.

It is easy work, twisting them from their refuges. We take only the biggest, for there are so many. Eldokwila ties a vine-twisted basket around my waist, as the other women wear them, and I throw in a mussel for every one I eat raw from the shell, salty and sharp.

It is like gathering oysters. My sister Dura, ahead of me, faster and lighter, diving low to pull them from the roots of the mangroves at the mouth of the river. We sucked the flesh from them raw and skimmed the shells across the water.

The breeze that rises off the water whips at my hair and I stand, to smooth it back. I watch the women as they work: their chatter and laughter. They throw the smaller, discarded mussels at each other, delighting when they meet their mark on a bent-over backside or shoulder.

This is what was stolen from me – among many other things. The company of women. Ease and comfort. Companionship and care.

Before the siege, before we were confined behind the barricades, we spent weeks at a time in the women's sacred place in the forest. No men, for they were barred from entering it at risk of death. They had their own place that was denied us.

There we learned what women must. Medicine, which herbs to use for healing and cleaning wounds. Those to wrap around a belly after childbirth. We learned the secret language for women's business. Musicianship and dancing. Later, when our enemies crept closer, after they had taken the villages upriver and encircled us, then the women who had served as warriors in their youth taught us to fire arrows at a mark.

There, we slept at night on the floor of a great hut, all the girls of learning age. And every day, a great feast: stewing-pots overfilled with the flesh of fowls, and beans and spinach. Food that never ended. A place of leisure and sanctuary.

A cry calls from behind me and I turn to see figures on the path coming down from the forest. The General is returned. My basket is full. I motion to Eldokwila that I am leaving and go back up the sands.

The Englishmen have been waiting for him by the smokehouse. Still, I see no Pyke. Carcy stands to greet the General, who grins from ear to ear.

"Well?" I ask, when I find Diego, unloading bags and baskets of tools by the king's dwelling.

He smiles a greeting and squeezes me to him. "It is everywhere – the copper. Barely does a man need to search for it."

I can imagine it. Flashes of green in the fast-running streams that bring the snow-melt down from the mountains.

"They take only what they desire for their ornaments," he says. "Much more is there they cannot carry out."

My heart sinks.

"And – something else, muñeca," he says, kissing me, his eyes sparkling. "That is not all there is in the mountain streams."

I close my eyes.

"Dazzling flashes of yellow. Little flakes of gold."

We return to the fort, my heart mighty heavy.

37

She comes early in the morning before the fog has lifted from the sea. Standing where the waves lap the posts of the fort, she sings my name, rising at the end like the call of a bird: "Maaaa-ccaaaii-yaa!"

The men do not ask why she calls me this. But when they hear her, they go to the gate, high in their lust. They give her valueless trinkets to get close enough to touch her – on the hand, the shoulder, on the curve of her hip. She fastens the bells they give her to her waist so she rings out as she walks.

The red hind, they call her. Since they think her deer-like in her beauty – and also so they may joke of what they wish to do to her behind. Englishmen are greatly pleased with a word that means two things.

I push my way through the men, taking my own manhandlings as I go, a hard pinch on my rear, a painful squeeze of my breast. Then we go, Eldokwila and I, fresh in the morning breeze towards her canoe, heaved onto the sands beside the rocks. Pyke and Collyns follow us out. I have a sense for them in the back of my head. I can see them watching her as she goes, her hips swaying with the music of her hawk-bells.

"Off with the savages, again?" Pyke calls to my back. "I see you. A full witches coven."

We pass the chaplain where he sits with the children of the village every morning. He has given up trying to bring the word of God to the adults. The new hearts and fresh souls of the children, he says, are more open to the Saviour of all men than the parents who have learned to go in sin.

He holds up his Bible and points skyward. I have seen this many times. I wonder when he will admit defeat with the children too, for they understand nothing. They climb over him, clamouring for the book he holds high to keep from them. One boy has a knee on Fletcher's shoulder, one hand square over his face, reaching to touch the gold engraving on the cover. A girl with blue-black feathers in her hair rides his back, gripping handfuls of his shirt at each shoulder. More run around him, jumping up with cries of glee, trying to hit the book with sticks.

Oftentimes we go alone, Eldokwila and I, out onto the bay. We paddle to mist-filled caves and little coves to collect seaweed or fish eggs, or into the forest, where she teaches me the words of her tongue. The names of the feathery needles of the vast trees they cut for timber, the closed pine-cones, the orange-furred creature like a cat, which scurries, teeth bared, along the forest floor.

But today we are not alone. Four companions wait at the canoe: the old woman I saw when we first arrived, a pale and timid girl who casts down her eyes, and two women of my age or thereabouts. One has a berry-red scar running down the side of her cheek to her neck, the other carries a baby strapped to a board on her back.

Save for Eldokwila, who walks unburdened, they carry baskets as well as bags and pouches hanging from cords across their backs and waists.

The canoe is brightly coloured in red and black, marking the broadsides and bow, circles like eyes and rolling lines like waves. The old woman and the mother step into it, and they motion to me to follow, while the others heave it from the sand, running alongside and leaping aboard in the shallows.

They take up painted paddles and steer the boat out into the bay, into the fog.

They sing: a chant they paddle to, to keep the rhythm. A little wind beats up white-crested waves. Light rain falls on my bare arms. I shiver and the old woman passes me a cape of feathers and bark, nothing so fine as the silver fur draped over Eldokwila's shoulders.

After the rocky headland we pass their village, where the children who are not with Fletcher are at play on the beach, racing against each other, climbing poles set up on the sands.

I thought we would stop here but we continue, past the village, and another rocky outcrop beyond. Close to the shore, where sea-wolves bask in the faint rays of sun. Such big eyes, all facing the same way, and back again, as if joined on a thread.

We alight at a wide bay. Bushes bright with yellow and orange berries cover the hills as they rise into the forest. The women spread out, throwing berries into their baskets, eating as they go. Eldokwila does not pick, but leads us to the biggest berries, and eats a great deal of them. I try one: sweet and sharp at the same time.

The pale girl picks as if she is possessed: taking as many as she can and eating as quickly as she gathers them. Her basket is empty, and the woman with the scar scolds her till her eyes brim with tears.

The fog lifts, the air warms. The bushes, covered in thorns, scratch at my bare arms and the cloth of my skirt. As we climb the hill, the trees grow higher and broader, trunks wide as a church door.

Soon we are in the dappled shade of the forest. Branches sway in the breeze. Songbirds trill. Running water trickles in the distance.

Life is everywhere. It cannot be contained. Musherons grow on the moss that grows on the trees. The cat-like creatures peer at us from low branches. Trees rise as far as the eye can see, giving off the scent of life and plenty. Roots stretch out, gnarled and knotted above the ground, plunging deep to anchor themselves below. Branches droop, like the arms of women dancing. High up, leaves glow in the sunlit canopy.

Never would you eat mouldy worm-ridden biscuit if you lived by such a forest: food is everywhere, in such abundance.

Regard Maria! The gifts of our bountiful God! Given freely to we, His children whom he doth love and preserve!

Por Dios, I thought I left him behind at the fort.

The baby is new and sleepy, waking only to whimper for milk. His mother swings round the board so he can suckle, still tightly bound.

The women move on to pick ferns and leaves. They dig for roots and break off bark from trees with little adzes.

I take for my basket fruits and seeds to bring away when we leave. The women have understood my aim, and help me gather red berries, and other plants they esteem, signing what each is used for. The woman with the scar breaks off a piece of bark from a tree, holds it up and touches her head, miming pain. The old woman digs out a root and holds her stomach in show of bellyache.

Eldokwila is changeable: sometimes stern with her companions, at other times soft. The other women yield to her command, save for the old woman who does exactly as she pleases and scoffs *ak ak ak* at the chatter she does not like.

Coming out of the forest, we reach a meadow with long grass and tall purple flowers that looks down upon a lake, still as glass. On the far side, the trees stand straight and narrow as needles on a comb, grey mountains rising behind them.

We stop here, on blankets laid out to flatten the grass.

The women take out pouches of hide, stitched close, from the bags they carry at their backs. They unpick the stitches with bone-handled knives each of them carries tied to their forearms. Inside is meat: strips of deer or goat flesh packed tight with berries and sealed with animal fat.

It is good, and we eat in perfect contentment by the lake, with the sun warming our arms and the breeze stirring the branches behind us. The baby suckles and sleeps. He whimpers. His mother rocks him on his board on her lap and he soothes and settles.

I put out my arms, asking to hold him. The mother scowls, and Eldokwila says words of anger to her. She puts him out to me, unwilling. He is rigid, swaddled tight in fur and skins, his body held tight to the board by cords of twisted hemp.

I hold him a while. As he sleeps, his dreams are written on his face. His brows shoot up, his forehead wrinkles, then smooths again. His tiny mouth yawns to show toothless gums. He has a blain on the bow of his lip, where he has suckled his mouth sore, and he works his lips in his sleep as though he suckles still. A whole world in a tiny body.

I had a baby like this. A boy. Perfect in every way, too. I had him only three days. I nursed him. I embraced him. I marvelled at him. Nor could I put him down, like this baby's mother, even in my sleep. I did not understand I would not be keeping him till Don Francisco brought the Spanish lady into the room where I was confined, above the custom-house at the port in Lima.

She put down the paper parasol she carried beside the door.

From the marketplace outside came the hum of everyday life. People bartering for maize and hides. The crowd jeering at a man being whipped. A dog barking.

Don Francisco closed the window. The lady put out her arms to take my baby. I thought she was there to bind my belly. To heal it, with a poultice of herbs. So I handed him to her. Not even a last kiss. And she left, running, her steps echoing down the stone steps and out onto the street.

I stared at Don Francisco. I was numbed, utterly. I stared at the parasol she had left behind in her hurry to be away.

The church bell rang out. It echoed through my body, tugging and jarring the torn parts of me still raw from the birth. I felt my mind slipping from its rightful place.

He waited for the chimes to stop, then said: "A ship is no place for a baby. We sail tomorrow."

I give back this baby to his mother who cannot hide her relief. Her eyes go back to him. She breathes him in. She caresses his tufted hair, his soft ear and plays with the tiny finger that has broken free of the swaddling. I was wrong. He is not a world in himself. They are a whole world wrapped up in each other.

My body aches, as it did that day. A sharp pain, below the breastbone, the pull of a cord.

Where is he now, my baby? Who caresses him? Not yet two. He will be walking, if he lives. I never even named him. I rub the top of my belly, and it passes.

Eldokwila takes from a pouch some small things like dice, carved from bone. She puts one in my hands when she sees my curiosity. The size of a kola nut, with carved patterns on its sides. Some are perfect circles, others notched and marked, each side different.

She rakes through the mossy ground with her fingers, picking up sticks and stones and tossing them to one side, then lays down a leather mat. She gathers the bones in both hands and shakes them. She says something, and the old woman drags herself to sit opposite her. They play, taking it in turns to shake and roll the bones, then see how they lie: on which carved edges, and where the smooth sides fall.

The other women watch closely, the pale girl on her knees leaning forward. They gasp and laugh with the rolls. Sometimes they dispute how the bone has fallen, and pick it up carefully, examining the underside. Then with much chatter and *ak ak aks* from the old woman, it is placed again where it fell.

They occupy themselves like this for a long time. The shadows of the trees stretch out towards the lake and the tops of the mountains retreat into a haze. The ever-changing mirror of the lake darkens from silver to black.

I am happy and content watching them: as much their faces, which tell the tale of who is winning the game, as the bones on the leather mat.

The baby wakes and looks at the clouds sailing across the sky. He flicks his black eyes to watch me, unblinking.

The sun is close to dipping into the water to the west when we paddle back to the fort. The sky is lit pink and orange, the mountains silvered with the last of the sun. The women take their leave of me on the far side of the beach from the fort.

What they can think of me I do not know. Where I have come from, what brings me here. They cannot guess at the world I left behind. Worlds, I should say, for I have known more than one. I am glad they know nothing of them.

The old woman touches my arm and says something in earnest as she holds my eyes. The woman with the scar touches my forearm with a word, then melts back into the canoe. The woman with the baby comes forward, and I bend my head to take in the scent of his head where he lies in her arms. I kiss him. He wriggles his nose in his sleep and she too sits back in the stern.

Eldokwila holds her head to mine for some moments. I step out of the canoe onto the sands.

38

In the east it is night already, the ten stars of the eagle sign shining bright and clear. Beyond, the moon rises, a thin fingernail of silver. The waning moon, she who brings new life and change.

I must get back to the fort – the wolves come out at night. One howls now, and I scan the darkness inland. Nothing. But as my eye falls along the line of trees blurring into forest, there is something. A commotion, a knot of movement. Staying still yet moving in the centre. A noiseless tussle.

Across the beach, men parade half-heartedly on the barricades of the fort. The smell of roasting deer drifts to me on the breeze. The bell rings out for evening prayers and the guards scramble, hurrying down.

The tide is high, and the waves come in fierce and black. They force me inland, where the sand is drier but it is harder to walk, each footfall heavy and laboured. I keep the forest in sight from the corner of my eye. The blur of movement stills. A flash between the trees reflects the moonlight. Metal glinting.

From the fort comes the low melody of a psalm as the men begin their worship.

By the rivers of Babel, we sat
and there we wept, when we remembered Zion.

I quicken my pace. The sky darkens, scudding clouds cloak the thin moon. A welcome sight to me, always, but they fear the moon, the Englishmen. Moonbeams kill, they say, should they shine upon bared skin.

Then they that led us captive required of us songs and mirth. Sing us the songs of Zion.

An owl calls out and flies low over my head towards the forest. I follow the line of his jagged flight. Just as he is swallowed into the void, a high, muffled cry pierces the air.

Madre de Dios, I should look closer. Perhaps it is one of the men struggling home with an injury – or a boy lost from the hunt. It could be Thomas. I am within calling distance if help is needed, the fort is not far. I pick my way, silently up the hill towards the forest, the psalm receding with each step.

O daughter of Babel, worthy to be destroyed.

I do not know why I did not guess what was at work.

I should have known. I know these men – I know all men.

Blessed shall he be that rewardeth thee as thou hast served us.

I should have expected it every waking hour.

Blessed shall he be that taketh and dasheth thy children against the stones.

For as I reach the edge of the thicket I see him on the ground. Struggling to keep something beneath him. A knee raised to pin down a kicking leg. Arms holding back flailing, punching hands. Little hands: a child. Blue-black feathers lie, quills bent and broken, midst a clump of torn-out hair beside her terror-struck face. His breeches are pulled down, his bare white arse raised in the air.

I drop my basket. Roots, bark and berries scatter into the grass.

"Let her go!"

It is Pyke. Of course it is Pyke. He turns to me, the greasy ropes of his hair masking his brutish face. "Fuck off, witch. Leave me to my business. Lest you wish to take her place."

"She's but a child!"

234

His hand goes for his dagger laid down above the girl's head, but he must let go of her arm to reach it, and she pummels uselessly at his jaw. I make a dash for the knife but he is quicker. He gains the weapon but loses his prey. The girl crawls out from under him and backs away, sobbing, into the dark safety of the trees.

Now he is angry. He stands, holding out the weapon to me with one hand, the other, pulling up his breeches. I want to get to the girl but he stands square and solid between us.

"You'll pay for this, mongrel bitch," he comes towards me. "The General won't save you when I tell him what I know."

I want to flee, but the girl is still behind him. Why won't she run?

"You're in league with these savages. I saw you today. I saw you with them. Gathering stuffs for your witchcraft."

"Merely... herbs for healing. For salves and suchlike."

"And I saw you all beside the lake. Summoning the Devil with animal bones."

"Just a game. Like dice," I keep my voice and my eyes low, to keep him calm.

I back away down the hill, hoping she will take the chance to run if he follows.

"And I saw what you did to that baby just now. Sucking the life out of him for your own evil purposes."

"I kissed him!"

I look behind me to the fort, a clear run downhill.

"Do not look for help," he sneers. "They are at prayers. They will not hear you."

I step back and stumble, my foot twisting deep into a coney's burrow. It fells me to my knees, and he laughs, coming to stand before me, my face to the piss-soaked canvas of his breeches. I cannot run now.

"And something else I've seen," his eyes drop to my belly. He pulls my head back, sharp to force me to look up at him. "And I wonder: Does the General know of it?"

Sweet Mother of God. I close my eyes.

He drops his breeches. The smell hits me. He puts his hand to my neck, choking the air from my throat, forcing my face to his foul-smelling crotch. He holds me there, laughing, his fingernails digging into the flesh at my neck to hold me still.

I cannot breathe. The ripe and rotten smell of him makes me gag. Vomit rises in my throat. I cannot see, but I feel it, his worm, nodding to life. Hardening into my face.

Then a cry. Something wet on my cheek. He stumbles back. Air to breathe. Someone else standing before me. I blink. My own skirt, rustling in the faint moonlight.

Eldokwila puts out her hand behind her back to wave me away. Her other hand, unseen, held forward.

I crawl back and wipe my face. Thick and black in this light, but the taste of metal on my lips: unmistakably blood.

Pyke crouches, his forehead on the grass. His breeches pin his legs together at his ankles. His arse shining bright, as the moonbeams burst through the cloud and fall upon it.

"Fucking devil whore," his voice judders.

She shouts something, not looking at me, waves her free hand. The knife in her other hand drips heavy drops of blood. She wipes it on her skirt.

She shouts again, this time my name, and gestures to the fort. I don't want to leave her. She takes the dagger from Pyke's limp hand and kicks him hard in the face so he sprawls back. I see the deep cut in his groin, the blood pumping out of it.

She hands me her knife, her eyes warning me to take it, and calls out to the girl still hiding among the trees. She comes running, holding together the torn cloth of her dress. Eldokwila embraces the sobbing girl, picks her up, and without a glance backwards, she runs fleet and silent down the hill to the canoe on the beach, where the other women wait.

I stand there, looking over him, watching the blood pump from his veins, wondering if a final blow is needed.

39

"Where was he?" asks Diego.

"Right here. See – there is the basket." I pick it up from where it was trodden into the grass during the struggle and take up the roots and berries the animals have left behind.

It was still dark when we crept from our beds, but the sky is lightening now. The mountain-tops emerge from the darkness in their daily act of Creation. The sun will rise over them soon.

Certainly it is light enough to see what is not possible to ignore: that Pyke is gone. I left him here last night, bleeding to a certain death, but he is gone.

"Perhaps he crept off to die?" Diego looks into the darkness of the forest. I think of the blood spurting out of Pyke's deep wound, and Eldokwila's fearless face urging me to run. I see the glint of her knife in the moonlight.

"What will the General do – if she has killed one of his men?"

He looks up the trail that leads over the hillock to their village. "We must hope he does not find out."

"He raped a child!"

Diego shushes me. "The General will not care to hear that either."

"And what if they come back." I nod towards the village. "To be revenged?"

"He didn't kill her," he shrugs. "Listen. Pyke is dead. Anything could have happened to him. Maybe he fell and dashed out his brains on a rock. A bear could have taken him. I will say I saw him going out alone at nightfall."

I nod, though I am far from comforted.

"We've gunners enough and their job is done," says Diego. "We don't need them for the voyage back. He won't be missed."

From the fort come the sounds of morning: men rising, stumbling from their beds, and washing at the shore. Someone pisses loud and long as a horse against a post of the barricade.

Diego's eyes sweep back into the forest. "This lake. Do you think you can find the way there?"

I look at the trees rising up the mountain. We came from further south but I know the direction. I nod, uncertainly.

"Then let us go," he says hurriedly. "There will be questions. Better to be gone. And I would see something more of this country before we sail."

I tie the basket around my waist and we go into the forest. I watch every step for a piece of Pyke's torn breeches, his blood – some sign of where he has gone.

The forest is waking to the day as we enter. Birds sing and swoop between the branches. Bracken crackles as the night animals return to their burrows.

Already, I am calmer. I breathe easier. How feeble are my worries and fears, how short they will last. These trunks are so mighty, the bark riven to such deep and gnarled furrows. These trees were here long before we came and will live long after we are gone.

Pyke, surely, is dead. The General will sail for the west and leave these people to their rightful lives. I think on it: of being on the ship, watching this land disappear behind the mists again. I find I can hardly bear it.

"Did he –" Diego pulls at my wrist from behind. "Did he – hurt you?"

"Did he fuck me, you mean?" I shake my hand free.

He tugs my skirt to punish me for pulling away, and I slip on a mossy boulder.

"If he's not dead already, *I* will kill him," he says, helping me up.

"There will be no need." I feel the weight of Eldokwila's knife where I tied it to my arm. The point of the blade presses into my forearm. I could loosen the cord, but I like to be reminded of it.

Has he observed the thickening of my waist, I wonder? My slowed walking, how quickly I tire? If he does, he does not mention it.

We climb higher. The early sunlight slants under the canopy, settling on a pale butterfly that flickers on the path.

The forest smells richer today: more alive. It must have rained in the night. The musherons unfurl. Underfoot, twigs snap heavy with moisture. A wide-leafed fern bows low as the dew drips from it.

Soon, we come to a clearing where the silver glint of the lake shines through the branches. The trees thin, the ground levels, and we emerge into the long grass by the shore. It tickles my palms as I walk through the swaying stalks. The mist is not yet risen. It sits over the water, cloaking the trees and far shore so the lake looks endless.

We stamp down the grass to make a place to sit back. For a long time we watch in silence as the mist clears from the lake, its full beauty revealed, moment by moment.

I think of the Hand of God the General talked of. That brought me not to *him*, but through him to this place. I imagine the Hand, wiping the mist from the lake to reveal its glories, just for me. I am blessed indeed. I am Macaia again, chosen by the snake to have rare good fortune.

Diego puts out his hand to mine. "There are lakes like this in Ireland," he says.

"What do you know of Ireland?"

"I have been there. With the General. Campaigning."

Of course: with the General.

A pair of black-necked geese glide low onto the water. I realise with a jolt, it is they: the geese that come to New Spain in winter.

To think that it is here they come! That I watched them, arrive from this place every year and knew nothing of it.

"Great green lakes and clear mountains," Diego goes on. "Empty land, as far as the eye can see." He watches a cloud shaped like a ship scud across the sky. "The Queen wants settlers there. Good Protestants."

"Why tell me of Ireland?"

"We could go there," he rolls onto his side, towards me. "When you are baptised. With my share of the fortune from this voyage, I can buy an estate. Land enough to farm."

"We?"

"Aye," his thumb presses into the soft flesh of my wrist. "We."

He pulls me to him. The lines at his eyes crease as he smiles.

"Together."

"Or –" I reach for him, feeling down the tight muscles of his back. "We could stay here."

The smile is gone instantly.

He takes my hand out of his breeches and frowns. "We cannot stay here," he says, as though it is the end of the discussion.

I lie back. The sun warms my face. The geese call to each other. It echoes across the emptiness of the lake and seems to come from all directions at once. How would it be for my baby to be born here? Far from want and savagery. Knowing no misery or despair.

"They would have us. In the village." I open one eye.

"My fortune is at Plymouth," he says. "Seven years I have laboured for this. I will be rich."

A leaf falls from a branch behind us and I watch it, spinning and floating on the breeze, drawn towards the lake.

"You said I would be free, but not free, there. Always different."

"Not if you have money," he says. "Everything is different with wealth."

He puts his hand behind my ear and strokes the sweat-damp curls of my hair there. I feel the pull of him. The want of him.

He leans in to kiss me. "We would be happy."

I can believe it.

We could live, we two, in a house: growing sorrel in the garden, keeping books upon a shelf. A cow out to pasture. How easy it would be.

But would I get there? With this baby? Would he want me, at all, with a child?

His knee rises and I press myself around him, to feel his sureness, his certainty: the solidity of him, body and soul.

What it is to live in hope. Should a person disregard everything they have seen and endured, in favour of mere hope?

The sun is at its height now. The lake is clear of mist. The mountains rise sharp and grey beyond the shore. Soon they will darken, through blues and purple to black as the sun dies, leaving only the outline of rocky peaks against the sky.

The geese take off, calling to each other, a rising bark of a call. Perhaps they are off to New Spain already. I think of them arriving. A girl like me watching them, amid the billowing sails of Acapulco. Wondering, as I did, where they came from. I wish I could send a message with them. To tell her of this place. The very notion of it.

We return in silence all the way to the fort.

40

We reach the beach at nightfall, as the first stars come blinking to life. It is strangely silent. No music, no drumbeat, no sound at all of merry-making drifting over the hill from the village.

We let ourselves in at the unmanned gate and creep towards the fire that flickers in the middle of the open ground.

The men are gathered around it, lying back on the blankets of fur and animal hair given us by the Indios. They pick at their teeth, the click of their toothpickers at work like cicadas in the eventide. Empty shells of mussels litter the sand where they have thrown them after their meal.

I scan each face for him, but Pyke is not there. Diego was right: he is not even missed.

Only the General looks up at us as we enter, his head to one side as he takes to his feet. Diego and I drop beside the men as if we have been there all along.

The General coughs, as he does to announce he will speak. He is not a speechmaker in the way of the Spaniards, finding his way to the subject by twisting paths of fancy words and fine phrases. He is straight upon it as a woman with a knife in the throat of her winter pig.

"Gentlemen, mariners," he starts. "I am a bad orator, for my bringing up has not been in learning." His eyes flick to Diego, as if he remembers something, and frowns. "But you know that I speak true – when I tell you that here – we have found our New Albion!"

The men cheer. I see now they are all some way into a double-ration of ale. Each man's cup is in his hand, many raised in salute. They drum cups against bowls, and the General waves for their silence.

"This is a fine country," he goes on. "It is temperate and bountiful. The Spaniards have never set foot here and know nothing of its riches. The forests and meadows are full of game. The seas throng with fish. The mountains yield treasures undreamed of. Tomorrow we sail—"

The men cheer fulsomely. My heart rises in my throat.

The General waits for the men to settle. Then he plunges in with the knife: "Who among you will put themselves forward to stay?"

His eyes shine, reflecting the flames. I look to Diego in alarm.

The men are bewildered also. There is silence, dismay.

"I will leave you with weapons," the General nods, pacing up and down. "Seeds to sow for the next harvest. Barrels for storing water, all other necessary things. And I will return within the year. With supplies, soldiers, and more men – yea and women too, for this will be a colony: our first of many in the New World. Great will be the glory for the pioneers who settle this country in the name of our sovereign Queen Elizabeth!"

One man stirs. "What is the reward?" calls Blackoller.

"The Queen will reward you. Every man in the colony will earn a share of the treasure taken by the fleets that will come through the passage and spoil the Spaniards' country in the south."

A murmur goes through the men. *Damn his eyes. God's blood. The Devil take the fucking passage!*

Carey stands. "But my General. In all faith, there *is* no passage!"

"Of course there is," returns the General, with a flick of

his hand. "We did not find it this time, but as sure as there are straits in the south, there is a passage here. I will return and find it when the ice melts next summer."

The men mutter and shift on their blankets. The fire crackles and spits. Sparks fly.

A colony of the English here: it will kill their peace, and it will kill them. Nor will the Spaniards rest in the south when they know of this land. This place will go the way of Guinney and New Spain, of Tierra Firme and Perou. Men in the mines and on the gibbet. Sold in marketplaces in coffles of iron. There will come a thousand Pykes to rape a thousand children.

Diego searches through the men, glowering at their disloyalty.

"Forty men," the General goes on. "That is the minimum to do the necessary work: the building, sowing and harvesting. A goodly number to found a colony – and it will lighten the burden on provisions for we who will cross the South Ocean."

The men look to each other and at the ground. No one meets the General's eye. Not a man among them would stay.

"Fletcher!" the General implores. "This is your chance! Convert the heathens. Bring them to Christ!"

"Aye – and die in the first winter!" Fletcher returns with fury.

The General frowns. "You, Doughty!" he calls to the brother of the traitor. "Stay and blot out the stain your brother brought upon your name!"

Doughty's eyes flash as he stares into the fire but he does not answer.

The men fall into anger and dispute. They talk, all at once, putting forward each other's names. A colony must have a blacksmith. Carpenters will be needed, gunners to man the defence. No man suggests himself. The General looks at them with disbelief.

"Those should stay," calls out Collyns, "who have no call to return to *Old* Albion." He stares at Diego and at me. I keep my eyes on the flames. A log spits sparks onto the nearest men, who shuffle back to escape them.

This is not how I had thought of staying. I would have them gone.

"Come, now!" The General's smile vanishes, dismay lines his face. "Will no one stay and found my colony? Will none of you do this for my sake, if not for the Queen?"

Complete silence. The fire crackles. The sea rolls in.

Then from the shore comes the one voice I had hoped never to hear again. The gate slams shut and every man turns towards him.

"Tis not safe to stay here," shouts Pyke. "Not lest we kill every last one of them."

He limps towards the fire, wincing with each step, eighty pairs of eyes fixed on him. "These are devils!" he points towards the hillock. "Tis no fit place for a colony till they are gone."

By the Virgin, I am for it now.

"Where have you been?" asks Carey.

"I was attacked," Pyke snarls. The firelight falls on him and I see his breeches are stained black with blood. "By a madwoman. An Indian witch."

The men curse and holler. *Give us the guns! We will show them no mercy!* They are delighted with the timely distraction.

"A *woman* got the better of you?" jeers Diego.

"There were two of them," Pyke growls, turning to me.

"And what did you do, Pyke," the General asks softly, "to provoke them?"

"Nothing," says Pyke. "Ask your whore." He points to me and holds my eye, daring me to tell what he did. "She was there."

I think about it. I think about telling him what Pyke did to the girl. But she counts for so little, a heathen child, I know that well enough. Then Pyke will tell him of my baby. And still they might march over the hill to the village, with guns and shot loaded. Destroy them all in a matter of moments. My mind crackles and spits like the fire. I cannot fix on a thought long enough to think clearly.

My eye rests on young Doughty. He sits straight-backed, staring into the fire. There is nothing the General would not do – has not already done – for the sake of his mission.

All men want is someone to rain their fury on. Pyke will be as happily revenged on me as on Eldokwila.

"I did it," I stand and address the General. "He is mistaken. It was I who stabbed him."

I pull back the sleeve of my shirt and loosen the cord. I throw Eldokwila's blood-stained knife at the General's feet.

Pyke says nothing. He watches me. The General picks up the knife and examines it. The men jeer and raise their cups and bowls into the air.

Foul Jezebel! Hang the witch!

Diego gets to his feet.

"Keep away, Diego," the General cautions, pointing the blade towards him. "Is this true, Pyke?"

Pyke narrows his eyes. I see it: the moment he decides to drop pursuit of the heathen woman and return to his original prey.

"It was dark," he says. "Perhaps I was mistaken."

"I will stay here," I tell the General. "Leave me here for my punishment. I will found your colony."

He stares at the handle of the knife. Carved from bone, skilfully shaped into the body of a bear, arms raised above its head. He turns it in his hands, examines the close and clever join of the blade and handle. He pricks the point of the knife with his finger to feel its keenness.

"But you are not to be trusted," he says, so quietly I can barely hear him above the crackle of the fire. "You are in league with the savages. How came you to have their weapons?"

"Eld – she gave it to me."

"So they have armed you. In our midst?"

"No!" I say. "I—"

"And you, Diego," the General turns to him, his soft voice

more menacing than angry. "Where have you been for the whole of this day?"

Diego steps towards me, but the General motions him back with the knife again.

"She's with child!" shouts Pyke. "You cannot leave her here. She has your baby – a Christian baby – in her belly."

The General turns back to him open-mouthed, cheeks flushed. He is stopped, utterly.

Malhaya Dios. My mind works, too slowly. All of them, looking at me. Diego steps back rigid, fists clenched. He holds me in his eyes with cold fury, all tenderness gone. What have I now? All that is left to women like me.

"It is not a Christian child!" I hiss. "I am no Christian! I renounce your God. Rather would I embrace the Devil than your unjust God!"

"Maria –" Fletcher stumbles towards me. The General holds his arm. He blinks at me, perfectly still in all other ways.

I cannot stop myself now. "I renounce five thousand of your Christs!"

I find in myself all the words I have heard screamed by men at the lash or the pyre – from girls hurling abuse as they are dragged from their beds or the marketplace. "I deny the Lord, his cuckold of a father and his whore of a mother. I forsake God who is dead, the Virgin, his mother, the Archangel and the saints."

Diego stares at me as if I have lost my mind.

I look into the sky and scream: "Devils, come take me now! I give myself to you." No one says anything. Even Pyke has lost his smirk. He looks to the General with alarm. The General does not flinch.

In New Spain, the filthiest of all the blasphemies are those that befoul the blessed Virgin. The worst I ever heard, from a man held down to be tortured with boiling oil, called for Her sodomy and ruin with a crucifix. But that would not do here. They worship instead the book. "I spit on your Bible! I shit on the Gospells!"

Finally, the General moves. He raises his arm and strikes me hard across the cheek. Shaking with rage, he orders the men to take me. They bind my hands with the same cords I used to secure the knife.

Mussel shells, wooden bowls and the tiny darts of toothpickers rain upon me, as the men throw whatever is to hand. They shout and jeer. It washes over me. I revel in the sting of my cheek.

I lie beside the dying fire, hands bound, coughing at the smoke. The men sleep, aided by the beer, like so many piles of tar-stained rags. The General slumbers in his privy tent, Diego, beside him. I cannot find comfort, my arms tied so tight and so painfully at the wrists. Nor can I shift on the hard and stony ground or stop the racing of my mind. What will he do? He cannot kill me – not till the baby is born.

Mayhap he will leave me here after all. It was offered to Doughty, a traitor, why not to me? But I know better than to guess at the General's plans. I might as well ask of the lightning where it will strike.

It is long after midnight. A cold and cloudless night. By the progress of the moon, I suppose it to be about three hours before dawn when they come. I am the only one awake – first to hear the signal, like an owl calling – then to watch them slipping noiselessly into the fort. Eighteen warriors, I count them. Eighteen women, each bearing a single bone-handled knife glinting at their forearms. They drop in on thick ropes thrown over the barricades, climbing swiftly and silently down, all at once. Eighteen bare feet feeling for the final step onto the ground at the same time. She is there of course, Eldokwila, chief among them. Without her finery, no cloak of silver furs, nor my skirt. She is dressed in a hemp shift, as they all are: indistinct shadows blurring into the night.

I look up to the men on sentry watch. Both are slumped

over the barricade, necks thrown back, broken, felled without a sound.

Within the fort, each woman approaches the nearest sleeping man. They do not discern. There is no search for deserving victims, save that they are all grown men.

Lit by the glowing embers of the fire, Eldokwila's face is fierce and sure. She makes a sign with her left hand and each warrior strikes at once. Eighteen knives in the hearts of eighteen sleeping men. A horrible gurgling sound, as the blood pumps out of them. Dull, low groans, a rasping sound in their throats. The thing is done so quickly I cannot believe it has happened.

They could kill every man here, but they have determined their number. With the sentries, twenty lives for the crime done to the child.

I could have called out. I could have warned the men. I chose not to.

She sees me just before she leaves. She doubles back and starts towards me when she sees my bonds. But I cannot go with her. They will follow more surely if they find me gone. I shake my head and urge her to go with my eyes. She understands. She retreats, as they all do, up the ropes, as silently as they came. The ropes are pulled up over the barricades and they are gone.

41

I do not know if I sleep. Only that I come to myself again at the sound of a terrible wail. The boy who lights the morning fire has discovered the bodies. The piles of rags stir, the men within them muster. They are up in moments.

The wail rises to a keening from every corner of the fort – men rocking and screaming, out of their minds with fear and horror.

"This is her doing," cries Collyns, pointing to where I lie bound and cowering by the remnants of the fire. "The blackamoor witch called on devils to do her murderous work – we all heard her!"

I inch backwards until I feel the barricade behind me, steeling myself for their blows.

"Fie!" says Fletcher. "There are no devils here." But even he won't approach me – none of them dare.

The men fall to their knees in loud and frenzied prayer.

Crouching beside a blood-soaked body, Diego examines the wound. "This is no devil-work," he says, rising. He looks pointedly at Pyke, who rocks and shakes upon his knees. "It is clear to see who has done this."

He will not look my way.

Finally, the General emerges. He sees instantly what has occurred. "Send runners to the village," he orders Diego.

"To watch – not yet to strike, and report back as quickly as possible."

Diego sends for the fleetest boys. Thomas and the cooper's lad take to their heels and fly out of the gate, across the beach.

The General comes to me. He helps me sit upright, for I cannot myself with my arms bound tight behind me.

"Well, Maria," he starts softly. "What have you done here?"

"I? What can I do, tied like this?"

"This is the work of the savages. And you are their agent."

"If I were their agent they would have freed me."

He makes a sucking sound with his tongue in his cheek and looks across at the chaos of the fort.

"Then why have they done this?"

Behind him, I see Pyke, holding his hat, shaking, to his chest. He knows what he has done. I decide to hold onto it.

The runners return, as I knew they would, with news that the village is emptied completely. Every fish-trap, each copper shield, the post and roof timber of every house packed up and gone, up into the forest. Returned to their winter homes, we know not where. I would wager they were gone long before the women came for their revenge. Nothing remains but the embers of their fire.

The General convenes his council under the sailcloth. He sits in a high-backed chair, facing away from me, while the gentlemen and officers stand, looking on. From where I lie, at the very edge of the fort, I cannot hear what passes. But I watch every man's face for some sign of what he will do. Carey toys with his moustache. Diego paces. Fletcher's face is deathly white, his lips mouthing silent prayer.

But what is there to do? The Indians will not be found easily in these wilds. The General cannot follow and risk losing more of the crew he needs to sail home. He is a practical man, cold-blooded, eyes and heart locked on his mission. There is nothing he can do.

The dead are buried at the bottom of the hillock. I am not

permitted to attend, but I watch them from the gate with a sentry standing over me. Twenty shallow graves topped with narrow mounds of earth. The General orders a brass plaque to be made and nailed to a post to record what has happened here: twenty names inscribed with the date of their deaths and their great sacrifice. It was not in vain, he says. For they died in claiming this land for Her Sovereign Majesty, Queen Elizabeth.

The men file back into the fort weary, replacing hats on their heads. Diego pauses before me and waits for the final man to pass. "Why did you not tell me about the baby?"

I do not like the way he stares down at me. "Because it is not your concern."

"Then it is not mine?"

Of course it is not his, can the man not count?

"Is it his?" he jerks his head towards the General in his tent.

"No. It is not his, and it is not yours. It is mine."

"You deceived me," he says coldly, eyes looking over my head and out to sea. "Seduced me with another man's child in your belly. I was right about you before: you are nothing but a whore."

He strides away to the General's tent, taking all the hopes I had in this world with him. He is like any other man, believing himself to be at the mercy of women, when it is clear as rain the other way round.

I watch as the men take down the tent. They load the guns, barrels, victuals; the sailcloth and their many stolen treasures onto the ship to sail with the tide.

As for me, when the fort is fully emptied, I am thrown roughly in the pinnace, still bound. They row me to the black outline of the ship at dusk.

So I will not stay here. And Ireland it seems, is no longer on offer. My heart aches to think I will not see Eldokwila again, and I have lost the only friend I had on this ship. But in a small corner of my heart I rejoice. For there will be no English colony in New Albion.

Book Three

MARE
PACIFICUM

August – December, 1579

AUGUST, 1579

MARE PACIFICUM

27°20'N

42

Twenty-eight days at sea again. Twenty-eight days in the Cage, with naught but a rough bench to sit and sleep on.

My belly grows. Every part of me to the smallest finger swells. I itch – all the time. Scratching as if at lice till the blood stains my linen. I pace. Up and down the small space of the Cage, three steps forward, three steps back, over and again.

Hard biscuit every day and New Albion deer on Thursday, salt-fish or pickled-pork three days a week, and other such tidbits as Thomas steals and brings me after nightfall.

A bucket for my needs, and plenty do I use it, for I am mighty sick again. A good sign, the midwife in Lima said. It means the baby thrives.

So close am I to the pumps, it feels like they are inside my head. Clanking, endlessly, day and night. Enough to drive away a person's wits.

I am freed to walk to the deck every evening for prayers, though I am kept apart from the men, and I speak to no one.

Diego does not come. He busies himself elsewhere at prayers. I thought to see John too, but no.

So other than Thomas creeping by at night, and passing me salt-meat through the bars of the door, some nuts and seeds, a lemon to keep off the scarby, the only soul I talk to in the long empty days is Fletcher. He comes daily. To bring me back to God – as he thinks.

As soon as I see his pale face at the bars of the door this morning, I ask before word of greeting: "When will he free me?"

As he comes in, more light falls on the dried grasses on the floor and I shudder to see something moving there. "When you have recanted your foul blasphemy, and begged forgiveness for your great sin and treachery."

The little light from the hold closes with the door behind him. But he has a candle, and he sets it in the corner. It flickers there, one kick from the tinder-dry grass.

He opens the door again to put the bucket outside.

"Take back your foolish renunciation," he says, coming to sit beside me on the bench. "Tell him you were not yourself. He is a forgiving man. He will believe you were not in league with the savages if you do."

"You did not think him forgiving when you were ill," I remind him. "You said then he was a dishonourable man."

He coughs but does not answer, instead making a great show of taking out his Bible from the inside of his shirt.

"Shall we go over your prayers, Maria? For your baptism?"

"I will not be baptised."

"Look forward," he puts my hands around the book. "You are lucky indeed to have stumbled across the true word of God. Never would you have heard it among the Spaniards. A full life in Christ awaits you in England – for you and your child."

"I do not want to go to England. I wished to stay in New Albion."

"When you give yourself to God, Maria, it does not matter where you are."

How is it possible to believe such a foolish thing?

"Don't look back, Maria. It will never profit you. Remember the wife of Lot."

Of all the grim tales in the Bible, this one I loathe the most. I tap my bare toes against the floor.

"I do remember, indeed. You gave the lesson only last week. Tell me, Master Fletcher: What was her name?"

"Lot's wife?"

"Did she have a name of her own? Esther, it may be? Ruth? Or Maria?"

His back straightens. "Undoubtedly she had a name. But it is not recorded."

"Mayhap it was thought not important?"

He misunderstands. "You are right, Maria. It is not important. The lesson is she looked back when she fled the wicked town of Sodom, and she was punished for it. Turned into a pillar of salt."

"Why is it so wrong to look back?"

The candle casts a shadow on the wall beyond, a long-nosed puppet that mimics him as he talks.

"Because God forbade it, Maria. That is why."

"And for this she was punished. For looking back at her home?"

The puppet flickers, close-mouthed.

"At the place where she grew from a child, and where she cradled her own children? Her home, which was burning and in the midst of destruction?"

Fast am I in my fury now, like a dog off the leash.

"And I think, in this story, Mistress Lot – I shall give her a name of her own, if the teller of this tale did not – I shall call her Lleni, after my grandmother."

"A pretty name, Maria, but—"

"Am I right, Master Fletcher, that Lot offered up his two daughters to the mob to suffer rape and violence, that he might save the angels from harm?"

"That is true, Maria—"

"And yet *he* is the good man of Sodom? And *she* is the one who is punished?"

He looks down. "God's ways are difficult for we mortals to discern, Maria—"

"I find rather they are very easy to discern."

"We are wandering from the… " He loses the words. "You cannot disobey God's command, Maria."

"Even if it is a cruel and stupid command?"

"God is never cruel, Maria, He is always just."

"You are wrong. He is not always just."

"Maria, my dear—"

"He is not a nice God."

"You know not what you say," he says, the trouble returning to his face. But it is he who knows not what he says. What can he know? Of being so lowly even your name is taken from you. Of watching everything you know and love destroyed.

"She should be honoured, Maria."

"Who?" No longer am I thinking of Lot's wife.

"The wife of Lot."

"Lleni," I say.

"Lleni," he sighs. He puts his hands to his knees to stand. "For the church was known in the early days of our religion as the salt of the earth because it will endure forever. So in truth, it is an honour that Lot's wi— Lleni was turned into a pillar of salt. She should be honoured by the comparison with the mother church. Glad that no longer was she made of corruptible flesh."

He leaves me, still tapping my toes on the boards. He closes the door, taking with him the candle so I am left in darkness once more.

Well, I am made of corruptible flesh. And so was my grandmother, who also, like the wife of Lot, looked back and wished she hadn't, when we ran from our burning town.

She saw things she wished she had not, and she told me not to look, but keep running. Eyes on the path, she said as she pushed me, stumbling, into the forest, and away from the swamp.

But of course I looked back, because I am a person and it was my home, and even if I had been commanded not to by the Almighty, I would have looked, and now it is not possible to unsee those things.

They are before me, still.

The men who came into my mother's house. Standing there, dripping the mud of the riverbank over the clean rushes of the floor.

They pushed us out with pikes and swords. Out of the house towards the village gates. From every other house came women and children with blades at their backs. Our men were long gone. They had taken to the barricades at dawn, oiled and perfumed for war, to the beating of drums and the cry of the battle-horn. Only women and children and old people remained.

The Englishmen plunged pikestaffs topped with fire into the tinder-dry roofs. Flames leaped into the sky. The air was hot and thick with smoke. The heat bent the light. Nothing looked real.

They forced us towards the sacred cotton-tree. The idols and offerings we had laid there, beseeching the ancestors for their protection, were trampled and broken. I thought I heard the spirits wailing, their screams raised in protest at such profanity and violence. Now I know it was the shot racing past my ears.

There by the tree, I was still with my mother and my sisters, holding tight to each other as we were pushed and pulled all ways. My mother carried Fode. He could not stop crying. The men pointed swords at him and shouted at my mother to make him stop. She started to sing. Midst the clap of the guns, the creaking of the high wooden gates, and the cries of children, she sang the song she had sung to us all in the cradle.

Someone wishes to have you as her child
But you are my own

Someone wishes she had you to nurse
But I have you
You are my own
You are my own

Smoke veiled the sun. Ashes fell like burning seeds. Timbers crashed. More screaming. The crowd moved as one. We were carried up, off our feet, towards the opening gates.

But in through the widening gap our Bullom enemies came running, wielding knives and adzes. They felled us where we stood. The ground ran with blood.

The Englishmen fired the guns and I saw for the first time what they did: an assault on the ears, people dropping as if by magic, blood pooling around them.

I put out my hand for my mother and I felt her waistcloth. But she was struggling, holding the baby. My sisters, screaming with fear, held onto her too.

I could not see where we were going. Someone pushed before me. I lost hold of my mother. Others sank underfoot, and still we were carried forward, through no will of our own.

Bodies closed in around me, dense as the underbrush. I heard my mother call my name, but she was too far ahead. Unreachable and lost to me.

Someone tugged my elbow. "Come, Macaia," my grandmother said. "This way."

She talked softly. I followed her. Away from the gates, towards the break in the barricade. There were fewer people here. It was easier to move. We heard the thunder of the guns behind us, the screaming and slaughter. We kept going.

Most were going the other way. Towards the swamp. When we looked back I saw the head of my mother, but not my sisters. Still she carried Fode in her arms. I saw the curls of his head. I called to her.

"Keep going, Macaia," my grandmother said. "We will find them later."

We reached the edge of the forest, where the path rises into the grove of sweet-smelling camwood trees. Ahead of us, people melted into the darkness. Behind me, a whistle and a thud. An old man fell. People ran over him, trampling his body.

I looked for my mother again.

From the higher ground we saw what they could not. That ahead of them, those who had run into the swamp, thinking to get to their canoes in the river, were stuck fast, sinking in the black mud.

But behind them, more people came, running from the gleaming knives of the Bulloms. They did not stop. Each one fell into the mud, which took them fast. Each downed and flailing body, crushed into the ooze by those that came after.

The Englishmen watched in confusion, shouting to each other, firing into the air. I did not understand then, but now I know. They did not want us dead – that was not their purpose. They needed us living.

I called to my mother to warn her. Nothing could be heard above the pitiful screams of the dying, the battle cries of the Bullom and the thunder of the guns.

She held Fode close to her breast. He was crying still, his eyes squeezed tight, his head thrown back, mouth wide open.

She fell. Like they all did, as more people came from behind and trampled them down. She held Fode high, as long as she could. I hope Dura and my other sisters were with her. I do not know. I saw only her hands and the baby, held above the black mud, when even she had sunk below.

I think of it often. Of the day the Englishmen came. I turn it over in my mind.

Ever since Fletcher was here, for he has not returned. There is plenty of time to think.

How after we got into the forest, my grandmother and I, we hid, trembling with fear. But the Englishmen found us and took us back to the clearing beside our village. The smoke still poured out of the roofs, flames leapt into the air. The stench was bitter: of gunpowder, burned thatch and charred flesh.

The cries from the swamp had ended. I did not look there. Two hundred and fifty of us in the clearing. On our knees, circled by the Englishmen carrying guns.

We had seen what the guns did now. No one moved.

Two hundred and fifty, that is all. Six thousand there had been behind the barricades when we were first besieged. Of my family, just myself and my grandmother. Aged Saba, who trained the girls in dance. Bala, who taught me to catch fish with a basket.

My grandmother stroked my hair. "Remember, Macaia," she whispered, "you are the Fortunate One. Chosen by the snake."

From the distance came the beat of the drums of our enemies.

We knew what this signified.

That they had taken captives of their own, as the price demanded of the Englishmen for bringing them here.

That they were parading them now at their war camp in the forest, before killing them, man, woman and child, as is their custom.

OCTOBER, 1579

MARE PACIFICUM

04°30'N

43

Eighty-two days in the Cage.

Still no sight of land.

It should not take so long. Something is wrong. Rations have been cut and cut again. Less water every day, and that stale and bad.

The pumps clank and whirr. The men working them grunt and curse. From the deck rings out the bell of Guatulco, sending men running to their duties. Steps slam the boards above my head.

The sounds echo through the caverns and passages of the ship, down to where I lie, hot and stifled in the Cage.

I am like my baby – kept close in the womb of a rolling, pitching ship. I long, as she must, to be out. To be done with the sickness and the closeness, never knowing which way is up or down.

A ship is no place for a baby, Don Francisco said when he took my child and gave him to another woman.

He spoke the truth, I had the sense to know it then. But nor is it any place for me.

It is all I can think of now: that we will find land.

I will beg his forgiveness, take back my blasphemy. Only to be let out of the Cage and off this ship.

There is nothing else. It is fixed in my mind always: the

solidness of land, earth beneath my feet. Fresh air to breathe. Water to wet my parched tongue.

And how it hurts when I stand – this body, growing inside me, pushing down so on my bones. I lean against the wall to let the weight fall forward. Down on all fours like an animal.

The ship's pitch grows more violent. I must lie on my side on the floor to keep from falling. The sickness will not stop.

She turns inside me. Struggling for room. I cannot think her a baby, it is something else. Something cankerous, growing within. She takes what little I have left. Imprisons me from the inside as well as without.

I start to hate her. He can have her. Do what he wants with her. Take this child from me too. Only to be out. Anything to be out.

A storm is fetching, I feel it in the roll.

And now he comes.

When I lie on the floor, retching into the bucket cradled at my arm.

Eighty and two days has he waited, the wretch.

He knocks at the door, as if I have anything to say about who comes in and who does not. He sits on the floor, legs stretched before him and puts down a bowl. I will not look at him or own his presence.

But it is not the usual ration. Rice and meat. No worm-ridden biscuit that must be eaten with closed eyes. Thomas must have husked the rice.

By the bowl, his feet. Booted, not bare. It makes me sit up and forget I would scorn him. "Is there land?"

"Nay. There is a storm coming. Eat. There will be no hot food till we can light a fire again."

"I can't eat," I wail, and retch again. Diego puts his hand to my back.

I wipe the vomit from my mouth.

He holds something out to me: the spoon the spirit-woman

gave me in the north. Stolen with everything else in my pouch when they put me here. I take it. I run my thumb over the figureheads on the handle, pricking at the sharp points of the antlers of a stag. On the beak of an eagle. It revives me to feel something new.

"A bad storm? Is the General worried?"

"Worried?" Diego sniffs. "He delights in it. 'Our God is with us! We have nothing to fear! We must fill our hearts and minds with the words of God! As he fills our sails with wind! We must trust in His Fatherly Providence. *Now* will we see who are the good sailors!'"

His mimicry of the General has improved.

"Let me out."

He stiffens. "I can't."

"Why have you not come? You are angry with me, still?"

"Nay, muñeca," he says softly. He looks at his boots. "I thought I could help you more. If I kept the General's ear."

"No one has his ear!" I slam my fist into the planks. He picks up my hand and kisses the palm.

He stands and I find I cannot bear to be left alone another minute. "Let me out!" I am crying now. "I will beg his forgiveness, I will recant. Please, let me out."

He shakes me from his leg like a dog. "I cannot. There is too much to be done –" He looks to the door, itching to be gone. "Bide your time. Eat – when you can. You are as safe here as anywhere on the ship." He leaves without a farewell.

Then his face appears at the bars. "The storm – if things go badly. Then I will come."

From here, where my head falls back upon the floor, I can see the dim light of the hold under the crack of the door as he closes it, and goes back up into the ship.

My mind returns, as it has often lately, to the words of the General's navigation book. They repeat themselves as if a devil whispers in my ear.

The purpose of navigation is this: What dangers are by the way, as Rocks and Sands and such other like impediments?

How to attain a port, if the wind does shift or change?

If any storms do happen, how to preserve the Ship and bring her safe unto the port assigned?

For I do have a port assigned to me now.

It is as real to me here in the Cage as if it is before me.

Very different it is from any I ever saw in the New World. There are no cannon, no batteries. No waiting officials nor soldiers with musket and sword. No crying women, weeping over children being torn from their arms. No men exposed naked in the midday heat in coffles of iron.

No friars nor men of religion who come to meet the miserable arrivals, checking each body for signs of oncoming death – not to save them, but to baptise them and win their souls. Who come to clothe the naked because their nakedness offends God, though their irons do not.

None who would take the blanket from a shivering child to cover a dead man, because *he* was baptised and the child was not.

The port I see has none of this. Indeed it has very little, save a curving beach of sand. A platform into the flat sea built from palmwood. Long, brightly-painted red and blue canoes tied to its stakes.

I raise my eyes, as if I am looking up, not to the bars of the door, but beyond, to the hills of green, rising from my port into fields thick with furrows and dykes.

Singing floats down from the fields, the song of women working. And from the wide river, which leads from the sea into the forest, the sound of children, splashing as they dive to the mangrove roots for oysters, laughing as they wash in the evening sun.

I have a name for this place now. It is Terra Australis, the land not yet known. That is my port. I assigned it myself.

44

At sea, the marineros say, never are you more than three fingers from death. Three fingers – the thickness of the timbers in the hull. All that keeps a person from the waves. Never till now have I known the truth of it, though I have survived many storms at sea.

Here, trapped in the bowels of the ship, with my head to the boards, the fury of the ocean pounding against the weak and rotting hull – now truly do I feel it with every sense in my heart and head.

I have curled into the corner to stop rolling, for the ship rises so high and so low with the falls, I am shaken, as if trapped within a wooden toy.

My back is to the hull, my feet against the bench to wedge it to the far side of the Cage. It takes all my strength to keep it there to stop it from rolling and crushing me. I cannot rest for a moment.

The bucket was long ago emptied onto the floor, and I hold that too to keep it from flying about the Cage. My own filth swills onto me with every roll. What does it matter? I retch now onto the floor and piss and shit my watery waste where I am.

Outside the Cage, the men work the pumps faster, continually now, to keep the water out. With the clank and the grate of the machine come their curses, echoing into my prison, such unholy prayers.

The wind whistles from all sides, screeching like the Devil himself sweeping through the ship. The timbers groan with every wave that crashes into the broadsides.

If it goes badly, he said. How bad must it be for him to come?

And what is the use of it? Only that I will not drown alone. For if we founder here, all is lost. We are but one ship alone on the vastness of this ocean.

Now there is hammering amid the panicked blasphemy and the cry goes up: *Bring mawls! More oakum!* I do not need to go to the bars to see what is happening. The holes are widening at the seams, the water is coming in.

The boys come running with tarred oakum they use to stuff the breaks, and hammers to beat lead thin enough to cover them.

The dread grows in me. It hums in my breast, deepening, strengthening.

Below, from the very bottom of the ship comes the most fearsome sound of all – the screech of the mainmast as it grinds against the keel. It shudders and moans, forced this way and that by the winds above. A terrible sound. It cannot hold.

I cradle my head with my arms.

How long I stay like this I do not know. Each minute is a fright, and there are hundreds of them running into each other. I know not if it is day or night, nor how long we have been at the mercy of the storm.

He has not come for me. None will come for me.

The water washes in at the door. Two inches, three. More with every minute.

Now do I long to hear the hammering and the pumps, but they have stopped. The men are gone from the hold.

I am quite alone. Locked in the bowels of the ship.

The mast grinds against the keel. The waves pound the broadsides.

In the darkness I see down, below where I sit, through the worm-ridden planks, to the moss and shells of the little creatures clinging to the underside of the ship. Below them, down fathoms into the bottomless depths.

Why delay what I know is coming? Why endure this fear without end? I could take the bench and hammer it into the weakened boards. Three fingers and I am free.

I think about it. I see myself, falling in the water, my hair fanning out, my skirts billowing as the sea claims me.

From the water of the womb we all came, and to the water will I return.

Not a bad death, Collyns said. No pain.

Everything comes from the sea. In Perou they say the world was born when the oceans were poured out of a bag, bringing all life with them.

That is not what we said in my country. We said evil comes from the sea. That is what we believed long before it did come, borne in on ships with sails like burial shrouds and men with faces pale as ghosts.

I see them now, those ships. At anchor in the bay at the mouth of the river. Vultures, sitting on the water. Six of them, as there were in the harbour at San Juan de Ulúa. I wonder now I did not make the connection sooner.

Such dread and shaking fear when first I saw them. Whole villages, they seemed to me, kept afloat by magic.

One smaller vessel – which comes to me now as sharp as a knife. I saw it first, not on the sea with the others, but on the river beside my village.

The day after the Englishmen came, we woke where we lay on the ground. The men with guns stood guard around us. My grandmother was sitting on her knees when I woke. She was watching them, her head moving by small degrees here and there, sharp-eyed.

The Englishmen gave us beans they had taken from our homes. We had not eaten since the morning of the attack. I was so hungry.

Then there came on the river the boat. A little bigger than the pinnace of this ship. Shallow enough in the hull to come inland to carry us all back to the sea.

And on the boat, its captain – a small man, with hair the colour of straw and a young man's beard. No sea-cap of gold – it was blue then. He held his hands behind his back as he surveyed us on the bank of the river. His nose, I thought, in its smallness, had the look of the beak of a hawk.

I did not know then the tongue he spoke. But his meaning was clear enough. And I can imagine him saying it now, in the breathless way he has, the stops and halting starts, his gunmetal eyes unsmiling.

Such a pitiful number of slaves. Barely worth the effort. Of the undertaking.

It was him. The General. I know it.

The fury fills every part of my body. It runs through my veins like poison. It tightens the drumskin of my belly around the baby. It fills my breasts with poison-milk and seeps into my swollen fingers, making fists of them so tight my nails draw blood.

All of this. All my misery in this New World – because of him.

He, who talks of brotherhood in Christ and the justice and the grace and the mercy of his God.

I slam my feet into the bench and it splinters, crashing and tumbling down the pitched floor. Without and within me everything roils and turns.

The ship dives steeply in the bow and the splinters of the bench come crashing back upon me. Barely do I feel them.

The baby fights inside me, kicking at my ribs from within.

The fury hardens. It is a real thing, molten metal cooling solid in my veins.

A thunderous crash booms up from the keel through my very body. Silence – then a fearsome creaking and splintering from all the way up into the top of the ship. Screams and cries from the decks above. An almighty roar as something vast falls into the water.

My rage makes of me harder stuff than this ship. I will not founder. I will not go quietly below the waves, to sink without notice nor sorrow.

The broken leg of the bench falls against my foot and I take it up, crawling to the door to smash against it. Barely does it make a scratch.

Through the bars, I see the empty hold in its dim light.

The mainmast that runs through all the decks is smashed in two. A great splintering of timber in the midst of the hold, the boards of the broken decks piled where they fell.

A hole gapes in the broadside, water pouring in. Now comes a fish, so wide is the hole. He washes across the boards as the water drains to starboard, and back again as we pitch the other way.

The patches of lead are abandoned – the oakum too, carried on the water like sea-grass.

I kick at the door, as well as I can with my swollen belly, smash at it with the broken timbers of the bench, swing the metal bucket wildly at the lock.

The lock. A lock can be picked. All I need is something sharp. I cast my eyes about the gloom of the Cage. Perhaps a nail from the joints of the bench. I feel for one in the rising water.

Nothing. Only the bowl Diego brought me.

I get on hand and knee and feel every inch of the flooded prison for the spoon. My fingers comb through the grass floating in the water, through the filth and the waste. Until something sharp pricks my thumb. The long handle, carved from bone into heads and faces. Near the top, the woman, and above her the final totem: a stag's head with antlers filed into curving, sharpened points.

It could be made for lock-picking.

I feel into the parts of the lock, pressing, searching for the machinery.

The ship pitches to the stern and I fall, tumbling to the back of the Cage.

My belly tightens in pain, and I crawl up the mountain of the floor.

I stab at the lock again. Barely can I see what I am doing. But I can feel, as if it is a part of me.

By the Virgin, by the Devil himself – by the spirits. I say it aloud, like a mad thing. *It must give, it must, it must – it* must.

And it does.

I wade through the hold, gripping the lifelines the sailors roped there before they went back up into the ship. Slipping, falling, trying to keep from the sheets of lead crashing about on the water. Silver coins when the water washes to one side. Hundreds of them, littering the boards. The General's precious cargo.

The stair is gone. A rope hangs there instead, with knots to climb. I pull myself up, unsteadily, into the gun deck.

By God's body, what a sight. The cannon have come unlashed, falling against the broadsides, smashing, wrecking whatever was in their path: barrels of powder, the makeshift boards that divided the deck – and into men. A body lies under the wheel of a gun carriage, his head smashed, his pulped brain open to the world. Others lie injured, groaning, whimpering like dogs. They do not concern me. I go through the deck.

Past the store, its door smashed by a fallen barrel. Past the manger, which is empty. Past a cupboard, which has been used by the surgion's boy, the floor beside it thick with black blood. An armless hand, its fingers curling upwards from the floor.

Past another man lying on his back, a blow to his head above the eye, the blood pouring from it into a pool around his head. His hand grasps my ankle, he whispers something, tries to pull me closer. I bend down and see it is Pyke. I do not care to hear what he has to say. I shake free my foot and walk on.

A skeleton remains of the stair. Enough to climb, pulling myself over the missing steps, up into the armoury.

The guns and the pikes and all their weapons are fallen all over the floor. I walk over them, stooping to put a hand to the floor to steady myself as they slip and slide upon each other.

Such a short distance, but it seems to take whole minutes to cross the sea of weapons until my hand finds the door to the Great Cabin.

45

Inside the Great Cabin are a dozen men. No one speaks when
I open the door. I stand at the threshold, observing them all.

John sits in the corner, head on his knees. Fletcher stands,
staring darkly at the floor, his Bible in his hands. Carey, arms
folded, looks out the window. Eyot leans forward on a stool,
hands on his thighs. Bosun Winter is seated at the table,
grasping the silenced whistle at his neck. The steward Legge,
his face like thunder, holds a browned and curling piece of
paper, which he drops to his side as I enter. Even Doughty, the
traitor's brother, is there. Never before has he been admitted
into the Great Cabin.

In the midst of them all is the General, arms outstretched
on the table. He holds my gaze without guilt nor shame. No
surprise in him – none at all – to see me there, though he left
me surely locked in his Cage.

"I see you are out, Maria," he says at last. "Come. You may
as well join us now."

I was prepared for malice. His indifference stuns me.

"Out?" I hear myself, dull as an imbecile. "Indeed I am
out! Though you would have me drown, locked in a cage as
if I were a dog."

"We will all drown," the General says. "The ship cannot

be saved. You were as close to Heaven there as you are here. Which is to say, in your case, not close at all."

John lets out a long wail.

"And you – all of you," I turn to each of the pitiless men in the room. "Not one of you came to help me. None of you would defy this *devil* to release a woman – a pregnant woman! – locked away in a sinking ship? What are you? Are you men? For you are surely not Christians."

None will look at me. The ship dives. Fletcher puts his arm to the back of a chair, and it gives, sending him stumbling forward. We are higher in the winds here than below and they race and shriek outside the windows like spirits come to claim the dead.

"But we *can* save the ship," says Legge, as though I have said nothing. He thrusts forth his paper again. He stabs at it – at a line-drawing of the plans of the ship, cut away to show the joints of the hull.

"Look," he pleads with the General. "The breaks are in favoured places. We can bind the hull with cables. You said yourself how close we are to land. All we need is two strong men to dive below—"

"We are in God's hands," the General says. "All we can do is pray. We must put our trust in Him."

"God's wounds, man!" shouts Carey.

The General glowers at him. "Blasphemy will not save us, my friend. Our only hope is in God. He throws down with one hand and raises up with another…"

"And you think God will look with favour on such a man as you?" I spit at him. "A thief. A slaver. A murderer! Do you think I don't know? You were there – in Guinney. I remember you. You were with the men who took us."

He laughs, a nervous sound, stretched too thin. "What of it? Of course I was in Guinney. Many times. And I have taken slaves, I do not deny it. Nor do I regret it.

"'Twas God's will, for we brought those heathens out of their ignorance and to the word of God. I brought *you* to

God, Maria. It is not my concern if you choose to disregard His word."

"You did *not* bring me to God." I am as cold as he now, the metal in my veins frozen solid. "God is not a man who seeks dominion over others. You have made your God in your own image."

He disdains me completely, looking to his men. "We must give thanks to God for this time given to prepare our souls for a better life in Heaven. Prayer is all that is left."

"You can pray. I want nothing of your God." I push the chair in my way and it falls clattering to the floor. At the door, I realise what has been whispering at my ear since I came into this cabin. He is not here.

I turn around. He is not seated beside the General. Not among the throng of men. Nowhere in this room.

"Where is Diego? What have you done with him?"

The General draws himself up in full mastery of his indifference. Only the rapid blinking of one eye shows he feels any discomfort.

"Where *is* he?"

The men look down. John sniffs. No one speaks.

Eyot raises his eyes to the cabin above.

I go out into the armoury. Only when I leave do I hear Fletcher find his courage.

"It is too late for you to make pretence at religion now! Far too late! This is your doing," he shouts at the General. "You have filled this ship so full of stolen treasure, she cannot float! We cannot withstand the fury of nature! Nor will God protect us for you have angered Him with your great sins.

"What chance has a ship with such a man at its helm? God punishes us – rightly – for your arrogance, your thievery and your sins. We do not deserve to live! We should all atone for our sins and make our peace with God and take whatever death He sends us."

"Silence, Fletcher!"

"I will not be silent!" Never have I heard him shout. "Now

is not the time to pray for mercy. We do not deserve it. We must repent and beg forgiveness for the great sins we have all committed."

As I step up into the maindeck, they are all shouting, a great hubbub of confusion and despair. I can no longer make out the words. Just the fury and the fear of men who know they will die.

The wind whistles sharp across the battered maindeck. I realise for the first time it is night. Warm, spite the rushing winds. The waxing moon shines through a break in the cloud lighting up the fallen spars and yards that litter the deck. Scraps of torn sail whip around the splintered foremast.

There is nothing left of the top parts of the ship – blown down or cut to save the vessel before the storm hit. She is naked, stripped of all her power. The mainmast is snapped like a twig, the top half gone into the sea.

I go unsteadily towards the cabin. The swell is high, the ship pitches sharply. I climb on hand and knee.

The water comes in with every wave over the smashed and broken gunwales. It washes over the boards, numbing my fingers, stinging the cuts on my hands I had not noticed till now. The wind drives into me. My belly tightens, over and again, the baby clamouring to be out.

The whipstaff is unmanned. Creaking mightily, it turns as it will, the rudder left to its own design. A barrel slams across the deck, a hand's width from my nose. A piece of carved timber from the lookout chases after it.

I reach the stair to the cabin – a miracle it is still here. Only five small steps but I fear I do not have the strength to climb them.

Inch by inch I pull myself to the top.

At the threshold the door is gone. I crawl inside.

Sodden papers and open books litter the floor. The General's brass globe rolls about where it finds a path through them. The pedestal, engraved with the arms of the Queen of England, broken from it.

The chest is lashed to the bottom of the bed. I pull myself up over it.

He is there. Asleep or dead I do not know.

His head is wrapped in blood-soaked sailcloth, the linen around him stiff and brown as rust. His right arm is strapped to his chest, a mess of blood and crushed bone. I climb in beside him and take his good hand. It is cold and wet.

I am numbed and I am empty. There is no fight left in me.

With the sound of the wind driving past the cabin like the Devil, the spray of the salt-water coming in at the window, and the clank of the globe rolling heavily through the maze of books on the cabin floor, I fall asleep.

46

I am woken by the sun streaming in through the window. For three months I have been denied it, and for a moment, I savour the warmth on my face. I fear to look about and find I am in the Cage again.

I blink open my eyes. The ship is calm. By some miracle, she floats. The sun is bright. The baby is quiet, all belly pains gone. Beside me, Diego lies still.

Through the open doorway I see the debris of the maindeck.

I climb over him to go closer. The brass globe has come to a rest by the doorway. Beside it, the sea-soaked bag carrying the fire-opal. I put them onto the high shelf.

Outside, it is but a graveyard of a ship. Broken barrels, timbers, pieces of torn sailcloth are everywhere. A gaping hole where the mainmast smashed open the boards of the deck when it fell, the bowels of the ship open to the sky, a mortal wound.

The jagged stump of the foremast points upwards, splinters like fingers accusing the heavens. Only one of its yards remains, a solitary sail hanging sorrowfully from it. The sea is flat at last. On deck, nothing moves.

The whipstaff is still. Lifelines stretch out all over the waist. At the foot of the stair to the maindeck, lies a body under a fallen yard. Thin and small. My heart sinks.

A lock of black hair lies across his face, and I sweep it back. His unseeing eyes look straight ahead. Poor Thomas. He lies where I saw him, when first I came on this ship, scrubbing the boards. Blood collects under his open mouth. His bare chest crushed by the timber.

Thomas who would never to go to sea again. Who would live up a mountain, far from the coast, when he returned safe to England.

Still so thin, though he stole food for me in the Cage. Fresh bruises and cuts on his face, a blackened eye since I saw him last.

Poor Thomas, who never chose this life. Unending toil in the frozen wastes and burning sun.

He is cold to touch. I cannot bear to look upon his eyes and his puffed and bloody face. I cover him with a scrap of sailcloth and go to the bowsprit, picking myself over the debris of the deck, skirting the gaping hole in the centre of the ship.

At the foremast, a little wind picks up. The tatters of the sail kick at the breeze. We sail south-east, I see from the sun. The wind raises the flat water to tiny peaks, foamy crests like snow. The bow cleaves through them. On we go, rudderless. Without aim nor design.

Something stirs in the wake. A ripple – a fish coming up. But the ripple widens – and poking at the air with a bottle-shaped nose, comes a dolphyn. She leaps into the air, soaring in a perfect arc before diving again below.

Another comes, competing with the first, soaring higher, diving deeper. And more – I do not know how many, all leaping and diving in turn. They smile, I swear it. One twists as she soars in the air.

Never do they collide, however fast they go. Each one in her rightful place, gliding, flying, skimming over the water – like dancers, each taking her turn to lead, showing off her grace and skill, before melting back into the sea.

They lead us. Onwards, into the pitiless ocean, towards the morning haze, that lies deep blue on the horizon.

From the east, a bird comes in, low over the water. Big-billed and sleek – a pelicane, my favourite of all the sea-birds. The first sight of one offshore near Acapulco meant the long journey from Manila was at an end. I watch the graceful line of her flight, so straight and clean. She veers out of sight flying south.

My heart leaps. A pelicane is never far from land. In the distance, where she is now a mere speck on the horizon: a cloud.

Solitary, and definite. A sign, a promise.

It can mean only one thing.

"Land!" I shout. It sounds like someone else's voice.

A dolphyn leaps beside me, turns in the air and chatters.

"Land!" I shout again. I fall back into the ship, running to the gaping hole in the waist. "There is land! Come up, come up for we are saved!"

Commotion from within, men stirring, calling to each other. Footsteps running, the slamming of a door.

But the first voice I hear distinctly comes from behind me, not below.

"Land?" he asks, his voice groggy from the pain. He stands at the threshold of the cabin, one hand to the blood-blackened cloth around his head, his crushed and broken arm hanging as he leans into the doorway. "Is there land?"

We limped towards the island, the dolphyns leading us on.

Legge won his fight with the General. In the night, while the storm endured and I slept like the dead, two men dived into the raging sea, down under the ship carrying cables to bind the hull. Three times they went down, feeling their way in the darkness. Three times they came up, gasping for air. Such crude and cobbled mending. But it saved the ship. She kept in one piece and afloat till we reached land.

We stitched together the rags of sailcloth, all of those still able. The carpenters fixed a makeshift mast and a rudder from the ruins of the mainmast yards. Like a toy made of scraps and garbage, we shifted, creaking mightily, towards the island.

Not just one island, we saw, as we got closer, but one of many. Sand-circled drops of green, forested hills rising to little peaks, each with a cloud at its summit. Beyond – land that stretches out both north and south: a main.

We put the dead into the sea, Pyke among them. I was not sorry.

A ship boy does not warrant a shroud, they said. So I wrapped and stitched Thomas into his sailcloth myself, weighed down with a cannon ball, for I do not want him to come back to this ship like Foster. Not now, at last, that he is free.

At the funeral service the General led the prayers. For Master Fletcher sits where he was chained the morning the storm broke. Shackled by the leg to a hatch on the maindeck as if he were a criminal.

We were summoned to watch it, all the people on the ship. An excommunication the General called it. On whose authority I cannot say.

"I denounce thee to the Devil and all his angels!" said the General, pinning a banner to his arm. "Never will you take this off! On pain of hanging. Here you will stay till we fetch home."

Francis Fletcher, the banner reads. *The falsest knave that lives.*

No one dares say any longer that women anger the sea. The mariners serve me like a queen, nodding low when they pass me by. "For did you not observe," I heard Collyns whisper, "the sea's fury and violence when she was caged. That it only abated when she was freed."

NOVEMBER – DECEMBER, 1579

ISLA MACAIA

0°40'S

47

The island sits on the line, a shade below the equinoctial. I took the reading myself. It no longer amuses the General to see me using his instruments, but nor did he take the device from me.

So here I find myself, neither north nor south. Directly between the poles of the world. A fit place for my journey's end – though nothing like the port I had imagined.

In faith, it is not a port at all. Merely a wild and lonely place. An empty beach. A forest that clings to the jagged hillside, rising to meet the solitary cloud I saw from afar. It sits there still, stubborn as a child, at the island's peak. Not a sign of a watering place, nor game to eat. Nor people.

Yet it is land. Solid land at last, after the misery of the raging ocean. And never, in all my life of countless returns to the shore, was I gladder to see it.

We anchor the ship in the calm waters of the bay and row towards the island. Diego lies with the other storm-damaged men on bales of ruined cloths brought up from the hold. John has lost his habit of chatter. He sits beside me, pressing hard against my leg, though there is space enough around us.

The wind rises against us from the south-west. The going is hard. The men, already exhausted, slow their oars.

The sun beats down so bright it blinds us. A shimmering

veil, keeping from us the sight of the island upon which all eyes are fixed. When I look again, I see God – or the Devil – plays a wicked jest on us. For as we get closer, we see the land is not solid at all.

It moves.

The sands shift and crawl. Moving over and around, like rice bubbling in the pot. From the shores of the water to the forest edge, the beach is in motion. A churning, angry sea on land.

Do we imagine it? Is it in our fevered minds?

The General frowns.

"What is it?" asks John. "Why is the beach red?"

I raise my hand to blot out the sun, but still I do not know if it is real. The men rest on their oars and stare in disbelief.

"No nearer," says Collyns, lifting his oar out of the water. "The place has some sorcery upon it."

Carey narrows his eyes. "Come, brothers. A trick of the light. A reflection from the sea."

He calls them brothers now.

"An earth-shake," says Legge. "I have seen it in Sicilia. We are safe on the water till it settles."

"Nay," says the General firmly. "The trees hold still. The water is flat. This is no earth-shake. Row on."

Grumbling and muttering, the men pick up their oars, and heave again, slowly through the water.

The spray cools my cheek as it falls back upon us. The air is heavy with the scent of trees and flowers. Of life again. The palms sway in the warm breeze, waving at us in welcome.

Closer, and we see gulls flocking down from the mountain peak. They swoop onto the beach, and rise again, circling in the air before descending once more with sudden speed. Still, the sands roil and turn.

When we are close enough, Carey leads the charge into the sea. He dives in, standing in the water to his waist to wash the sweat from his face. He wrings out the golden hair that falls to his shoulders. The men watch him, hesitating.

I drop uneasily, backwards from the boat. It is blissfully cold. I fall, turning, slowed by the water. I am light again, freed from the burden of my belly.

The sounds of the men – their nervous chatter, their fears – are gone. All that remains is the muffled rattle of oars against the boat and the rush of waves breaking onto the shore. My heart beats louder in my ears. I think of the second heart, beating alongside it.

My feet find the bottom. The sands underfoot shift. Time seems to stretch out forever. For a moment, in the lonesome silence underwater, I wonder if I will continue – sinking through the sands, my whole body passing through the earth. How would it be, to emerge far from here, on the other side of the world?

The sands settle over my toes, tickling between them. The fancy passes, and it occurs to me how glad I am to be here – where I never thought I would come again: back to solid earth.

I stand into the world. The water runs down my back. The hubbub of the men continues as before. Time is restored to its usual pace.

I blink away the water and look at the island. From here, lower than the pinnace, the beach seems steeper, the mountain peak higher.

The sands still shift and roll. But I see now it is not the sands that are moving, it is what is on them. Crabs. Thousands of them. Red-shelled, scuttling ceaselessly from the water to the trees. Waves of them, breaking onto the shore of the forest.

As they go, they step out of their hardened shells, leaving the husks upon the beach, where the waves pick them up and carry them back into the shallows. They bob there, breaking onto the shore like flotsam from a wreck.

I laugh. The sorcery the men were so afeared of is life itself.

When I reach the shore, barely is there room to put my feet. I wade through the discarded shells. The crabs scuttle over me, pricking at my toes.

The men wade in from the pinnace and see as I did what

stirs on the beach. They find their voices again, calling out in delight.

"We shall not starve here, brothers!" Carey calls to those behind him, holding up a crab in each hand. "An island of plenty! An Eden no less."

The men roar in their great joy. They stoop to their knees, pouring water over themselves, washing away the sweat and the grime. They run through the waves, as well as they are able, taking up crabs to put in pockets and pouches at their waists, laughing when the crabs pinch them.

The General stands among them, thigh-deep in the water, his arms held out to the shore. "Behold the mercy of God! He who brought us to this bountiful land."

The men lift up their smocks like children, to carry the crabs within. John lies on his belly, watching one dig into the sand.

The General smiles benevolently at them all. As if this bounty is by his careful provision rather than luck.

The pinnace is tied to a stake set into the sand, and it bobs in the waves behind us. The injured men are brought ashore and laid on the beach. The tide of crabs coming out of the shallows thins. They race to the forest, the men chasing them, picking at the laggards.

From above, the gulls swoop. They carry up the crabs in their beaks, dropping those that still have shells to smash upon the rocks. The salty smell of crab flesh fills the air.

The crabs quicken their race to safety. The gulls caw in the frenzy of their slaughter. The men call out in their great delight and relief. Until the final wave of crabs breaks onto the ferns at the forest's edge. They disappear, scuttling into burrows in the shade of the trees, under roots, beneath rocks, and down into the dark and tomb-like places of the forest floor.

The gulls take up the last of the broken crabs from the rocks and retreat. The exhausted men fall where they stand, onto the sands, into rest and slumber. The land is stilled at last.

48

We raised the cross in thanksgiving for our deliverance. Carved from the broken mainmast, it stands five yards high on the rocks that tumble into the sea at the northern tip of the island. It towers above the breaking waves, mocking their power.

A lie, I think it. Made from the very ruins of nature's fury. It pretends to mastery over that which we cannot govern.

After the service on the rocks, we walk back, skirting between the forest and shore to the camp beside the beach.

There is the rough timber shelter at its centre, crude tents of sailcloth raised around it. They do little to keep off the rain when it falls, every afternoon, at the same time.

Smoke rises from the little forge by the sea. It has not ceased since we arrived: the smith and his boys at work, day and night, making nails and rivets. Melting the pitch for caulking. The bitter smell of tar is everywhere. Even in this Eden, we cannot escape the stench of the ship.

The heat of the day is dying. The sun drops into the sea to the west, but still the sweat runs in little rivers down my neck and back.

It is hard to walk for my belly and the grinding of the baby against my bones. Each step is like a knife in the groin. I fall back, behind the men, to where Fletcher limps, holding up the chains around his feet. He looks thinner than ever.

"How goes it, Master Fletcher?"

"Very slowly, Maria."

We walk in silence. I must look where to put my feet on the sharp rocks, and Fletcher walks uneasily, his feet chained by a short length so he must shuffle.

Little pools collect from the rain that fell earlier, staining the rocks dark as wine. Ahead of us the General has reached the camp. He strides directly to the tent where Diego recovers.

The rocks soften into sand before giving way to the forest ferns, and it is easier on my sore feet. I nearly did not notice the snake in my path, sand-coloured, concealed. I step over her, carefully.

The snake that chose me for my luck when I was a baby was not so easy to miss: bright and terrifying, the leaf-green amoofong that spits blinding venom in the eye. She was found in my cradle coiled alongside me. She left me untouched and unhurt, a sure sign of great favour and good fortune.

"We honoured snakes in my country," I tell Fletcher, for something to fill the heavy silence. "They signify great wisdom."

"Nay, Maria. They must not be honoured. Snakes are evil, cursed since Adam. They brought Man to his Fall."

How differently we see this same world.

"What will you do when you fetch home?" I ask.

He makes a sound like an angry hog, but nothing I can take meaning from.

"You counselled me to beg his forgiveness. Why don't you?"

"And did you?" his eyes flash at me.

"I do not need to." I bend, uneasily, to pick up a piece of driftwood. A twisted, gnarled thing, yet beautiful. Carved by the terrors of the sea and cast upon this island.

"Why not?"

"Because I will go no further with him. I don't need him to take me home."

He sighs. "We have talked of this before, Maria. He will not leave his own child here." He looks pointedly at my belly.

"But it is not his child."

He looks at me with disbelief. I pick at the driftwood. Little splinters come away, soft and rotting between my fingers.

"I was pregnant when I came on his ship, and he will know it for the baby will come very soon. He will be glad to be rid of me then. And the baby."

He drops his chain to take my arm. "But you, Maria. You cannot stay on this island. It is death to stay here alone."

"And death for me to go on. I will not go back on that ship, Master Fletcher."

I point, my finger stiff with fury, at the ship at anchor in the bay. Still is it a crippled wreck of a thing. It has not the power now to be a prison. The carpenters have cut a new mainmast in the midst of the island, but it is still being worked where it was felled. There are many more days of work and repairs – weeks maybe – before she can sail.

"There will be other ships, Maria – a fleet. We are near the Moluccas. He talks of returning here to trade for spices. I will make an appeal. To the Queen herself, if need be. That you are a Christian woman, and must be collected and brought to England."

"No!"

"You cannot stay here."

"I am not a Christian woman, and I will not go to England!"

He shakes his head wearily.

Ahead of us, the final group of men has reached the camp. They return to their duties, stoking the smelting pot, setting out for the forest to gather wood. Carey runs into the water to leap aboard the pinnace with a handful of men. They are headed for the watering-place on the larger island to the north, a light in the bow twinkling as the boat rises and falls over the waves. The low sun throws out a long shadow behind the boat, its ghost following them.

"There is something I ask of you, Master Fletcher."

He looks up.

"That when you write your account of the voyage—"

"He has taken my journal," Fletcher sniffs. "He said he would not suffer such a false and snivelling piece as I, to write the history of his glorious venture."

"But you still have your cipher-journal?"

He pats the pouch around his waist.

"You said he who has the pen writes the story. He cannot take away all the pens in the world, Master Fletcher. You can still write it."

He looks down, fearful.

"Because when *he* writes the story of his voyage, I fancy I will not be in it," I tell him. "I want you to tell about me in England. About what was done to my village. To the people they sold, he and his cousin Hawkins, in Isla Margarita and Cartagena and Rio de la Hacha. And to the people they left on the ships they abandoned in San Juan de Ulúa."

"Maria—" he starts, weary again.

"And you will not call me Maria!" I throw down in anger what remains of the driftwood.

He stares at it where it falls.

"Rather – you will say that Maria died on the ship, in the storm. It was another woman you left on this island, alone and pregnant, to test her fortune."

"What other woman?" he asks. "There is no other woman."

"Indeed there is, Master Fletcher. You will call her Macaia."

He blinks and swallows. I think, at last, he understands.

49

I was right. The General is mighty glad to leave me here.

He would return home to be thought a great man. But he would rather forget the manner in which he achieved his greatness. Easier to forget if there is no one around to remind him: of driving women and children to their deaths in the mud, of bartering people like cattle, the lowness of it all.

It is not for shame. He thinks slave-taking righteous enough if he makes believe it was done for his God. Rather, I trouble his sense of himself. He can think himself so much nobler if I am omitted from his legacy.

So we are in perfect agreement. That I shall stay here, on this island – as I would have stayed in New Albion.

On that score, at least, he shows regret – even to an apology, when I came to him this morning.

I said it too quickly. I had practised many times, but it did not come out as I prepared when I found him returning from the thanksgiving cross not long after dawn. "General," I stopped him. "The baby will come soon. I would have it here, on this island. I will not go back on the ship."

He flicked up his eyes to see who else was around. The men were up and about at the camp, carrying more timber to the fire. Tapping the barrels for rainwater. Too far away to hear us.

"Is it—"

"No," I say – too quickly again. "I was pregnant already when I came on your ship."

"It is the Spaniard's?"

I nod. Though it is not. The baby is none of theirs. She is mine, and she will not be taken from me.

He swells visibly with relief. "I am sorry, Maria. I should have left you, as you wished. In New Albion. Pyke was not a man to merit justice."

I blink at him in astonishment.

"You know? What he did?"

"He confessed to me. At the height of the storm. Poor man, he thought the tempest Divine Retribution."

Poor *man*! "And still, you left me in the Cage?"

"And still, you are a traitor," he smiles.

"Nevertheless –" he waves his hand as if he wipes away the charge, and the punishment. "All is well. God saw fit to punish Pyke and preserve us. Here we both are. By Divine Providence."

He toys with a cocoa-nut he carries in his hands, the size of a new baby's head, and smiles, saint-like, upon me.

"Did you ever go aboard the *Angel*?" I ask.

"The *Angel*," I repeat when he does not answer. "The smallest ship in your cousin Hawkins' fleet. That carried me to Cartagena in the year 1568. And was sunk at San Juan de Ulúa."

He tosses the cocoa-nut idly from one hand to the other, looking up into the lightening sky. "I don't believe I did," he says at last.

"Did you ever see a woman on its foredeck? An old woman. Taken with me, from Guinney. She prepared the food."

He looks to the side of me. If I did not know him better I would say he felt shame.

"I did not," he says, firmly. He does not ask me why.

"Did they all drown? Those – people," I will *never* call my grandmother a slave, "on the ships you left in the harbour?"

"I cannot say," he blinks, rapidly. "I – escaped. With my vessel. Before the other ships were sunk."

Fled, Fletcher told me. In disgrace. Abandoning his Admiral, and the fleet. I work my toe into the sand.

"But... could she swim? This aged woman?"

I look up. "Yes."

"*If* she was on deck. Some of those... captives –" It seems he will not say slaves, either. "Who were not chained in the hold. Some swam to shore – when the traitorous Spaniards attacked. Then – if she were among them. She may have lived."

I hate myself. For feeling gratitude to *him*. But I will hold it – and imagine my grandmother safe, escaped into the hills beyond Veracruz in the heat of the battle. There to find the Cimarrones, and live out the rest of her life, free. Perhaps she lives there still.

He plays a game with his cocoa-nut, dropping and catching it, as if to test his reactions. He smiles to see how quick he is. "What will you do for water?" he asks. As if I plan a merry cruise. A journey overnight to visit a friend in a nearby town. It catches me off guard.

"I will – may I? – take some barrels... from the ship? To store water – till I can paddle to the watering place again." I pat my belly to remind him why I am indisposed, for he gives me no allowance for my condition. Indeed – he cannot look below my neck now.

He nods, a very slight movement.

I did not expect so much. Worth asking for more.

"And – if I may – take some seeds and some grain? To sow a harvest."

"Aye, you may," he sighs. "Take what you will." He pulls strips idly from the husk of the cocoa-nut. He watches the little waves rolling in from the open sea. The crabs, their new shells hardened now, scuttle between the sea and the forest.

It strengthens me, that I embarrass him.

"Pray – assure me of something, General."

He looks sharply back to me.

"That you will let those people in New Albion alone. They were provoked, sorely. Give up the notion of a colony there."

A moment passes. He studies my face. I hold still, waiting for the storm.

It does not come.

"As it happens," he says, "I have given it up." He smiles, to see the surprise on my face. The man has a genius for confounding a person.

"For this place is far better." He sweeps his arm along the length of the beach, up towards the green peaks of the mainland across the sea to the north and west. "Such bounty in these islands. The Moluccas and all their riches are merely some days' sail from here. That man – he from your ship, the *Cacaplata*," he winks at me, at the memory of the shared jest, "the Spanish pilot. He told me the savages there are at war with the Portingales. I shall return – with the Queen's commission. Bring them guns and shot to fight the papists – and make trade for their spices at better terms."

His eyes shine at me in the early sun. He weighs the cocoa-nut in the palm of one hand. "I picked this to give to the Queen. A crude promise of the riches to come from this place."

Without a word, I turn onto the sands, and walk towards the camp. I feel my way by the lap of the waves at my feet, closing my eyes to the images that bubble into my mind like water rising to the surface in a barrel.

Of houses afire, with black smoke curling into the air, and palm-thatch falling in upon them. Of the men sent down into the earth to mine for silver and their precious stones. Of the children violated without retribution, when these men arrive to make their trade.

50

After the rain, and before the sun sets, I go to the ship on the south of the bay. It lies there now like a beached whale, heaved over to one side, so the hull can be gotten at, scraped clean of shells and weeds, repaired, caulked and greased.

Blackoller stands guard at the boarding ramp, his hand resting on an ancient arquebus. "What's your business, wench?"

"General said I could take some grain from the ship," I tell him, shielding my eyes from the sun.

"And you will carry it yourself – with that belly?"

"I shall mark what I need. And it will be fetched," I say, holding up the brush and the pail of tar Legge gave me.

He stands aside.

I walk unsteadily up the planks. Pitched to one side, as though the ship is stopped forever in the midst of the storm, I crawl up the maindeck, just as I did in the tempest.

The steps, rails and broken boards are repaired. It is fresh and new, the smell of tar mixed with the sweet odour of the timber from this island.

Below, in the steward's store, the barrels and boxes have been piled to one side.

The rice, I will have. They will not miss it. No rice has been husked since Thomas died. I dip my hand in the sack and let it run through my fingers. I tuck some grains into the hair behind my ear, as my grandmother did, to send me into the New World with a piece of my homeland.

Here are the baskets of the Indios in the north, still full of the dried leaves and berries of that frozen place. These I shall have also, for they were given to me. I put them with the barrel of rice and daub my mark. Empty barrels too, to fill with water. The seeds of New Albion, wrapped in cloth, and put in a box.

Here is the image of the bird-god of the people from the north. I shall have this, a spirit to watch over me. I mark everything I would have and climb out of the open doorway.

The sunlight slants in through the gunports, lighting up the gun deck as I have never seen it before. The guns are all ashore. It seems bigger. Certainly it is brighter, with the ports opened high to the sky. I shudder to think how it will be when it is full of the men again, jostling for a space to unroll their beds, pressing against each other at night – the boys huddled together for protection from the men who seek them in the dark.

I climb the stair to the maindeck.

On shore, the carpenters are finishing the new mainmast. They have brought it out of the forest and onto the beach, where they sit upon it like ants, each with his adze or plane, working his own section. Smoke curls up from Cook's fire. Blackoller has wandered to it, lured by the smell of roasted crab-meat that drifts downwind.

Above, a flock of sea-birds is in flight. Long-necked and wide-winged, they dip and soar with the wind, bearing off towards the south-east.

My eye falls down to the headland. The General and Diego are there, walking towards the thanksgiving cross. Their backs to me, I cannot see if they talk or pray. Diego puts his good hand to the General's shoulder, as if in supplication. The General looks at him and takes it. He grasps it with both his hands and kisses it. Such tenderness in him. A curious sight.

They are intent on something. I know not what. But whatever it is, they do not watch me. No one does. I turn back to the General's cabin, and creep inside.

The pictures are gone. The instruments are onshore. John's sea-chest too.

All that remains is the bed, stripped of its linen, and fallen against the beached side of the ship and the stool, which lies fallen against the window.

I sit on the bed, lying back, against the pitched cabin wall.

I am trying to think of a baby here – crying in this cabin, angering the General, or worse, below: she and I banished to the gun deck, defenceless, as open to attack as poor Thomas – when a curling piece of parchment catches my eye.

I go to take it from the shelf. It is a chart, small and brightly-coloured: a copy in miniature of the chart the General showed to the Alcalde of Guatulco. I trace my finger along the equinoctial line.

Fletcher said we are near the Moluccas. Then we are here, by these islands, north of Java. In the Cage, in the darkness, I dreamed of reaching Terra Australis. How close it is on this chart, somewhere out there to the south-east, beyond New Guinney. I have made it closer than Gonzalo – or any of the marineros on the Manila galleons – ever dreamed.

As I go to put the chart back upon the shelf, I see it was covering something. The men missed it when they emptied the cabin. A yellow silk bag. A ribbon of crimson velvet to tie it. She did not call to me this time. She did not need to.

51

The ship sails tomorrow.

Tonight, we feast. By the light of the stars and the fire, and the little flies that light up the air like flying candles.

The men are merry. Fat on the endless supply of crabs, and the plentiful fish.

Diego sits beside me wrapped in a New Albion blanket. He is mended in body, save for his crippled hand. A bare patch surrounds the wound on his head where the hair will not grow.

The full moon rises behind us, emerging from the shadow of the mountain peak. As she begins her journey into the west, she lights up the ship at anchor in the bay. The sails shine in the silvery light. Barely can the patchwork be seen.

The sea is calm. It breaks onto the shore in little waves, a restful lulling sound. Shells of crabs lie on the sand. The men are quiet after the meal, at work with their toothpickers. A bat flies out from the forest, a void against the starry sky, and comes low, sweeping over the fire.

Some things are the same the world over, I think as I watch the stars. I believe it true what Fray Calvo told me: that the same God is everywhere, for the heavens are surely the same. These are the same skies I saw from Guinney, from New Spain, and New Albion.

There is the pole star, lower in the sky than it is in the

north. There is the sign of the dog. The same heavens. Merely shifted somewhat. The three stars, Las Tres Marías, that the English call the Hunter's Belt, are upside down here, as they are in the southern part of the globe.

Everything is there – but in the wrong place.

Orion the Hunter leads the eye to the brightest star, and I point it out now to Diego. "You see this one. It is the most important star in the sky."

"The dog star," he murmurs, settling back onto the sands beside me, his good arm thrown behind his head.

"The canoe star. Sigi tolo, we called it."

Fletcher stirs. His shackles have been removed, but still he must wear the banner around his neck. "Is it used for navigation?" he asks.

I nod. "And it is a calendar. On the first day it rises before the dawn, it signifies the season that brings the rains. But that is not why it is important either."

"Why, then?" asks Fletcher.

"It is where all the other stars come from."

Diego watches sigi tolo. Fletcher watches me.

"And though it is the brightest star in the sky," I go on, "the important part is that which you cannot see."

John creeps over too, and curls beside me like a cat, looking up at the sky.

"What part of a star is there, but cannot be seen?" he asks, as though it is a riddle.

"His companion. She is with him always. And it is she who gave birth to all the other stars in the sky."

"How do you know?" asks Fletcher.

"It is known." That is all I can say. But then I remember what my grandmother whispered in my ear at night, as we lay on the hard boards of the open deck of the slaving ship.

"If you watch it long enough, you can see how she affects the bright star."

"How so?" asks John.

"They circle each other. It takes a lifetime: threescore years, or thereabouts. And when she is near sigi tolo she makes him brighter, and when she is further away, he twinkles – to signal to her across the heavens."

"I see only one star," says Fletcher, searching the heavens.

"*Everyone* sees only one star. But the second star is there. Unseen and unknowable – save for her power over the bigger star."

"Like God," he sighs, happily. "Known only by His works."

Something else I remember now too. "When she is closest to sigi tolo, every threescore years: that is when she is celebrated. A feast that goes on for many days. It comes only once in a lifetime, and it is something to remember until you die: such food, such dancing."

The sorrow is I don't know how to tell when is the time for the feast. Nor is there anyone who can show me.

"What is she called?" asks Diego. It surprises me to hear his voice, and I turn to find his eyes fixed unblinkingly on the star. "The companion of sigi tolo?"

I cannot remember that either. I look up, as though I can find her among the tiny pinpricks of light in the sky. But of course I cannot. And then it comes to me as if she whispered it in my ear herself.

"Po tolo," I tell them – for she is the source of all life. "The star of the deep beginning."

52

All good things come from the east. Like the sun, every morning.

East is where the ancestors came from, long before we settled in the land beside the river. Would that they had stayed there – far from the evil of the ocean.

East is where spirits rise again, after a body is buried, and its soul must travel, out of its tomb and far into the west, through the land of the dead, to be reborn.

So it is fit, I think, as I watch the ship disappear, its shroud-like sails slipping into the void between the sea and the sky, that that is where they go. Into the west. Towards the underworld.

So long have I sat here that the sun descends to follow them too, dropping from above, slowly, towards the same spot on the horizon.

I came up high, so I could see them for longer, from the island's only peak. To this pleasing flat rock, where the branches of the sweet-smelling trees have parted, to allow the sun to warm it, just for me.

It is hard to walk now, for the bigness of my belly, and harder still to climb the steep forest trail, which is wet and crumbles underfoot. But I wanted to see them go. Till the sails had gone, until I saw them disappear myself, still did I fear he would turn back.

What if he found it missing?

My thumb strokes the fire-opal in my palm. I would wear it down I cannot stop from feeling it.

Dull now in the full glare of the sun, like embers in a dying fire. Too much light seems to deaden it. It flashes and marvels at its greatest, the fire leaping from the stone to escape, when it sees only a small portion of the sun.

No one will call it the Glory of Cortés again. She called to *me* through it and led me here. It is *my* stone now and I shall name it. It is the Eye of Mansarico.

Has he noticed it gone – among his shipload of treasures? Has he forgotten it already? As he has forgotten me, no doubt. I do not care to be remembered by him. But when Fletcher took his leave of me he pressed his Geneva Bible into my hands, blessed me and kissed my forehead. He showed me the page of his cipher-journal that he will put abroad when he is home. His sketch of these islands. The measurements of each, carefully recorded: the degrees and minutes in which each lies, south of the equinoctial line. His estimates to the degrees east and west. And this one small island, waterless and barren, with the words *Isla Macaia* etched above it.

I should go back to the hut on the beach and light a cooking fire. The sun shines directly in my face now. So hot, though it is late in the day. The sweat drips off the tip of my nose, between my swollen breasts and onto my belly. I think about the cool walk down through the forest: the giant ferns brushing my feet, the sweet smell of the trees, the march of the beetle-sized ants carrying aloft their prizes of cut leaves. But still I cannot move. The blood throbs in my legs. Everything aches. My belly feels like it will burst. I am so full, and so weary of feeling full.

She must come soon.

I lie back so my head is shaded by the branches, and I look

through them into the sky. The solitary cloud is there, ready to send down its rain, which now I think about it, is late today.

What will I tell her? If she survives. If we both survive her tearing out of me.

How will I explain why we are here, alone on this island?

The first person ever to live was born in the sea – fully-formed, a woman. She stepped out of the waves onto land, a child in her womb.

My grandmother told me this. *Do not fear the sea*, she said, as it assailed us on all sides, throwing us down and up in that alien first ship, every which way in its fury. *Do not fear the sea, it is where we all came from*.

I think of this plenty, since I came to this island, stepping out of the waves myself, a child in *my* belly.

She – the first woman – was the mother of all people, everywhere in the world.

I shall tell my child that.

That we are the first people. We are fresh and new.

I will start again. As crabs leave their old and outgrown shells to float away on the sea.

She need know no different. Nothing of the miseries from before. Nor that they endure, far across the ocean – behind me. Where all life, like the sun, begins in the east.

She need not know I brought her here, against all possibility and reason, on the only ship that sailed out of the land of the dead.

Epilogue

Terra Nondum Cognita

OCTOBER, 1580

3°30'S

The boat is little more than a canoe. Outriggers carved from a single large trunk on each side, a solitary sail unfurled from one mast. One yard and a canopy of sailcloth to keep off the burning sun. But she is seaworthy. We skim over the waves like a pelicane. Barely do we seem to touch the water.

I sit under the shade, on a fur-and-feather New Albion blanket, with the chart on my knees. There is little room, wedged as I am between sacks of rice, water-filled barrels and everything else we brought away from the island. The corners of the little chart curl in through their habit. As I smooth them back, the parchment rasps my skin.

On the map, the islands stretch out towards the south-east, leading to the mainland rising up to meet it.

Difficult to tell how far now, and the light blinds when I look into the haze of the horizon. If I could measure the declination, I could be sure. I thought of it when I was in his cabin, and I saw the fire-opal and the chart for the taking. But his astrolabe was ashore, and in any case, a risk too far. *That* he would have noticed.

No matter. I know the distance. I know the direction: the same way the sea-birds fly, always heading towards the main. I know how the roll of the water on the flat hull changes when the swell of the ocean meets the rising land. At night, I know to keep the setting moon at my right shoulder and sigi tolo, which rises in the south-east, direct ahead. We aim for unseen po tolo. The deep beginning.

A cry, that tugs sharp at my breast. I look down to see she is waking.

I pick her out of her cradle of woven vines and palm leaves. She blinks and wriggles to free her arms from her wrapping of blue-and-white striped shipcloth. The moment they are free she stretches her hands for the gleaming stone hanging at my neck. So like my mother. I remember her face now, for they are so alike. I named her Yalie, for her memory. The same high cheekbones. The same arched brows. Long toes, good for balance, slim fingers for the spindle.

How strong she is already. I peel her fingers from the jewel and tuck it back under my shirt. Through the linen, it glows still: a flickering fire she watches keenly.

I pick her up, this child of mine. She reaches for the light that filters through the sailcloth canopy. She curls and uncurls her fists, delighting in the new-found power she has over them. She gurgles, grabs my hair, and pulls at it ferociously.

She looks over my shoulder and laughs when she sees him.

"Yaaaa-liiiie," says Diego, drawing out the syllables low and long in mock chastisement. "Let go your mother's hair."

And she does, still laughing.

I turn to watch him. He settles beside the tiller onto the bench he carved himself, and looks to the south, at the empty, forested coast slipping past.

Once again – as I have every time I have seen him afresh since the ship left, and I struggled down from the island's peak to find him, to my everlasting surprise, sitting in the little hut on the beach – once again, I feel the overwhelming joy of the bare facts of him. Of his sureness in everything. Clear in his easy grasp of the tiller, his good arm holding it steady, thick-muscled to make up for the other withered limb. One leg rests, the other poised, should he need to rise of a sudden to balance the boat, or steer sharply to weather a high wave. The papagayo-red cap against the deep blue sky announces with such conviction that he is there.

The first time I ever saw him, I thought he had damped the charge – put out the fizzling line of gunpowder. In truth, he lit it. He is the spark that brought me back to life.

"How many days do you think?" he asks.

I bounce Yalie on my knee to see her laugh. "A week? Maybe two. We can skirt the islands for much of it. But the last part..."

I leave it there. He knows. We have talked about this many times in the months we readied ourselves on the island. Building the boat, harvesting the crops grown from seed.

"And tell me again, muñequita," I can tell he is grinning, though I am not looking at him. "Why Terra Australis?"

"Because it is not theirs." I put Yalie to my breast. "The English want only what belongs to the Spaniards. The Spaniards must defend what they have. They will leave it be. An old world. Unspoiled and free."

Yalie locks her eyes on mine as she feeds. Her fist beats rhythmically against me to test I am still there.

I sing softly to her.

Someone wishes to have you as her child
But you are my own
Someone wishes she had you to nurse
But I have you
You are my own
You are my own

Such completeness. Such perfection. The joy of being all that she needs. The relief that I am here to give it.

Author's Note

This is a work of fiction built upon the bare facts of Francis Drake's circumnavigation voyage. I have taken particular licence with events during the summer of 1579, for which the official accounts of Drake's exploration of America are far from convincing. I have placed Nova Albion, for example, not at 38°N (California) as is claimed today, but at 48°N (Canada-US border). This is where it appears on multiple maps linked directly to Drake in his lifetime and where John Drake reported it under interrogation in 1584.

The bloody conclusion to the establishment of Nova Albion is entirely my invention but was sparked by the mismatch in reports of 80 sailors on board the *Golden Hind* in early 1579 and the 59 who returned home in September 1580 – though no deaths or desertions were recorded during this time. It is also inspired by the violence of the colonisation of this part of America in later centuries.

The historical Maria lived aboard the *Golden Hind* for nine months, though we know little more of her than the dates she joined and departed the ship. But recorded history is only one version of events and recovering the stories of women who appear only fleetingly in the records requires imagination. I present this novel not as a history but a possible life: a fiction in which I have privileged Maria's story over the accepted facts of Drake's circumnavigation.

Acknowledgments

Among a huge number of historical works that helped me build Maria's world, I would like to mention in particular *Afro-Latino Voices* edited by Kathryn Joy McKnight and Leo J. Garofalo, *Colonial Blackness* by Herman L. Bennett, *Dangerous Speech* by Javier Villa-Flores and Nicole von Germeten's edition of Alonso de Sandoval's *Treatise on Slavery*.

Maria's original name Macaia comes from Emory University's *Trans-Atlantic Slave Trade Database*, which collates all known information on 36,000 slaving voyages, including the African names of 91,491 men, women and children liberated by the International Courts of Mixed Commission and British Vice Admiralty Courts in the final decades of the slave trade. The six ships in John Hawkins' slaving fleet of 1567–68 can be traced here, including the *Angel* (voyage ID 98849), in which I placed Maria.

The lullaby Maria remembers her mother singing is inspired by an Akan folk song published in Margaret Busby's anthology *Daughters of Africa*, 1992.

I am indebted to Zelia Nuttall, who published the Spanish documents relating to Drake in *New Light on Drake* in 1914. Nuttall discovered the depositions of John Drake in the Spanish archives, providing the confirmatory eye-witness account of Maria in the historical record.

The character of Fletcher in this novel is greatly inspired by Richard Madox, the ship's chaplain on Edward Fenton's disastrous voyage to the Americas in 1582. Madox's witty and humane diary was published as *An Elizabethan in 1582*, by Elizabeth Story Donno in 1976. From Madox I borrowed for Fletcher the use of cipher to record his impressions of a dishonourable captain.

Though two hundred years after Maria's time, *The Interesting Narrative of the Life of Olaudah Equiano* describes encounters with English sailors from an enslaved African's point of view. From Equiano I borrowed for Maria his belief that it was the book itself speaking, when he first saw people reading aloud.

The real Diego probably died in the East Indies in late 1579, although some reports say he died earlier, in Chile, while others confuse him with different Africans aboard the *Golden Hind* at various points. Given this contradiction, I chose to keep him alive for the sake of the fictional Maria. To read more about the historical Diego, see Miranda Kaufmann's *Black Tudors*, published 2017.

Thank you to Dr Paul Evans for his help with details of Elizabethan life, Arelis Diaz for help with colloquial Spanish, Matthew Bradbury of Bonhams for terminology of early modern art, to Laura Marmery Shiels for Latin translation and Wim van der Horst for Dutch translation.

Thank you to my agent Ella Diamond Kahn, editor Lauren Parsons, Lucy Chamberlain and everyone at Legend Press for bringing this book into the world.

Thank you to Lucy and Louise, who know all anyone ever wants for their birthday is a tour of the British Library.

Thank you to the British Library, and all libraries.

Thank you to my first reader, Paul.

Thank you to all my friends and family for your unflagging enthusiasm for this project, particularly to Bethany for library-based support and encouragement and to Sarah for being an exemplary research trip companion.

Last but never least, thank you to Tom, Ben, George and Guy for allowing me a day here and there to write this book.

If you enjoyed what you read, don't keep it a secret.

Review the book online and tell anyone who will listen.

Thanks for your support spreading the word about Legend Press!

Follow us on Twitter
@legend_press

Follow us on Instagram
@legendpress